Dilemma In Yellow Silk

An Emperors of London Novel

Lynne Connolly

LYRICAL PRESS
Kensington Publishing Corp.
www.kensingtonbooks.com

Lyrical Press books are published by
Kensington Publishing Corp. 119 West 40th Street New York, NY 10018

First Electronic Edition: April 2016
eISBN-13: 978-1-61650-573-8
eISBN-10: 1-61650-573-7

First Print Edition: April 2016
ISBN-13: 978-1-61650-598-1
ISBN-10: 1-61650-598-2

Printed in the United States of America

Ever ready to do the right thing, The Emperors of London act bravely—
and when it comes to matters of the heart, impetuously...

Despite her cover as the daughter of the land steward for Lord Malton, Marcus Aurelius, spirited Viola Gates is tied by birth to the treacherous Jacobite legacy. Not that this keeps her from falling for the dashing Lord from afar. Despite his staid demeanor, Marcus is devastatingly handsome—and hopelessly beyond her reach. Then Viola's father is mortally wounded and her secret identity revealed, sending her straight into danger's path—and Marcus's arms...

For years, he'd only known her as a wild child, the tempting—and forbidden—daughter of his trusted steward. But when Viola's life is threatened, Marcus must act as duty—and his barely contained passion—dictates. Ferrying the bold beauty on an eventful journey to safer quarters, he offers her the protection of his name. Their tempestuous union might succeed in vanquishing their enemies, but will the chivalrous lord and his unsuitable wife surrender to the power of love?

"Lynne Connolly writes Georgian romances with a deft touch. Her characters amuse, entertain and reach into your heart."
—Desiree Holt

"Plots, deviousness and passion galore...a truly enjoyable read."
–*Fresh Fiction* on *Temptation Has Green Eyes*

Books by Lynne Connolly

Emperors of London
Temptation Has Green Eyes
Danger Wears White
Reckless In Pink
Dilemma In Yellow Silk

Published by Kensington Publishing Corporation

Chapter 1

A cloud of dust puffed out of the window of one of the state apartments at Haxby Hall. It was about time someone shook out the rugs.

Standing at her drawing-room window, Viola Gates had a good vantage point of the great building, the pride of the neighborhood. By her reckoning, the cleaning team had reached the double salon.

She turned around to face the other occupant of the room.

"What are they doing, girl?" her father asked.

"Bottoming," she said succinctly. "Nobody bottoms like Mrs. Lancaster." She cast a backward glance at the hall. "I should go and help, since it's your fault the marquess is coming."

Her father chuckled. "They didn't expect him for another month. More fool they. And do you know why he is coming?"

She turned her attention to his heavily bandaged foot, wondering why he was stating the obvious. "To see you, Papa. You're an old retainer."

He snorted. "I'm a bit more than that, my girl. I'm related."

"In a way." He was a cousin of a cousin of a cousin. Her father had used the nebulous connection many years ago, and the previous marquess had given him the position of land steward here. Well, not land steward immediately, but he'd gained the position, and he wasn't about to give it up any time soon.

Situations like his often ran in families, but since she was the only child, they weren't about to give her the job. "Do you think they'll use your broken ankle as an excuse to force you into retirement?"

Her father shook his head. "Not a chance." He fidgeted, wincing when his foot shifted on the padded footstool. Mrs. Lancaster had brought it from the house for his use while he recovered. She'd always been a bit sweet on Viola's papa, but he wasn't buying her careful solicitude. Not yet, at any rate. She wouldn't surrender her position at Haxby yet. If she married him, she would probably have to retire, and she was queen of the hall, except when the marchioness was in residence.

"His lordship is sick and tired of London. Any excuse will serve to get him back. He's probably made out I'm at death's door. That's the actual reason he's coming."

The Gates household had heard the marquess was coming yesterday. From what she knew of the current incumbent of the Strenshall title, that information meant he'd arrive soon.

Her father was right. The family had lingered in London this year. His lordship was probably aching to get back to the country. Viola should really go to the hall to help.

The drawing room she currently stood in was beautifully neat and tidy, its comfortable furnishings inviting guests to take their ease. They did not want for visitors, especially since her father's recent fall. Nobody expected George Gates, who was perfectly at ease on a horse, to fall, much less suffer a tumble bad enough to cause his horse distress. However, he had, and now both participants were recovering in their respective residences. The land would hardly go to rack and ruin in the two months it would take her father to fully recover.

The great hall drew her. Mrs. Lancaster would need all the help she could get. Her father was comfortably ensconced in his favorite armchair with the newspapers that had been brought to the hall fresh off the mail. After tomorrow, the staff would keep them at the hall for the use of his lordship. Her father would only receive them in the afternoon.

Apart from that small hitch, estate managers at Haxby tended to live well. They even had the use of this house for the duration of her father's tenure, though he owned a perfectly good one in nearby Scarborough. Too far to travel when his impatient lordship required his presence.

George Gates hated fuss and bother. The fewer people who disturbed him, the better he liked it. And while he was off his feet, he said, he could concentrate on going through the books. He had the overview of not just Haxby Hall, but all his lordship's properties. That made for a lot of paperwork.

"Perhaps you should open one of those books, Papa," Viola said.

He scowled at the stack of account books on the side table awaiting his attention, as they had for the last week. "Perhaps. Account books have never held much appeal for me, but the sooner I start, the sooner I'm done. Your dear mother always proved of signal help there."

"She was more dutiful than I am, I fear," Viola confessed. "But if you wish it, I'll take half." She heaved a heartfelt sigh, letting her shoulders rise and fall.

Her father chuckled. "You could never abide adding up, but be warned; I'll make use of you later." He made a scooting motion with his hand. "Go, girl. Make the housekeeper happy."

Laughing, Viola hurried from the room, making her way to the front door before her father could change his mind.

Had she been in the city, she'd have had to don gloves, shawl, cloak, bonnet, fan, all the accoutrements of required outdoor wear, even on this glorious summer day. Instead, she crammed on her old straw hat to protect her complexion from the sun, shoved her feet into her sturdy leather shoes, and set off. Her small hooped petticoat kept the fabric of her gown away from her body. When she ran, holding on to the hoop to keep her skirts from swinging, a comfortable breeze gusted around her legs.

The hall was less than half a mile away, a distance she accomplished in very little time, around ten minutes by her reckoning. The side door to the hall was never locked, except when the marchioness took it into her head to have every door and window secured. Viola went in and grinned at the footman standing inside.

Tranmere was in full uniform, the blue-and-silver livery blinding in the sun.

"That must be hot," she commented.

"Don't want his lordship to catch me out," Tranmere said, his deep voice booming across the spacious hall.

"You could always take the coat off and then put it back on when you hear he's arrived. He won't come in this way."

Tranmere grimaced. "I can't. Mrs. Lancaster's orders. She wanted to inspect us all, although it's not her place."

"Don't let her hear you say that."

He grinned, the expression revealing the severe lack of teeth on his lower jaw. In his chequered past, Tranmere had engaged in prize fighting and had, so he claimed, won a trophy and a purse for each tooth. "She's all right, as long as you do what she says."

While they spoke, Viola was unbuckling her heavy outdoor shoes and putting on the light slippers she used inside the hall. Haxby had too many treasures to risk damaging the floors or the rugs. Mrs. Lancaster would have her hide if she caught Viola indoors with outdoor shoes on.

With a cheeky wave to the footman, who had taken her advice and slipped off the heavy coat, she ran up the wrought-iron staircase. It was built on a cantilevered spiral, one of the wonders of the house, based on the Tulip Stairs at Greenwich. Not that Viola had seen the Tulip Stairs, but she'd accompanied Mrs. Lancaster on so many guided tours she knew the words by heart. Almost without thinking about them.

Along the corridor, she opened a jib door and scampered up the servants' staircase. The only stair she was forbidden to use was the grand staircase in the main hall. She rarely went that way, and in any case, she had no desire to use it. If anyone asked, she'd touch an imaginary forelock and tell them it was too good for a servant girl like her. But in reality, the estate manager was more than a servant.

If Viola had insisted on her consequence, she'd have found herself very lonely indeed. She preferred to let everyone forget she was a daughter of a cousin of a cousin. There might even be another cousin in the way there.

Upstairs she opened the door at the top and entered the great state rooms. These were the absolute pinnacle of the house's grandeur and wealth. Public openings centered here, and when the family were in residence, they would hold balls and gatherings here. Viola had attended a few, but always standing at the back, not drawing attention to herself.

In the first room, she paused. The covers were off here, the glass, furniture, and china buffed to a fine dustless sheen. From the Meissen figures on the elaborately carved marble fireplace to the glittering crystal drops on the chandelier, the room looked pristinely perfect.

The rooms were set in a line—enfilade people called it—and when all the doors were open, a person could see right to the end. At the moment, the staff were opening the doors as they moved to the next room in the sequence.

The second chamber was the huge double room, so called because it could be split into two spacious rooms by using the panels embedded into the walls on each side. The current marquess preferred to keep it open. He only used it for large gatherings and when he wanted to impress people. A couple of maids were dusting, holding each ornament carefully while plying the feather dusters. Both greeted Viola with smiles, and she nodded back before moving on. The cleaning army had finished with the music room, too, so she passed on.

Mrs. Lancaster and most of her cohorts carried out their duties in the library. The family only kept precious books here, the ones they rarely read. Between each bookcase was a marquetry wooden panel depicting a literary figure. Mrs. Lancaster was applying a liberal amount of honey and lavender polish to Chaucer's nose. "Ah," she said, looking over the tops of her spectacles at Viola. "I wondered when you'd get here." Since she was standing at the top of a stepladder, she could look down at Viola. The rest of her staff, half a dozen maids, all sweeping, buffing and dusting. "Could you go into the music room and check the instruments? The tuner came last week, but nobody else can try them."

Viola had undergone torturous music lessons because one of the marquess's daughters, Lady Claudia, had hated learning, and Viola had to help her. Claudia still avoided musical instruments when possible, although her twin, Lady Livia, could hammer out a piece if forced to it.

Viola had hated the lessons, but once she could pick out a tune, she changed her mind. Not that she would ever make a professional musician, but she was at the level of a decent amateur. None of the maids could play.

Delighted she was spared the dirtier work, she went into the music room.

The instruments here were precious. A gold-encrusted harp stood in the center of the Aubusson carpet. She padded over to it and tested the strings. They sounded all right to her, but she didn't play the harp. Such a lovely instrument, with nobody to play it.

The room also contained an old set of virginals dating back to the time of James the First. Viola knew better than to touch that. It was a relic, not a real instrument. The king had presented it to one of his gentlemen as a token of his thanks for some favor long forgotten. A case contained wind instruments, but they would be fine. A mandolin stood in one corner.

Viola turned to the harpsichord. The inner lid bore a painting of a woman dressed as the Muse of music, Euterpe. Viola lifted it carefully and put the prop under it. The strings gleamed, daring her to touch them.

She dared.

Sitting on the broad padded bench-like seat, she ran her hands over the white-and-black keys. They trilled. She did some scales, up and down, the automatic movement of her hands lulling her into a state where she could link with the keys. Each note sank into her. She absorbed them and made them hers. She could have stopped there. It sounded fine.

The piece of sheet music propped on the stand was a two-hander. She could always play one part of it, but mischief led her into doing something else. The locals had a wonderful collection of music, some of it scurrilous, some quaint. She started with a few quaint ones, and when she sang the verses, a few voices rose in song from the next room.

How far could she take them? An urge took her to hear the ditties in this beautiful treasure-chest of a state room.

Viola began with a few more local songs, the innocent kind about lovers losing their ladies, ladies losing their soldier lovers and running away with the gypsies. Moving closer to her goal, she played a tune about a poacher and his boy.

The song described poaching from a more innocent age, when peasants snared creatures for the pot instead of gangs of organized ruffians stealing animals by the dozen. It bled innocence. Except in the last verses, when the song revealed the uncomfortable punishment demanded in those days—the stocks, where a man could die if the crowd took a dislike to him.

She grew a little bawdier in her choice. Not all the way, or Mrs. Lancaster would call a halt to her playing, but the maids would work well for a little entertainment. Mrs. Lancaster would not have been the superb housekeeper she was if she had not understood that.

They sang. She joined in, singing of maids lying in the fields, tossing up their skirts for their swains and paying for their sins, or simply marrying. The keys, cool to the touch, warmed, the ivory taking on the heat from her fingers as she progressed.

She'd played with the notion of finding someone who could help her assuage the need she occasionally felt, but then dismissed the notion as foolish. At her age, she would probably never marry. The prospect didn't worry her as it might another. In fact, she had agreed with her father that she was probably better remaining a spinster. She would inherit a comfortable income and a house, the one her father owned in Scarborough, so she would not want. But sometimes, when she allowed herself to think about it, her body heated and the memory of kisses seared her.

Several people next door joined in, so she continued on to a local song she'd found in a gossip paper recently. At first she played just the tune, a folk tune from another part of the country. Many people hereabouts considered Yorkshire the only part of the country that mattered. Although loyal to the county where she lived, Viola was aware of what was going on elsewhere. She had to be. Her father and she shared more knowledge than most, and they had to maintain a certain level of vigilance.

This tune spoke of the King, and the other king—the one in Rome— and the confusion between the two together with the futility of choosing one side or the other. The cheerful jig-like tune belied the underlying cynicism in the words.

This one took some concentration, for she had only just learned it. She failed to notice the silence that had fallen until too late.

* * * *

Marcus loved coming home. He always regarded Haxby as his home, not the London mansion his family occupied during the season. This time he'd come with his father alone, a fast journey to see Gates and arrange affairs for the estate manager's period of infirmity.

The gatekeepers barely got the huge iron gates open in time, but the coachman was stopping for no one and he swept through. Any faster and he'd be taking the corner on two wheels.

The impetus pressed Marcus against the side of the coach. "You need to tell Harrison not to travel so fast," he said to his father.

"Ah, but his thoughts of seeing his sweetheart engross him," the marquess said, smiling. "He left her behind to take us to London. We'll find someone else to take us back."

Marcus groaned. "Do I have to return? It's the end of the season. Surely there is no need to have me there."

"Your sister is marrying, and your mother is on the verge of betrothing two of your sisters. What do you think?"

The curse of being the eldest of a large family. They expected Marcus to wish them well and substitute for his father, if necessary, when he'd prefer to stay here. He'd had enough of London and its intrigues. With the season nearly over, he'd hoped to remain at home, one of the main reasons for accompanying his father.

"Could they not marry from home?"

"If they marry at all." He cleared his throat. "Besides, I have something particular to discuss with Gates. It seemed an opportune moment to do so."

Another sweep of the drive and the house came into view. As always, Marcus feasted his eyes on the place. The central structure boasted a tower in the middle capped by a lantern dome. It was not the largest of the great houses in the county, but to his mind it was the most beautiful. The central block rose a story above the side wings, the huge pilasters fronting the façade creating a grand display.

When his father died—may that be many years hence—Marcus would inherit this and all the responsibilities that went with it. The notion of becoming the marquess had always shocked him, an emotion he kept to himself, as not worthy of the heir to the marquisate. Hundreds of people would depend on him for their livelihood.

They swept up the elm-lined drive, the spaces between the trees affording glimpses of the parkland beyond. The occasional sheep, kept here to keep the grass down between scything, lifted its head to watch the coach going past. The sight warmed him. This—not the house in London—was home for Marcus.

"Your mother says she will look out for a likely bride for you," his father said.

Marcus sighed. "I would like nothing better than to select my own bride. I swear I will choose someone suitable."

"She has eyes and ears that penetrate further than ours. She knows the most promising young women about to make their debut in society." Lord Strenshall shifted in his seat. "Devil take it, these seats are damnably uncomfortable. I'll have this carriage reupholstered when we return to town."

"There are people perfectly capable of doing the job locally," Marcus pointed out. "Then you won't have to pay London prices."

"But we need to get back in it." His father sighed. "Perhaps I can wait until the summer."

Considering this was June, Marcus considered summer well under way. The day was fine, and they had come home. It had taken three days, since they could move faster without the ladies to cater for. Both Marcus and his father preferred to travel for longer and eat quickly rather than linger on the road.

"We'll have a shooting party, come August," his father said.

That gave Marcus a clear eight weeks until he needed to concern himself with entertaining guests, including the ones who wanted to marry him. He didn't fool himself. They wanted his title and his family name as much, if not more, than his person. While not exactly unprepossessing, he wasn't the kind of person who enjoyed dallying with ladies when there was work waiting for him.

There was always work. Mostly Marcus told himself he didn't mind, but sometimes he fretted at the bit. When he dreamed, he soared free, but he rarely remembered his dreams. Just the sensation of flying remained for a few moments after he woke.

While here he'd talk to the gamekeeper, and ensure the coverts were well stocked. "If Gates is—" He couldn't finish the sentence. He'd known Gates all his life—and his daughter, although they had drawn apart recently. Necessary, because they lives were destined to take different paths. His duty took him somewhere she couldn't join him. Much to his regret. But he would not burden the free spirit he remembered with the duties that belonged to him.

She didn't deserve that.

The carriage drew up outside the front door and the efficient machine that ran Haxby Hall clicked into action, its cogs running to the inevitable conclusion. When the liveried footman unfolded the steps of the carriage, Marcus got out and stood before the magnificence of his house with his hat in his hand. The butler stood at the top of the stone staircase. As his father climbed down to join him, Marcus took his first step, and then hesitated.

The spirit of rebellion stirred within him, as if it had remained dormant until now.

"I'll go around the side way," he said.

"Trying to catch out the servants?" his father said with a grin.

Marcus returned the smile. "Something of that nature."

He would avoid going through the "Good afternoon, my lord" ritual the footman, and then the butler, and then the maids would go through. His father enjoyed it as little as he did, but Marcus didn't have to endure it yet.

He strode off to the side of the house. That in itself was a fair walk, but one he enjoyed, as he reacquainted himself with the place. He'd been in London too long. In November he would refuse to rush to town at the start of the Parliamentary season. What was the point? They never got anything done.

Scents assailed him as his feet crunched on the gravel path. Flowers, mostly, the kind women enjoyed, but they made a fine show in the beds at the front of the house. His mother had decided to remodel, and they were looking into replacing the formal Tudor gardens with a more informal stretch of parkland.

While the house would appear more à la mode, Marcus would miss the bright displays. Perhaps they could keep something. He wanted the flowers.

The stone walls were not entirely even, partly from design and partly because the Palladian façade covered a much older house. Parts of the central block dated from Tudor times, when a courtier of Elizabeth won the land for singular service to his queen. Marcus's grandfather had extended the house, making the E shape into a closed double quadrangle and adding to the wings on either side. He'd created the grand enfilade of state rooms from a hodgepodge of salons, creating the house Marcus had grown up in.

Marcus descended a staircase, opened a door, and entered the servants' quarters. He looked to neither right nor left as he took the well-remembered shortcut to the side door. That cut out traversing the wings. He wasn't in the passage long enough to create a commotion; in fact, nobody saw him as far as he knew. He was into the inner courtyard before anyone could register his presence.

A short walk along the stone paved path took him to the side entrance, and the shortcut to his rooms. His valet had set off early that morning, so he could arrive early and have everything ready for his master. Marcus prayed that included a decanter of burgundy and something to eat. Freshly baked bread and local cheese would not come amiss.

Then, fortified, he'd return to being the Earl of Malton and join his father for whatever duties awaited him.

Entering the side door without ceremony, Marcus enjoyed the sight of a large footman scrambling into his silver-laced coat. "My lord!"

"Good afternoon, Tranmere. How is Gates?"

Tranmere stared at him and then found his voice. "Broken ankle, my lord. He's resting at his house."

"Ah." Well. That was one concern dealt with. Gates had fallen from his horse and hurt himself, but the messenger had left in such haste they had not ascertained precisely what was the matter. Marcus had been glad to use the excuse, but worry for the estate manager had also driven him to discover for himself.

Leaving the man stammering, Marcus climbed the stairs two at a time, not giving the poor footman a chance to sort himself out. His childish amusement was not worthy of him, he knew that. But the welcome had suited him in his present mood more than the ceremonial one awaiting his father.

Pausing at the state rooms, he decided to go through them. His rooms were equidistant if he took the corridor with guest rooms or the state rooms.

He opened the first door. He recognized the sign that maids were about. The door at the end was closed, but the others were open. That meant they'd finished up to the closed door.

Marcus grinned. Mrs. Lancaster would be furious he'd caught them working. She preferred the family to think that fairies dealt with their needs, invisible ones preferably.

Notes of music drifted to him, so delicate his fanciful notion of fairies became real. Through the first salon, the anteroom, and then the main salon, the huge space that never got warm in winter unless they packed it with people. Then the third. The music room.

He paused. The maids chattered in the library. Some sang along with the music. Smiling, he tiptoed across the parquet floor to the connecting door and closed it as silently as he could.

Chapter 2

Concentrating on her music, Viola nearly jumped out of her skin when a large body plumped down on the stool next to her. She shrieked, spun around, and closed her eyes. "You!"

"Why, weren't you expecting me?"

His expression of innocence did not fool her for a minute.

"Not here, not like this. Did you run from the last staging post?" she demanded. She should not talk to the Earl of Malton like this. Right now he was less the earl and more Marcus, the boy she'd known so long ago. "Oh, my lord, sir, I'm sorry!"

She should recall her place, but she was finding the task difficult when he was wearing the same mischievous grin he'd used at nine years old.

"I couldn't resist. Do you know what you were playing?"

The heat rushed to her face. "Yes." No sense dissimulating. Of course she knew.

"And if you don't stop 'my lord' and 'sir'ing me, I'll have you sent home forthwith. When we're alone, it's still Marcus."

What had happened to him? Marcus had slowly moved away from her, gone from a childhood friend to a dignified, proper aristocrat. She understood the move, because he would have responsibilities to take care of, but sometimes she missed him. He'd remained a distant figure ever since, growing more pompous every time she saw him. Now he seemed to have cast all that off.

"I thought—that's not right."

Sighing, he shook his head. "And I've stopped you playing. A pity—I was enjoying that. Carry on."

"Is that an order—sir?"

He growled deep in his throat, such a small sound she'd have missed it if he were not sitting so close to her. "Stop it. I'll be Malton in about an hour." He pinched the bridge of his nose. "I've spent the last three days in a closed carriage with my father, and I want to forget the stateliness. He would, given the chance. But with outriders and men riding ahead to warn innkeepers we were on our way, we had little chance."

"So they commit the great crime of ensuring the best bedrooms are free. The cook is bursting from his waistcoat, trying to cook the best meal he's capable of making. If only my journeys were so tedious!"

His laugh rang around the room. "Exactly. But we're welcomed with 'Good evening, my lord,' and 'How can I serve you, my lord?'"

"You poor thing." She should guard her tongue, but she delighted in reacquainting herself with the man she used to know.

He rewarded her with another laugh. "I know. It's such a hardship." Lifting his feet, he spun around on the bench so he faced the keyboard, as she did. "You got a phrase wrong. The tune is based on the traditional one, but it's varied in the last line of each verse. Slightly different each time. Like this."

When he demonstrated, Viola understood exactly what he meant. But with the amusement, her heart ached. She had missed him so much. At the delicate age of nine, two years after his breeching, Marcus had begun his training, and since then, he'd become engrossed in his life's work. Before then, the laughing boy had had no cares, and they'd played together.

Until someone remembered their different stations in life, and she did not think it was Marcus.

"Your turn."

After giving him a doubtful glance, she copied the phrase. He sang the verse along with her, his baritone blending with her untrained mezzo. At the end of the verse they continued with the next one. Then he added one she hadn't known about.

By the end of the song, she was quite in charity with him. The years slipped away. Or rather, they did not, because never at any time did she forget that a man sat next to her, not a boy.

Viola hadn't been this close to Marcus for years. In this lovely room, with sunshine streaming in through the windows, they could be in another world—one of their own, a place out of time.

Playing scurrilous songs on a valuable string instrument seemed part of their world. Eventually she joined with him as his infectious laughter rang around the room.

"Do you remember this?" She played a few notes. A two-handed exercise taught to children to help them accustom themselves to the keyboard.

"Ha, yes I do."

He joined in, taking the upper part of the tune. It was simple but capable of infinite variations. At the end of the piece she changed the pitch and they continued. Four times they went around, until she stopped with an emphatic chord.

She rested her palms on the edge of the harpsichord. "This was tuned last week. I was only supposed to check it, not play it until it's out of tune again."

"Do harpsichords lose their tuning so easily?"

He really didn't know? "It's a harpsichord. The strings are delicate. Even damp can send them completely wrong. Each quill has to be checked and replaced if necessary. Don't you know anything?"

He shrugged. "I know how to address a duchess and how to dance a minuet. I can shoot straight and use a sword."

"So can I. The last part."

He widened his eyes. Such a perfect shade of blue they were. She hadn't seen them this close for years. Far too long. "You can fence and shoot?" he said, his voice rising.

"I shoot better than I fence, but I know one end of a sword from the other. I know how to stop someone taking it off me." Considering her position, her father had considered the training useful. The daughter of a land steward, especially an only child, needed to know how to take care of herself.

"I will certainly test you on that." He patted his hip. "But I don't generally travel with a sword at my side. We have them in the carriage, though. Shall I send for them?"

She bestowed a jaded smile on him. "No. Or fetch them yourself, come to that."

His cheek indented slightly, as if he were biting it inside. Stopping laughter? Then she was a source of ridicule? No, he wouldn't do that, not the Marcus she'd known.

But she had not known him for years. Only seen him at a distance and occasionally exchanged polite nothings.

He shook his head as his smile faded. "Why did we not tell my tutors to go to the devil, Viola? What harm did our friendship do?"

"They were teaching you to be an earl, and eventually a marquess."

"Ah yes. That. But you continued to play with my brothers and sisters."

She lifted one shoulder. "I hardly missed you at all."

That was a lie. She had missed him very much. His way of talking, the way he would say what he was thinking without hesitation—but he would hardly do that any longer. People hung on his every word, at least some people did. The people wanting the ear of his father, or for Marcus to do them a favor.

"I missed you," he said softly. "I would like us to be friends again, as we used to be." He covered her hand with his own.

Startled, she stared at it, but she didn't move. His warmth seeped through her, heating more than her fingers. He'd been her childhood sweetheart, but they had both known they were only playing.

He did not mean it in that way. Occasionally she'd allowed herself to dream of him, but never allowed her fantasies to creep through to real life.

Marcus had grown up tall and handsome, and unlike most men she knew, he wore his own hair tied back in a simple queue. He rarely powdered, his one concession to his wishes rather than the dictates of fashion, but he would consent to wear a wig on ceremonial occasions.

The first time she'd seen him dressed for a grand occasion had served to distance him completely from her. Without those glossy dark brown locks, and dressed in the finest London could provide, Marcus appeared a different person, one Viola didn't know at all. So when he said he missed her, he probably meant the carefree days of his childhood.

Viola could not pass this opportunity by. She turned her hand and curled her fingers between his. He clasped her hand warmly.

She stared at that symbol of friendship, as if it weren't her hand. "I missed you, too."

"You've grown up a beauty, Viola," he said softly.

She shook her head vigorously. "No. I'm ordinary. You're—" She cut off her words, fearing she would give away more than she meant to.

"Your hair is darker than mine, and it shines like a raven's wing. Your eyes are fathoms deep."

His words made her laugh, but that was to prevent her heart cracking. Once she'd dreamed of a man saying such things to her. But now she knew better. She would never hear that in love. Friendship would have to serve. "My face is too narrow, and I'm too tall."

"You are only too tall for short men," he said. "I'll show you. Stand up."

His voice did not ring with command, as she knew it could. Nevertheless, she pushed against the floor and got to her feet, rounding the end of the stool to avoid stumbling. She wanted to put something between them, because her emotions rose until she was barely able to keep her features still.

Their hands were still linked. "Satisfied?" She made to pull her hand away, but he only gripped it more firmly.

"Not nearly." He stood too, and then stepped over the bench so they were close.

Far too close. In his simple traveling clothes he had the appearance of a gentleman rather than a great lord, but that did not fool her for a minute. She could not think that way. Must not, if she wanted to keep her peace of mind. This close, closer than he'd been for years, he devastated her senses.

"See?" he said brightly. "You come up to my shoulder. Far too few ladies do that."

"It makes me stand out too much," she grumbled. She was not freakishly tall, though. Lanky Annie, the woman in the village who took in sewing from the hall, she was oddly tall. Six feet, her father said.

"Not at all. It makes you graceful." He touched her chin, tilting her head up.

This close, the little black pinpricks of beard under his skin were apparent. The way his eyes shaded darker at the edge, to the brilliant shade inside. She stared in wonder, reacquainting herself with him this close.

Something else sparked in his eyes, passion and heat, passing from him to her and back again.

"A kiss of friendship, Viola," he murmured, and suited words to actions.

Viola lifted her hands, grasping for purchase, and found his coat. She clutched it gratefully as her world spun, realigning into a new space.

When he touched her lips with his tongue she opened for him, and he tasted her. Delicately at first, licking softly, like a cat at milk, but then stronger, he entered her mouth with a mastery that made her helpless under his onslaught.

Nobody had ever kissed her like this.

She had thought he meant a kiss of friendship, a sweet salute, but this was so different as to be from a different place. He hungrily pressed his mouth to hers, and she responded in a way that came instinctively to her.

He held her in the circle of his arms, her breasts pressed against his chest. Although layers of cloth and whalebone lay between them, she felt the heat of his body. His closeness overwhelmed her, heated her from head to toe. He made those secret, private nooks and crannies of her body tingle with new awareness.

Was this, then, what Mr. Ridley had meant at the New Year's dance when he'd told Viola that she excited him? She'd barely escaped his clumsy caresses, whereas she had gone willingly to Marcus, eager to learn whatever he wanted to teach her.

Danger!

Her mind whispered the word, and then it grew louder. Recklessness took her soul, the same kind of heedless joy as when she kicked her horse into a gallop or danced in a field at midnight, barefoot and all on her own. When she dared fate to do what it would.

She dared it now. Nobody could stop her.

Marcus led her through the blending of not only their mouths, but a forbidden closeness. She yearned for more, even as he gave it to her, and deepened their kiss. He spread his hands wide over her back, encompassing her.

A sound from the room next door pierced her senses, reminding her they were not alone. These rooms were the public rooms, for heaven's sake!

She jerked away, breaking the kiss with a clumsy unsealing of their mouths.

Her breasts heaved as if she'd run around the house ten times, breath sawing in and out of her. Tentatively, Viola touched her lips. They felt tender, swollen, and hot.

Marcus stood completely still and watched her, his eyes wide and dark, his hair disheveled. Dimly she recalled thrusting her fingers into the silky mass, holding him to her.

He said the one word bound to push her away. "Wanton."

Indignation swamped her arousal. "Me? What are you talking about?" How dare he speak to her like this?

"The way you attacked me."

Had she? Honestly she couldn't be sure, but his response to her was anything but reluctant. "So you're the poor, helpless victim. Is that what you're telling me?" She curled her lip. "Truly?"

"How else would you explain it? Who have you been practicing with?"

* * * *

Marcus heard his words as they left his mouth. Tendrils of jealousy curled their green fronds within him. She kissed as if she'd done it many times before, so if not with him, then who?

She tasted sweet, and the moment he acquainted himself with her taste, he realized once was not enough. He could stand here, in this gleaming polished room and kiss her all day.

A movement gave him pause, and he glimpsed his reflection in the large pier-glass hung between the two big windows. She had turned him into a lover, although he had never thought of Viola in that way before.

Liar. Of course he had. He'd carefully kept his distance until the way they behaved with each other had changed. She'd left his life when he'd left the nursery. But he'd seen her at a distance, watched her grow into the lovely woman standing before him now, her breasts swollen under the clean but no longer neat fichu tucked into her bodice.

In another moment that fichu would not have been tucked into anything. Need to the point of agony had come to life inside him, roaring for its release. He'd have had her across that bench on the silk-tufted carpet. Hell, on the gravel path outside if someone had not moved next door.

He'd heard it too, the telltale shift of furniture, reminding them where they were and what they were doing.

What had started as a kiss of friendship, of re-acquaintance, had served to push them apart again. Because as sure as Styx rowed the dead to Hades, he could not come anywhere near her again. She was temptation personified, a reminder of what he wished for when he awoke alone in the middle of the night in his luxurious bed in Mayfair. A symbol of everything he could not have and should not want.

What was that woman's name, the one he'd danced the quadrille with a week ago at Lady Costigan's ball? Ah, yes, Lady Myra Smedley. His mother had introduced them. On paper Lady Myra was his perfect match, a woman of taste, refinement, and no passionate emotions. Just the kind of wife he needed. Not a wanton like this one. And unlike many of his compatriots, he did not intend to cuckold his wife before the sheets on the marriage bed had cooled.

He could not afford to get close to Viola again. She was dangerous to him, and what he wanted to do with her was dangerous to her. He would take what steps he could to get her to stay away. Unfair accusations should do it. He curled his lip into a sneer. "Have you been practicing on the nearest ploughman, Viola?" No, of course she had not. Her kiss had been tentative, unpracticed, and utterly delicious.

He would not debauch the daughter of the estate manager. Such behavior was below them both.

"No!"

"While I'm here," he said, keeping his voice low for fear it would shake, "Do not approach me. Spend as little time in my company as possible. I don't know where you learned those tricks, but you will not use them on me." Clearly he could not trust himself around her. The discovery made his head spin.

A woman of sense would have gathered her skirts, held her head high, and walked out of the room, keeping her dignity intact. Not Viola. He might have known she'd retaliate. She was always a spitfire.

Instead of retreating, she advanced. "How could you say those things, Marcus? My first kiss—my first grown-up kiss—and you think I've been doing it with every footman and farmer who comes my way?" She waved her hand. "Do you really think I would do that with anyone? How do you imagine I could do that? Oh, wait, because you do it?" Her eyes sparked fire. "Do you kiss every half-decent woman you come across? Does it lead to more? I heard you had a good reputation, but you just put the lie to that, did you not? Perhaps you keep your affairs to yourself, unlike your brother Val!"

Marcus gritted his teeth. How dare she compare him to Valentinian, who chased anything in a skirt and then lost interest the next day? "How else do you explain…?" Lost for words, he gestured. "You, me, the way you know what to do?"

Her first kiss? He'd given her her first kiss? Deep down, the knowledge staggered him. Surely she could not have reached the age she was—mid-twenties? Yes, she must be that—without kissing someone. Not fond kisses, friendly kisses, but passionate ones? How had the local gentry kept their hands off her?

He spun around and headed for the door to the library. "Remember what I said. Do not come near me again!"

A dry, "Yes, my lord," followed in his wake.

He didn't regain his senses until he'd arrived at the relative privacy of his chambers. Dismissing his valet with a request for coffee, he strode to and fro, eating up the floor and carpet with his restless walking.

He was a fool. The sight of her pinched white features as he left told him that. She'd retaliated, and so she should after he'd hurled so many insults at her. How could he have destroyed their tentative friendship that way? Kissing her, proving his lack of self-discipline. Of all things he was proud of, his self-control came first.

He was afraid. No, not afraid. He had nothing to be afraid of. Her sweet, innocent kiss had taunted him with the things he could not have, the foolish boyhood dreams he'd put aside. Love, happiness, and friendship were all tainted by his position. His damned responsibility.

He drove his fingers through his hair, dislodging the velvet ribbon tied neatly at his nape. "What is wrong with me?" he moaned aloud, but it didn't sound any better in words than it had in his head.

Marcus was born to a position most people would give their eye teeth for. It involved nothing he could not do and no life-threatening duties. As a soldier, his cousin Antoninus had stared death in the eye. Marcus would do no such thing. Instead he'd be master of great estates, have the attention of the greatest men in the land, and control the country. Why would that fill him with terror in the dead of night when he couldn't sleep?

When his valet returned, the well-trained man didn't blink at his master's restlessness. Instead he put down the tray with the coffee, picked up the ribbon, and stood by the dressing table, ready to apply a fresh one when Marcus was ready.

Viola had given him a vision of freedom he had no right to expect or even consider. He owed her an apology, but he did not know how to deliver it without putting both of them in peril.

He must regain control of the emotion that had broken free when his mouth had touched hers. Viola deserved better than what he could give her.

* * * *

How much better Marcus had not realized until his father called him into the meeting with Gates later that afternoon. Expecting to discuss estate business, he went down to the estate office to discover his father and the estate manager sitting at the large circular rent table. But none of the usual account books and bills littered the table. Only a few papers.

"Close the door, Marcus. Come and sit."

Marcus did as his father bade him. Lord Strenshall pushed the papers across to him. Marcus perused them in silence and then closed his eyes.

He'd seen similar documents before—copies of a marriage certificate, a birth certificate and a letter written in Italian. He did not need to know the language to know what it said. He'd seen one of those before, too.

The birth certificate was for a baby girl, born in Rome in 1729 to a woman named Maria Rubio and a father named as James Francis Edward Stuart. The marriage certificate was dated 1719, wherein it stated James Francis Edward Stuart and Maria Rubio were man and wife. The letter was from Maria Rubio, certifying the accompanying documents were genuine and asking the bearer to care for the baby girl.

Maria Rubio had married James Stuart, otherwise known as the Old Pretender, and borne him God knew how many children.

"It's Viola," his father said. "We've kept the secret since she was born, but we have to do something about it now."

Marcus didn't want to believe what he was seeing. "No. It's not true."

"It is," his father said quietly.

"Why didn't you tell me?" He knew as much about the affair as his father. At least he'd thought so.

"Because the fewer people who knew, the better," the marquess replied. "Until recent developments, we thought the marriage certificate at least was false. But now we know it is not." That discovery had brought the children into danger. It made the Young Pretender, Charles Stuart, and his brother, Henry, bastards, and it gave remaining Jacobites a new cause.

Marcus and his relatives had discovered two children so far and a bastard girl, the product of another of the Old Pretender's liaisons. Viola made three legitimate children.

"Does she know?" he demanded.

Gates grimaced. "She discovered the papers, but she believes it's a fanciful legend. Indeed, until recently we considered the marriage part to be false. The rest?" He shrugged. "Kings and pretenders have bastards."

Marcus dropped the certificate as if it were steeped in poison and addressed his father. "So that's why you wanted to rush here."

The marquess nodded. "I needed to tell Gates of recent developments and get his permission to tell you. His accident was a good excuse. We need to keep Viola safe. That is why I elected not to tell anyone of this. I still believe secrecy is our best defense."

"But what about Viola? Doesn't she have a right to know?"

"Why, when it would only upset her?"

Marcus needed to talk to his cousin Julius, who knew much more about this affair than he did. But every sense went against him leaving Viola here in the country, unsuspecting. Enemies were gathering on the horizon, and with the current state of affairs in London, very little would urge the more hotheaded amongst them to action. "Viola is a grown woman," he insisted. "She should know."

Her father shook his head. Or her foster-father, more like. But as her guardian, he had more rights than Julius to say how his daughter should be treated. Marcus hated that, but he could not go behind Gates's back and tell her. He'd try to persuade the estate manager his daughter should know.

"We will continue as normal," Gates said now. "Behave as if nothing has changed. Because if people are watching and they see unusual activity, the game will be up."

At least Marcus could agree with that decision.

Chapter 3

"His lordship wants us to come to dinner," Viola's father said the next day.

"Why?" Viola demanded.

"The usual reasons." Her father smiled at her mildly. "To catch up on local gossip, to ascertain that I'm recovering properly, to speak about the weather, I have no doubt. The day after, he will have me conveyed to the offices, and we will spend the day closeted with Lord Malton, going through the accounts. Quarter day is not far off."

"Quarter day is never far off." With four a year, the seasons tended to be marked by the quarter days. Rent days, the days when magistrates were busy, and country life coalesced into a mild climax. Then on to the next one. The process was comfortable, never-ending and reassuring. Only the seasons were different. Now they headed into summer, and after that came the frantic activity of harvest. But first, mellow days when plants were tender.

Mr. Gates shook out his paper, which the marquess had sent over once he'd done with it. She should see to ordering one for her father while the marquess was in residence, but cancelling it could be more trouble than it was worth. Making an order was always easier than cancelling.

Fear rose in her throat. She had not seen Marcus since he'd told her to get out of his sight. In fact, whenever she'd heard his voice or sensed his presence, she turned around and went the other way. She would not face such humiliation again willingly. He was the lord. He could do as he pleased, but he could not have her.

They had guests due today at the house, local visitors—another reason for her not to venture forth. Many of the local residents knew her well. The village held two houses of reasonable size, and a little farther off, Scarborough and York held people who knew them. Once the marquess and his son had let people know they were in residence, the local gentry had sent in their cards. The marquess had announced an open day.

"While you were out this afternoon, the marquess sent a note. He wants you to act as hostess for a few days," her father said. He gazed over his spectacles at her, his brows drawn together in a frown.

Her immediate reaction was, "No," but she should have known better.

"I accepted on your behalf," he continued, as if she hadn't spoken. "What else could I do?"

"I cannot." Frantically she searched for an excuse and came up empty. As well born as many of the gentry hereabouts, she had acted as the marquess's hostess before, when the marchioness had been absent. Ladies could not visit gentlemen on their own, even to accompany their husbands, so her presence was necessary. Her status as distant relative made Viola the most eligible.

"Yes, you can. And you will." Her father picked up his cane from its perch at the side of his chair. "Viola, what has happened? You came back from the house the day before yesterday in an agitated state. Has something occurred?"

She had not realized he'd noticed. Nothing of note had happened, after all. Only her first kiss from a man she should never consider as anything but her father's employer. "No. I was merely surprised to see Marcus again. Lord Malton," she corrected herself. Too late. Her father would have noticed that slip. "We spoke, but Papa, he was insufferable!" She could tell him part of the truth, at least. "Arrogant and behaving as if my only reason for being present was because he was there."

"Did he touch you?" Her father's voice turned hard.

"No." She hated lying, but she could do nothing else. She rushed on. "But the thought of pandering to him, after— We were friends, Papa!"

Marcus had faced her, white-faced, drawing his cloak of arrogance around him to accuse her of monstrous injustices. He had the right, as her father's employer, to treat her that way, but not as the friend of her childhood.

That was the truth. She had lost her friend. Even though they had grown apart, she'd always known she could turn to him if she needed help. But now—no. She wouldn't turn to him if he were the last man on earth.

"You will do your duty, daughter."

When her father spoke in that tone of voice, she could not argue with him.

Viola curtseyed and said, "Yes Papa," in as obedient a voice as she could muster.

* * * *

Despite the sunny weather, Viola set out at ten for the hall the next day with a heavy heart. She was to preside over afternoon visits and a dinner.

She took a dinner gown packed in a bandbox, as well as her best wine-red day gown. She had few gowns that were presentable to company, but what she had served her well. Her father would have bought her more, but she couldn't see the point. She spent most of her days in more practical clothes in fabrics she could have laundered.

For all her stout declarations, she had to admit silk felt better against her skin in this hot weather.

As she rounded the side of the house, a sound made itself apparent—a horse being walked, the clop of its hooves melting into the sounds of an English summer day. Birds chirruped, and the breeze made the trees and bushes rustle as if they were gossiping. About her, no doubt.

Why had the marchioness not accompanied her husband? Was London so fascinating she could not tear herself away?

Tranmere was on duty again. He touched his finger to his powdered wig as she entered. His face was gleaming and flushed.

"You look hot," she said.

"I'm fine, ma'am," the footman said, obviously on his best behavior. What a shame he could not doff his coat and wig, but he was in full blue-and-silver today.

She passed on, climbing the stone steps, the iron rail cool to her touch. Today she adopted a sedate walk and set a polite half-smile in place on her face. She would go through the day by rote and try not to think about anything. Or anyone, come to that.

They would open the Blue Saloon. It was not one of the state rooms, but a cheerful, sunny drawing room on the east side of the house that caught the morning sun. Mrs. Lancaster usually kept the curtains closed for fear the carpets and furniture should fade, but today the sun blazed through the sparkling windows.

The marquess was already sitting there, his legs crossed over the knee, a newspaper in his hand, and his spectacles perched on his nose. At her entrance, he rose and smiled at her. "You are looking in good heart today, Viola. You did not linger when we arrived, so I could not greet you. You are well?"

She dropped a curtsey. "Yes, my lord, I'm in good health."

"Unlike your poor father."

"He is immensely gratified by your visit, sir."

The marquess cleared his throat. "Yes, well, I could not leave him to handle matters. The message we received in London merely said he had suffered a fall from his horse and he'd taken to his bed. At first I thought him at death's door. It was a relief to find he was not."

His lordship was as tall as his sons and easily controlled his boisterous and numerous family members, although they would have daunted a lesser man. Dressed fashionably in a green coat and waistcoat, his garb was nonetheless appropriate for the country. "I appreciate you stepping in today," he said affably. "Since your father is about as far from his last breath as I am, I plan to return to London on Thursday." The day after tomorrow.

She tried not to allow her sigh of relief to disturb her too much. That meant Marcus would go too, and with matters between them, it was better so. "We were very pleased to see you, sir."

"And we are working on a few matters. In a way, your father's enforced rest will help. The books need checking before quarter day. I don't know if I will be here for that. There are matters in town clamoring for my attention." He motioned the chair opposite his. "Please take a seat. Do you wish for tea?"

"No, sir, I had sufficient before I left home."

He nodded. "Very well." Being a man of impeccable manners, he waited until she had sat and disposed her skirts before he retook his seat. He plucked his glasses off his nose and placed them on the table by his side.

The door opened. Marcus appeared. He wore riding-dress, but a lady leaned on each of his crooked arms and two gentlemen walked behind.

They were early. The Stewarts lived closest, barely five miles from the Haxby estate. The marquess and Viola rose and made their greetings. Viola rang the bell for tea and received a sharp look from Lady Stewart. Her husband, a baronet, made Viola well aware of her position in local society. When the marquess and his family were not in residence, they led local society.

Sir Henry Stewart had a certain solidity about him the marquess lacked, although the two men were equal in age. His wig sprinkled fresh powder on the shoulders of his velvet coat. The ladies also wore their hair powdered. While that was a valid choice, Viola disliked the fuss of having her hair done that way and frequently avoided it, as she had today. His lady was as thin as he was not, and Viola was hard put not to mouth their nicknames—Jack Spratt and his wife, only in reverse.

Fortunately, she refrained, but in the tedium of settling them and attending to the tea, she caught Marcus's direct gaze. She flinched, an instinctive reaction she could not stop. Fortunately nobody saw the tell-tale twitch and her sharp intake of breath.

He was staring at her. Snared by him, she could not look away. She could not read what he was silently telling her, but at least he did not appear hostile. Still, her senses went on alert. In her imagination, she felt his lips on hers, his hands on her back. This time her shiver was not one of revulsion.

She hated herself. Why, especially after his unspeakable behavior to her, could she not resist his gaze and force herself to be indifferent in his presence?

A thought struck her. The marquess had said developments. Did that include Marcus? Did he know her darkest secret?

Surely not. Lord Strenshall had always told her he would inform her if he found it necessary to tell another person. Not even his wife knew, because she'd asked him not to tell anyone. He would not have betrayed her with Marcus, surely?

When the maids came in with tea and all the accoutrements—the china dishes, the deep saucers, plates of bread and butter and other delicacies—Viola busied herself helping them. She tried not to worry about Marcus and what he did or did not know. She handed around tea and offered tidbits on the delicate plates that were part of the Dresden set Lady Strenshall had received as a wedding present.

When she met the eyes of the younger lady, Miss Emma Stewart, the woman looked away immediately. Her attention skittered from Viola to Marcus who sat next to her on the sofa. Marcus's lips thinned, but Miss continued with her artless chatter.

She had just cut Viola, treated her as a servant. Her brief word of thanks was no less than a servant deserved, and certainly no more. Did she resent Viola, or more likely, viewed her of little importance?

Viola's ire rose, but that smile she'd fixed on her face remained firmly in place, if a little harder at the edges. When she would have returned to her seat, she discovered her ladyship had taken her place next to the marquess. She glanced at Lord Strenshall, who raised a brow but said nothing.

Viola found somewhere else, a seat near a young sprig and Sir Henry's heir, Mr. Jeremy Stewart—a likely youth, just returned from Oxford, only a few years younger than Viola. With none of the attitude of his sister, he engaged her in chatter about the city of Oxford. She found his talk restful, even though his boyish enthusiasm, when he swept his arm wide to express a point, nearly cost Lord Strenshall one of his precious tea dishes.

This being an informal visit, they could stay longer than the prescribed half hour. Soon Lord Strenshall bore Sir Henry off to his study to discuss business matters. That included a land dispute they hoped to settle without the help of the courts.

When Marcus suggested a visit to the gardens at the back of the house, the others agreed.

"It is too lovely to be cooped up indoors," Viola said. She received a response from Lady Stewart that she would have said was less than friendly.

"Indeed, Miss Gates, you are often abroad, are you not? It is surprising you are not brown as a nut from your outdoor excursions."

True, she spent much time outdoors at this time of year, but Viola always took care to wear her gloves and hat. At least, when people were watching. "It would be wrong to suggest that I don't care what color my complexion is, would it not?" she said sweetly. "So I won't."

A snort told her that Mr. Stewart had caught her remark. "I've never noticed your complexion any other but clear and healthy," he said. "But I'm afraid I rarely look further than a lady's address and figure."

That was nicely said. Marcus remained silent, but she felt his temper as if it were her own.

After a necessary respite while they donned outer gear, they met again on the south terrace. The gardens sloped before them, and by mutual consent, they headed for the rose garden. "It is at its best," Viola said. "Lady Strenshall was considering sending for a yellow rose."

"I did not think there was such a thing," Lady Stewart said. "Is it not a legend? The fabled yellow rose?"

"I have seen them," Marcus said, "in London. But it is true. They are passing rare." He glanced at Viola, who was tying her hat ribbon. "Precious."

"I have never seen one," she said briskly. "But I have never seen a giraffe either, although I know they exist."

"I shall ensure you see one," Marcus told her.

What was he doing? He had said he never wanted to see her again. She could not believe his cordiality was due to anything other than common politeness. As soon as the guests had left, he would probably disappear.

Miss Stewart pouted and put her gloved hand on Marcus's sleeve. "Will you not show me the maze?"

Where they could get conveniently lost. Her mother shot her a warning glance. "I doubt the maze is ready to receive visitors."

"The gardeners need to clip the hedges," Marcus said smoothly. "Else the overgrown twigs would tear your charming gown to pieces."

Miss Stewart indeed wore a fetching gown of pale pink silk with rosebuds embroidered in relief rioting around the hem—not entirely practical for outdoor walking, but undoubtedly becoming to her porcelain complexion. She must sleep with lemon juice on her face to achieve that effect.

Viola castigated herself for her acidity. Why should she care if Miss Stewart was intent on flirting? It was none of her business. She should be glad, because it took Marcus's attention from her.

She walked behind them, her hand on Mr. Stewart's arm, conversing comfortably on the subject of roses. "My father loves the blooms. Our small garden has a number of bushes."

"You live on the estate, do you not?"

"Yes," she said, for they did not advertise the presence of the Scarborough house. Her father regarded it as a retreat and a safeguard against his old age. If the marquess should take against him, they would not find themselves sleeping in a ditch, he said. "The house is charming, perfect for my father and me."

Miss Stewart's voice floated back to them, her piercingly crisp accent sending sparks flying. "I should hate to live as someone's pensioner. However, I can understand people who do. It must be so convenient, living on the estate. Mr. Gates has hardly any distance to go to work."

"Since he has the managing of all his lordship's estates," Viola replied, doing her best to keep her tone level and reasonable, "he sometimes has to travel a great deal. His lordship has extensive holdings."

Miss Stewart turned her lovely face up to Marcus. "Have you seen them all?"

"I believe so. The larger ones, certainly, and most of the smaller holdings. There is a small estate in Devonshire I'm particularly fond of."

"Oh, but there's nowhere as lovely as Yorkshire!" Miss Stewart exclaimed.

Marcus flashed a grin. "Spoken like a true Yorkshirewoman."

The gravel path was doing no favors to Miss Stewart's skirt. Her maid would curse when she saw the increasingly ragged hem and the rosebuds that had picked up tiny stones. Not that Miss Stewart appeared to notice. A lady did not deign to pay attention to such trivial matters. Viola couldn't help thinking of the poor seamstress who'd worked through night and day to produce the pretty effect.

They turned off on to a harder packed gravel path to stroll between the roses. Lady Stewart, leading them, paused to sniff a pink rose. She made a charming picture, the cream color of her gown setting off the velvety petals. Her fingers cupped the bloom gracefully. She stood and cast a smiling glance at her daughter, and Viola realized the mother had just demonstrated a lesson to her daughter. The older lady's gaze passed on to Viola and hardened a fraction, although Viola retained her smiling mien. Her jaw was beginning to ache.

The scent of the roses wove around her, soothing her. She had always enjoyed their perfume. The warm day, the roses, and the lush grass all worked their magic on her. A dreamy sense of wellbeing filled her as they slowly strolled around the lovely garden. She strove to keep their little garden pretty and neat, but it did not have the magic that this one always evoked in her. She loved to sit on the bench against the old stone wall at the side of the house with a book. A house cat would often join her and wash itself before stretching out to bask. She'd do that tomorrow, when Marcus and his father had gone. That would give her something to look forward to.

Not that the prospect of him leaving filled her with anything but resignation. He would return in a month, in any case, with a houseful of guests for the shooting season. She would see him then, unless she could devise an absence. She was not without friends. Perhaps she could go to Harrogate and do a little shopping or visit her aunt Charlotte in York. That would keep her out of his way.

After what she was now categorizing as The Kiss, she could not look at Marcus without recalling how she felt in his arms. He'd controlled their embrace so well without overwhelming her. She badly wanted to try it again, but she would not. As he'd said, they'd had an aberration and nearly lost what friendship they still had.

Rather than watch him with society ladies and his friends, she'd take herself off.

Mr. Stewart held her arm rather firmly. When she made to follow the others along another path, he led her in the opposite direction. No harm in that, so long as they kept the others in sight. "Miss Gates, I am so glad to see you again," he said as they walked. "I trust I may bespeak a dance with you at the next assembly."

"If I attend, I would be delighted, thank you." Assemblies were held once a month in York and in Scarborough. The assembly rooms in York were housed in a particularly fine building. That was her excuse. She could visit her aunt and attend an assembly. "I was thinking of going in August."

"During the house party?" He sounded scandalized, his voice rising in tone and pitch.

"It has little to do with me. I am only hostess here today because nobody else may serve."

"But you are a relative of his lordship?"

She waved her hand. "Only distantly. The connection is hardly worth mentioning."

"I don't believe that." He was holding her very firmly now and rather alarmingly leading her toward the maze. Ostensibly built to afford people a chance to exercise without going too far from the house, it had become a trysting place for the younger members of any gathering here. It had formed the backdrop to not a few downfalls of young maids. Lady Strenshall had more than once demanded it razed to the ground. Perhaps that was behind her desire to remodel the gardens. The work would give her a chance to rid herself of the hated maze.

Hedges rose higher than her head, the box-trees so dense she could not see through them. Too private. But Mr. Stewart was a boy, barely capable of overcoming her.

Once inside and a few paths in, he turned and backed her against a hedge. Her spirits sank. She had no mind to upset his lordship's guests. But if she had to, she knew how to bring her knee up and depress a few pretensions.

"You should not allow my sister to speak to you in that way," he said.

She liked him for that. "She is a guest, and young besides."

"So are you, but you never traduce anyone."

She smiled. "Not within their hearing, at any rate."

His smile broadened. He was a good-looking man. In a few years he'd be a heartbreaker. "So we're to dance. What if I want more?"

"You will have to want." Her heart beat faster. He was becoming too bold. If he tried to kiss her, how would she deter him without offending him? "Sir, we should be seeking your mother."

"We will, in a moment. You know my sister means to have the earl?"

Viola tried not to laugh. "Why does she think she will succeed when so many have failed? The whole of eligible London seeks his hand."

"She means to trap him before that time."

She would not tell him Marcus was leaving the next day. Otherwise he might tell his sister, and then she might do something foolish, like try to entrap him. Marcus would be adept at avoiding his fate.

That made their kiss even more inexplicable. Why would he kiss her alone in a room where they could be interrupted at any minute? What had pushed him to take that step? Not hard for her, because she had wanted to kiss him for a long time. But him? She doubted he thought of her from one end of the year to the next. Not half as much as she thought of him.

If she hadn't had on her full armor of gown, stays, and petticoat, the hedge would be pricking her back. Mr. Stewart was pressing too hard. "We should really return." Ah, now she understood what was going on. "You're helping your sister now, are you not?"

His smile turned wry. "I'm afraid so. She bribed me with five guineas and time alone with you. You're worth more than the guineas."

"I should hope so." If she tried to leave, she'd have to get past his body. He really had grown since she'd seen him last. Should she risk getting close to a man twice in two days? This time with none of the eagerness she'd experienced with Marcus.

As if she'd summoned him, his voice drifted over the hedge. "Miss Gates?"

"Here!" she called out before Mr. Stewart could prevent her. "We are trapped in the maze!" It seemed like the most expedient explanation, although she knew the place better than she knew her own bedroom. Oh, no, why did she have to think of bedrooms?

"If you follow my voice, you will find your way out. It's really not difficult." He continued to talk, probably because that assured them that he was doing nothing he should not. And so that Miss Stewart could not claim anything of the kind.

Within five minutes, including a detour she took for appearance's sake, she'd left the maze. Miss Stewart had her hand on Marcus's arm, but he appeared unharmed, positively cheerful.

Miss Stewart glared at her. "You are quite disheveled, Miss Gates."

Viola plucked a twig from her hair. "So I am. When we return to the house you must excuse me while I right my appearance." And change into a gown more suited to dinner, although she would not say that. She stuck her chin in the air and walked past them. "Thank you for rescuing me, my lord."

"Think nothing of it," he said, humor coloring his voice.

He must know she needed no rescuing from the maze. She had rescued him just as much.

Chapter 4

The other dinner guests had arrived by the time they returned to the house. Excusing herself, Viola raced upstairs and into the red bedroom, the one she usually used when she visited here. Once the room had been a grand showplace. Now the lovely silk on the walls hung in shreds, the floor was bare, and the paintings had gone from the wall. It was even emptier than usual, only the bed remaining. The marquess must have decided to deal with the room at last. Viola would have to find another room to use in future.

Tranmere had brought up her bag. Viola wasted no time shrugging out of her red gown and shaking out the yellow silk she used for dinners. A modest gown worn over a small hoop, it was nevertheless a reliable one, its cheerful color making up for its deficiencies in other departments.

Hastily she pinned the lace ruffles to her sleeves and shook her petticoat. She was about to push her arms through the sleeves of the gown when a tap came on the door. "Come in!" A maid would be useful. She could help pin the gown to her stays.

But it wasn't a maid.

Viola shrieked, then clapped her hand over her mouth.

"Maidenly modesty?" Marcus said, strolling into the room. "I never would have thought that of you, Viola."

"You're doing it again!" She clutched the gown to her chest.

"What?"

"If they caught us, you'd be compromised. I'm a lady, you know. Kind of."

He smiled. "Kind of?" He advanced on her. "Ladies don't compromise gentlemen."

"And gentlemen don't compromise ladies!" She was still angry with him for his behavior in the music room. "What are you doing here?"

He lost the smile. "I came to apologize."

"What for?" Not that he didn't owe her an apology, but she wanted specifics.

"For yesterday."

"For kissing me?"

He shook his head and a trace of the smile returned. "Not that. I can't regret that. But for what happened afterward. I should never have accused you of something that was my fault. I should not have come near you."

He spread his arms wide. He was in his shirtsleeves, and the pose gave her a view of the powerful muscles. That shade of intimacy sent a small shiver through her.

She gripped the yellow silk. She wouldn't admit she'd enjoyed it too. "You made me feel cheap. As if I were yours for the taking."

"Aren't you?" He clapped his hand to his forehead. "No, I didn't mean that, I swear it. I do apologize for everything. For the kiss if you need me to. Could we go back to the way we were before?"

No. "Barely knowing each other?"

He shook his head once more. "I want to be your friend, Viola. In truth—no, I can't say anything on that score. But what I said afterwards?" He placed his hand on his heart and bowed. "Please forgive me."

Of course she forgave him, although she wasn't quite ready to say so. "Why did you say it?"

He regarded her solemnly, dropped his chin, and sighed. "Because I was angry with myself. I want to remain your friend, Viola. You're a woman alone in the world except for your father, and you may need my help in the future. I want to be in a position to give it."

"My father is an extremely healthy man." Marcus was right, though. "He will live for years yet. By then I could be a matron with children of my own. Plump and content," she added because she wanted to see his reaction.

He didn't disappoint her. "You will continue to be lovely no matter what you do."

She let a smile curve her lips. "And I heard you were not a lady's man."

"I'm not, but I am a truthful man."

His words unnerved her. She could not afford to believe him. He was not for her, and such talk would only lead her down paths she should not even think about, much less dream about.

But those eyes, gazing into hers fearlessly, and his soft hair, worse since she had felt it for herself, were enough to push her mind to places she had never explored. The thought of touching those arms, sliding her hands over them, and more—was his chest as strong? Under the elaborate waistcoat did he have muscles to rival the ones on his arms?

Likely she'd never know.

She released her grip on her gown. She was perfectly well covered, after all.

As casually as she dared, she slipped one arm into the sleeve and dragged it up. "I need to finish dressing."

"I like what you have on now." He sounded half-strangled, as if he had something stuck in his throat. That was not true, but then she realized her action had pushed her breasts up in her stays. She was still decent, but barely. The stays fit her well; she'd had several new pairs made last year. The shoulder straps prevented them slipping, but her décolleté was extreme.

"Thank you. Marcus, you should not be here." Thus she broke her resolve to call him by his title. He should be "Malton" or "sir," but she found it so easy to call him by his given name.

"I know. I'll leave in a minute." He glanced around. "You can't be comfortable here."

"No." She followed his gaze and pushed her other arm through its corresponding sleeve. "It used to be better, but Mrs. Lancaster must have stripped it ready for its refurbishment."

"Ah, I see." His attention went to the big old-fashioned four-poster bed. "We'll find you somewhere better to use."

"This serves." She glanced to where she was used to seeing the dressing table. Of course it was gone, and the mirror that lived on top of it. "Ah." She would have to dress by guesswork. "The mirror's gone."

"You could use my room."

Her incredulous laugh rang around the bare walls. "You are joking, aren't you? Of course I cannot! But I would appreciate the use of a bedroom for a few moments so I can put my hair to rights. Just wait while I fasten the front."

She set to fastening the gown, hooking it together. Fastening the decorative ribbons over the top proved more difficult. She was used to accomplishing that task with the help of a mirror. She sighed. "Well, at least I'm decent."

"More than decent." He cleared his throat. "Do you have everything? Let's find another room you can use."

She cast a wistful glance back at the room. She liked it; it was at the end of the corridor with easy access to the side stairs. Convenient, when she'd helped with dirty work like cleaning the attics and she wanted to make herself clean for the walk home. However, she could not use it when it was so bare. He picked up the bag with her day clothes in it and held out his arm. "Let's hope nobody sees me in this state." Her hair was loose and tousled, and her bows done up any old how. She could not appear at dinner like this.

Unfortunately, as they strolled along the corridor, a door opened and Miss Stewart popped out as if she'd been in waiting for them. She glanced at them and blinked. "Why, my lord!"

"Indeed," Marcus said, at his most urbane. "Good evening, Miss Stewart."

She curtseyed. She must have brought a change of clothes too, as she wore a delightful white silk gown sprinkled with embroidered forget-me-nots. Her elbows sported double ruffles of finest Nottingham lace. Her hair was dressed up, a couple of curls left to tease and tickle the bare skin of her shoulder. "Shall we be seeing you downstairs, Miss Gates?" Her voice was frozen.

Emboldened by the man next to her, Viola smiled and agreed. "Indeed. I merely have to find a mirror."

Miss Stewart did not offer the one in her room. If she had any sense, she would have, and then she would have had Marcus to herself for a while.

With a nod to Miss Stewart, Marcus led Viola on.

Viola could have died of shame. But Marcus showed no reaction as he led her into a room at the end. This was furnished in a much more modern style, with little Chinese people going about their duties all over the walls.

The Chinese Room with its precious wallpaper was one of the best guest rooms in the house. "Oh, but I can't!"

Marcus raised a brow. "I fail to see why not. Feel free to enjoy it, Viola."

At least one of them appeared to have recovered his sang-froid. He released her and bowed. "I'll go and make myself decent. If I appear at dinner in my shirt sleeves, my father will have my blood."

Alone in the lovely room, Viola allowed herself a skip of glee. The mirror sat on top of a draped dressing table, its three leaves artfully angled to allow her to view herself from most angles. Retrieving her packet of pins, she secured her bodice and then put her bows in order. Now she had a mirror, she took but a few moments to brush out her hair. She twisted it and secured it into a bun at the back of her head. Once accomplished, she tilted her head on one side and studied herself.

She'd never make a London beauty, but she'd do. She touched the place where she could, if she wished, pull out strands of hair to make curls, as Miss Stewart had done. No, as Miss Stewart's maid had done.

Viola did not have a maid to adjust the lacings under the skirts of the gown that made for a perfect fit. But the gown would not disgrace her.

After popping her brush and the remainder of the hairpins in her bag, she made her way downstairs to the drawing room.

Dinner was unexceptional. The marquess had invited the prominent local gentry, most of whom Viola knew. They accepted her presence unquestioningly, but few treated her as an equal. More as one might treat a companion or a poor relative. The subtle distinction was not lost on Viola. These people might talk with her, the men dance with her at the local assemblies, but here she was most certainly the hired help.

But she refused to behave like one, to retreat and behave deferentially to everyone. Graciously she offered food. She sent the buttered potatoes, almost marble-small and tender, to the marquess at the other end of the table because he liked them.

He shot her a grateful smile and a nod. She watched the hake in parsley sauce go unused next to Miss Stewart and had the dish exchanged with the apple pie at the other end of the table. She discussed politics with the gentlemen—gently, the subjects of local interest rather than national—and listened to the Stewart ladies discuss the latest fashion.

She learned something she had not been aware of before. Miss Stewart, in a bid to attract Marcus's attention said, louder than she needed to, "Although we spell our name differently, we are related to the royal house of Scotland."

Silence fell, but only briefly. "We must assume not the disgraced branch," Viola said.

"Of course not." Miss Stewart picked up her fan and snapped it open, fanning herself so vigorously the candle nearest to her was nearly blown out. "But our own dear King George is himself a relative, is he not? The Stuarts once had a benign influence. Before the Catholics gained the upper hand with them."

Ah, yes, the Catholics. Blamed for everything in certain quarters, especially with good county Tories. Because of her peculiar and distinctive background, Viola had always sought more than simply blaming someone else for her troubles. She wanted to know reasons, not excuses.

This time she understood because she'd read widely on the subject. "The Young Pretender converted to Protestantism a few years ago," she said. "Nobody cared."

"It's too late for him," Mr. Quick, a local magistrate, said. He held up his glass of wine, the red liquid wavering in the candlelight. "And since he has only a bastard daughter and his brother is a man of the cloth, we may see the end of that branch of the family soon. Certainly they are finished as monarchs."

He turned his attention to Miss Stewart and her mother and raised his glass to them in a silent toast. "However, the legends are romantic, if inaccurate. The Stuarts have a long and distinguished history far beyond the current generation and the one before."

"We all have our black sheep," Lord Strenshall said. "Even the Emperors of London have their wicked side."

Thus he deftly moved the conversation on when it appeared to become mired in controversy. His own family—or rather, his wife's family—was known as the Emperors.

Viola toyed with the food on her plate. She had not eaten much of the delicious offerings, but her appetite had fled long before she sat at table. "Lord Malton is Marcus Aurelius," she reminded them.

Marcus groaned and clasped his forehead. "Don't remind me."

"It could be worse," she continued. "Your cousins Nicephorus and Antoninus have interesting names."

Mrs. Stewart tilted her head on one side. "I did not know your family was blessed with such unusual names."

In an age when men were often known even to their wives by their surname or their title, the remark would not raise brows. Except the Emperors were famous, if not notorious, and the gossip sheets loved to spread news about them, however scurrilous or defamatory. The worst of the papers rarely paused to check such trivialities as facts.

"My siblings are Valentinian, Darius, Drusilla, Claudia, and Livia," Marcus said, twirling his empty glass, watching the facets flash. "I have cousins called Julius Caesar and Poppea. Surely you knew this?"

"I did not think the matter was relevant," Mrs. Stewart said. Her jowls shook when she moved her head. "Why a gentleman is given as his first name is hardly apropos. But now you mention the names, taken together I understand the way you are referred to by the Grub Street press. My education did not include the ancients of Greece."

"Rome." Viola mouthed the word but did not say it. That would have been rude, but the correction lay there. She couldn't have been the only person here tonight to think it.

Glancing up, she caught Marcus's gaze. He was not smiling, but the tiny lines at the corners of his eyes revealed his amusement.

He picked up his wine glass and tilted it toward her, the toast for her eyes alone. "My namesake was a great Roman emperor and a renowned general. I have no intention of following his example. He was also a philosopher, something I bear in mind in my less…philosophical moments." The slight pause gave his words a wicked innuendo.

Her face heating, Viola glanced down at her empty plate. No conversation was safe with Marcus. Why did other people not see that? It appeared only she had noticed the warmth in his eyes.

Candlelight added warmth to features, of course, but it was more than that. It was as if his blue eyes were lit inside with a tiny flame of their own.

She got to her feet. "Ladies, shall we leave the gentlemen to their port?"

Although the ladies had finished eating, some demonstrated a reluctance to leave the men. Viola wanted to get away, to compose herself for the next part of the evening. Although the clock chimed seven as they went into the drawing room, it felt like much later. It wasn't even fully dark yet. "Daringly late for a dinner," a lady remarked.

"They eat at this time and much later in town," Mrs. Stewart said airily, as if fully conversant with the ways of London. She had probably never been there in her life. Neither had Viola, come to that, but she never pretended she had.

They were using the Blue Drawing Room as it had windows that opened on to the garden. The scent of roses and honeysuckle drifted through the air. The maids had been in to light the candles. They sent a warm glow over the blue-upholstered sofas and chairs set in an informal arrangement.

"Are we not to go into the state drawing room?" one lady asked. Viola was in danger of causing insult, so she gave the answer she'd heard the marchioness use once or twice before.

"This is a private family room. His lordship thought you would enjoy the intimate atmosphere more," she said and received a gratified smile and gentle agreement.

Mrs. Stewart took control as much as she could. When the maids brought in the tea-trays, she organized them on the tables and took charge of one, while Viola took the other. Soon every lady was furnished with a dish of tea or a sweet cordial. Viola took a small glass of the elderberry wine.

"Darling Emma, sing that new piece for us," Mrs. Stewart said. The harpsichord in here was not as fine as one in the music room. However it had been tuned at the same time, and it sounded just as good.

Her daughter stood and went to the harpsichord, where her sheet music lay ready. *Quelle surprise*, Viola thought.

"I would rather concentrate on singing the piece," Miss Stewart said, leafing through the pages. "Is there nobody who will play for me?" She glared at Viola. Hardly a gentle hint.

Taking her glass with her, Viola stood and went to the harpsichord, taking a moment to go through the pages. "Would you prefer to start with something more traditional?" That was a kindness, because the piece Emma Stewart handed to her was fiendishly tricky to sing. Viola sang indifferently, and she would never have attempted this piece. Perhaps Emma had been taking lessons.

After Emma decided on a sweet popular ditty, Viola played the introduction and Emma began to sing. She had a pretty voice, better than Viola's for sure, but not opera standard. But Viola had to give her credit for singing the song about a soldier leaving his lass at home with feeling and intonation.

When the gentlemen came in, Emma did not stop. She bowed her head at the patter of applause and nodded to Viola, just as if Viola was hired for the evening. "The new piece, please."

Viola did not argue, but began to play. She had to concentrate on the unfamiliar air. That meant she didn't notice anyone standing behind her until an arm clad in figured green velvet reached over and turned the page for her. Even if she had not been aware what Marcus was wearing, she'd have recognized him from his distinctive male aroma. Spicy and slightly peppery—that was Marcus.

The ruffles at the end of his sleeve brushed the bare skin of her neck as he withdrew. Viola suppressed a shiver of response. As always, her senses went on alert, although she tried to conquer her reaction to him. Every time he had that effect on her she swore he would not again. But here she was, responding as if he'd taught her body to do so.

Determinedly she turned her mind to the music.

Emma began to sing. She'd given Viola the music, so she must have been working on this piece for some time. It was Italian, an aria from one of the newest operas. At first Emma made a fair attempt. She hit all the notes and even managed a trill or two. However in doing so, she lost the meaning of the piece. That was a shame, since the song was a lament that the lady was waiting for her lover, the one man she could never openly give her heart to.

As the song wound its way along, Emma lost her way. She missed more notes and forgot the trills. She was obviously finding it hard work. She should have kept to ditties.

And all the time Marcus stood behind Viola, turning the pages.

Relief filled Viola when they reached the end.

While he leaned over to gather the sheets together, Marcus murmured to Viola, "How on earth did you allow yourself to be maneuvered into this?"

Lady Stewart had taken charge. She was dispensing tea and leading the conversation as if born to it.

"I gave up the fight," Viola confessed.

Marcus straightened but remained by Viola's side. "Why don't you give us the piece you were playing the other day?" he said mildly, when the applause was done and compliments given. "You remember, the one you used to test the other keyboard."

What was he doing? She glared at him. "It's just a local song." She began one of the innocent airs, but he interrupted her by touching her hand. Immediately she stopped.

"Not that one. The one you played last."

The scurrilous one. Could she remember the words for the sweet version? No, damn him, she could not. Only the other rang through her head, mocking her.

Stepping over the bench, he joined her, sitting by her said. "Perhaps just the tune," he said softly. His eyes gleamed, but with wickedness.

She wanted to hit him, but all she could do was glare.

They played the two-hander. Over the tinkle of the notes, talk swelled and then faded. Someone laughed. At her, no doubt. She kept her head down as she finished the piece. Despite the smatter of applause, she felt tainted, as if caught out playing a trick.

"Goodness, that was clever," Lady Stewart said. "My lord, I did not know you played."

"Everybody plays," he drawled. He turned toward the lady, allowing Viola a moment to recall herself. "Do you not?"

"No," her ladyship said shortly. "I do not. I take it Miss Gates learned with you?"

"We learned together," he said, "But my sisters spent more time in the music room. I believe at one time they formed a quartet, but after my mother begged them to stop, they went their separate ways."

The marquess laughed. "Oh, yes. Each played their own version of the piece. Only Viola ever kept in time."

"And Drusilla," Marcus said quietly.

Dru had been a solitary child. Sandwiched between two sets of twins in birth order, she had spent much time alone. Viola recognized something of her own situation, except that Dru was alone in the middle of her family, and Viola was an only child. However the two girls had not gravitated together. For some reason their fathers worked to keep them apart, even when they were small.

Viola sometimes wondered if the cool and collected Dru had ever found someone as a particular trusted friend. Viola had her father to keep her company.

Tonight Dru's brother was tormenting Viola, sitting next to her much closer than a gentleman should, but the cramped stool they shared necessitated that. He must know that, surely. Would he tease her so if he knew what he was doing to her? Probably not, and he must never know. She would die if he discovered how deep her feelings went for him. He'd marry a grand lady and become a marquess in the fullness of time. His wife would give him a quiverful of children for the title and estate, and they would most likely remain content.

She would be happy for him; she truly would. Heartbreak did not last forever.

Marcus got to his feet and held his hand to help her up. "Yellow suits you," he said softly. "I like this gown. Will you wear it again for me?"

She swallowed and smiled. "Of course. You'll see it again without a doubt. I only bought it this year, so it has to last me for a while."

"It is extremely becoming," Lady Stewart said, seemingly heedless of joining in a private conversation. She must have ears like a bat. "A little simple for my taste, but if you need it to last a few years, it is best to keep the style simple." She made the decision sound like a sin. She shook back her triple ruffles. "Come and take some tea, my dear. You must be parched."

"I find singing fills me with inspiration," Emma said. "I shall take out my sketchbook tomorrow."

Only Viola was close enough to hear Marcus's soft groan. No sign of his unspoken comment appeared on his face, a skill she would dearly love to emulate. He made her smile. Far too much, if truth be told.

The party did not decide to call for carriages until nine o'clock. All that time Lady Stewart had animadverted on her daughter's skills and their plans for the year.

It took until ten before they all left.

In the now quiet drawing room, the marquess turned to Viola. "I must thank you for this evening," he said. "You showed a great deal of fortitude. Lady Stewart can be a little wearing. When she began on the family tree of the Scottish Stuarts, I thought she would be here all night."

Viola dropped a small curtsey. "It was my pleasure, my lord."

"I doubt that." But he raised her and kissed her cheek. "I will leave first thing in the morning, probably before you are awake. You will stay here tonight?"

She had not expected that. "Oh, but it's not far. Only half a mile. It's a fine summer evening."

"And full dark," the marquess said. "I insist. Do you need a maid to help you?"

When he spoke in that tone she knew better than to argue with him. And, she realized with a flip of pleasure, they had put her in the Chinese room. They could not mean her to use that. "I can manage perfectly well, my lord. Should I find a room?"

"I took her to the Chinese room," Marcus said. "She should be comfortable there."

His lordship smiled and nodded. "Yes, indeed. Since I intend to leave at dawn, I'll bid you goodnight." He bowed over her hand. Enchanted, Viola loved it, even the wink he bestowed on her when he straightened.

She could smile back, none of the reticence she felt when the Stewarts patronized her tainting her mood. "If you will excuse me, then, I'll make my way upstairs."

"Of course. Feel free to ring for whatever you need."

As if she would. But with another word of thanks, she lifted her skirts to run upstairs.

His lordship said to Marcus, "A word with you before you retire."

So they were leaving in the morning. Gloom settled on her. They would go back to London, and she would return to her father and spend her days caring for him and his house, as she always wanted to. Why should she not be happy with the prospect?

In the room, she lit the candles in the sconces and pirouetted in front of the mirrors. The light played over the gleaming folds of her skirt. But her enjoyment had faded with the prospect of losing her friend so quickly. Yes, her friend. It was all Marcus could ever be and she should feel glad. He might write this time, now he had the opportunity. She'd like that.

Reluctantly she took off her clothes, plucked her day gown from the bag, and laid it out for the morning. The yellow silk she folded carefully and put away. Perhaps she'd attend the assembly next month in York and give it another airing. If the Stewarts deigned to attend, no doubt they would remark on the reappearance.

Hot water sat in a can by the door. She washed with the finely milled white soap on the dish and finished undressing.

She had no night-rail with her, so she climbed into bed in her shift. The sheets were fresh and the room smelled of lavender from the sprigs used to preserve the linen. What would it be like to live this way? To have the best all the time?

She'd be bored in a month.

Determined to enjoy her night of luxury, she snuggled down and laid her head on the pillow.

Chapter 5

Viola opened her eyes to the sound of carriage wheels bowling along the drive. Dawn filtered through the windows, but she was awake. She would not sleep any more tonight. Today.

Turning her head, she could just make out the little clock on the mantel, but she could not read the time. She didn't really need it. With the light at this level, it must be around six. Time to get up.

She could get some food in the kitchens here, but Mrs. Lancaster would tut at the disruption. The housekeeper's formidable counterpart in the kitchens would most likely do the same. They'd be serving breakfast at her house, so she'd get up and work up a fine appetite on the walk over.

Besides, with Marcus gone, she wanted to get back to her real life as soon as possible.

Her decision gave her the impetus to swing her legs out of bed, wash in fresh water—cold now—and dress. It did not take her long. The only sign of her presence was the not-quite-straight cover on the bed and a few hairs in the brush on the dressing table.

Time to go back to normal. Her deflated spirits would revive in no time.

Downstairs, she was surprised to find Tranmere standing in the hall, in full livery. They usually had them in storage when the family were not in residence.

"So his lordship left in good order?"

"Yes, Miss Gates, he did."

"Back to normal then," she said, swinging her bag as she left the house.

She could probably walk back to her house blindfolded, but she decided to enjoy the day. Until a voice hailed her. "Viola!"

Spinning around, she nearly stumbled when her skirts tangled around her legs. "Marcus?"

He was close enough to speed up and catch her, but he put her on her feet as soon as her skirts settled. "You're up early. I was looking forward to sharing breakfast with you."

"I thought you left with your father." She blinked, not sure he was really there. She'd set her mind to her normal life, and seeing him again had thrown her senses. When he'd steadied her, the brief touch of his hands had sent her senses spinning.

"I decided to stay behind. The Stewarts cannot visit me when I'm alone in the house, can they?"

"I thought you quite taken by Emma."

He laughed. "No, you did not. You knew what a bore she was. Oh, she's pretty, and she'll do well, but I desire more than looks in a wife. And that mother of hers… I have no wish to saddle myself with such a creature."

"You should not speak so of her. She means well."

"No, she does not. At least she doesn't where it concerns you." His voice lowered. "I need to speak with your father. My father gave me some information last night that I'm eager to discuss with him. Do you mind if I walk along with you?"

She glanced down at him. He was dressed for riding. "Will those boots take to walking?"

"Yes, of course. What, you thought I was the kind of coxcomb who had boots for different occasions? Sometimes when I ride I like to get off my horse and stroll apace. How could I do that with boots I could not walk in?"

He fell in by her side, although thankfully he did not offer her his arm. But he did take her bag. She knew better than to argue.

They enjoyed their walk, chatting about the countryside and the estate and their neighbors. Nothing of consequence. But oh, she'd miss him, if only as a friend. At one point she said, "Shall I write to you?" Then unaccustomed shyness seized her. "No, no, I should not."

"I would like that, but I will return next month."

"With a houseful of guests." Who would keep him busy.

"Indeed, but I will make some time for you."

"You don't have to." Looking anywhere but at him, she lengthened her stride.

* * * *

Since Viola was pointedly avoiding his gaze, Marcus had an opportunity to study her. Now his father had let him into her secret, he could see the resemblance to the disgraced royal family plainly.

According to the marquess, Viola spent little time worrying about it, instead preferring to believe it was a falsehood. Indeed, everyone had believed it a falsehood until recently. Yet another political lie put out by the enemies of the King to try to dislodge him from his throne.

Slightly taller than the average female, Viola was built on slender lines, which also fit with his information. Her black hair was darker than others he'd seen, but his cousin Tony's wife resembled her more than somewhat.

How would Viola feel when he told her the legend was real? Once he had confirmed the details from her father and acquired his permission, he had every intention of telling her. She should know; she had every right.

But for this brief twenty minutes they had peace and companionship. He longed to make it half an hour and stop to kiss her, but he had no idea how she would take it. Their kiss should never have happened, but now it had, he wanted more.

He could not make her his mistress. Would she even consider the position of wife? She was uncomfortable in society, not herself. He would not be the leash around her neck, holding her back when she wanted to run free.

His parents would be bitterly disappointed if he threw himself away on the estate manager's daughter. Society wouldn't approve, either, and that could prove tricky.

With regret, he discarded the passing thought.

He'd read a poem that reminded him of Viola recently. Ah, yes. He recited it aloud.

"*Noli me tangere*, for Caesar's I am
And wild for to hold, though I seem tame."

She stopped, turned and faced him. "That's pretty. Who wrote it?"

"Thomas Wyatt. He wrote it for Anne Boleyn." He should have remembered before he quoted the poem. That affair did not have a happy ending.

But she smiled. "It's pretty."

"So are you." The words emerged before he could put a cap on them. But it was true. She was pretty. Very much so, her lively personality showing through when she danced, or smiled when she thought nobody was by. Or with a tranquil expression lost in reading unfamiliar music.

He was not sorry he'd spoken. But he could not allow any more. They were on their own, and she was vulnerable. So was he, the way his mind was going this morning.

"I'm returning to London soon," he said, as much to remind himself as her.

"Yes." Her face lost a little of its animation, her eyes slightly duller.

That made him happy, although it shouldn't have. It meant she would miss him when he was gone. He was a selfish bastard for thinking that way, but his spirits, unlike hers, lifted. He would see her again in August, and despite what she obviously believed, he would ensure he had time for her.

Marcus no longer bothered denying he desired her, but the knowledge his father had imparted complicated matters. He would have to force patience on himself and bide his time. As she was right now, she was safe. As safe as anyone in her position could be.

Impotent fury filled him, as it had last night when he demanded to know why the marquess had not told him before. "It's getting obvious that we are racing to discover the children before the Dankworths. Viola knows nothing of this, or of our struggle. How could you not tell her?"

"Her father knows," his father had told him calmly. "He is keeping her safe."

She should know, and today Marcus would ensure she did.

The news would distress her, that the father who had cared for her all her life was no blood relative.

Her father's house came into view. Not far now, and then all hell would break loose. Marcus didn't imagine for a moment Viola would accept her fate meekly and let the men take charge of her life. Oh, no, she was more likely to do something completely unexpected and shock everyone.

"You nearly made me laugh at the most inopportune moments last night," she said abruptly.

"Why?" Shocked, he stopped walking once more. "I don't make anyone laugh. What did I do?"

"You make me laugh. You looked at me just so, and when you suggested I play that tune for the guests, you very nearly overset me."

She had noticed? "I shall have to guard myself closer. Everyone is convinced I'm a most staid, ordinary fellow. I am considered one of the safest prospects in London."

"I have noticed that in you, of course." She skipped over a molehill and back on to the path, her skirts swinging indecorously. Her plain stockings and stout shoes flashed into his view. "Not the safest prospect, I wouldn't know that, but you think of yourself as ordinary. You are definitely not ordinary, Marcus. But people treat you with the greatest respect and the kindest consideration. They defer to you."

He shoved his hands in his breeches' pockets. "Yes, I know. It's a bore, but if I tell them not to, they do it more. Or they become embarrassingly close. Overdoing it. I do have friends, of course, but most of them are in the same situation I am."

She clucked her tongue. "Poor boy!"

So of course he laughed, and she joined in, which eased the situation considerably. Nobody made him laugh as much as Viola. Or sweat, like the time she'd taken the worst-behaved horse in the stables for a morning ride.

She'd explained to his father later that she didn't realize she'd taken the gelding, mistaking him for another. He only half believed her. Viola had a restless streak, and every so often she had to release it or burst. Or that was how she'd explained it to him after the incident with the horse, one of the few times he'd sought her out. Killing herself was not the answer, he'd told her firmly before walking away.

He'd spent far too much time walking away from her. He would make an effort not to do so any longer. Time to face whatever waited for him here. To claim something for his own, in spite of his responsibilities. If their relationship deepened into friendship, he would enjoy it, but in his heart, he wanted more.

They had reached the gate. He swung it open and waited for her to go through. The land steward's house was what his father had termed a "comfortable" size. "I'd have enjoyed living in a house like this."

"What? How can you say that?" She paused in the act of finding her key for the front door. "We have four bedrooms and three servants, no more. How could it compare to what you have?"

"That's the point." He halted abruptly. "What was that?" Had that male shout come from inside the house? He laid a hand on her arm. "Go back. Go back now."

A shot rang from inside the house, and someone yelled.

He didn't even have his sword. "Where does your father keep his weapons?"

"In a locked case in the study." Typical of her to keep her head. Thank God.

He pushed her behind him. "Stay out of sight."

Two men rushed out of the side door and along the path, heading for the copse of trees nearest to the house. Marcus's first instinct was to give chase, but if he did, he would leave her unprotected, and who knew how many men were inside? He had to let the ruffian go and hope someone remained in the house for him to beat senseless. Anything to assuage the fury seething through him.

"Papa!" she cried, and would have rushed inside, had he not seized her arm and held her back.

"Don't do that. Wait for me." They would go in through the side door. Likely he might find a weapon there.

No person stood inside. He spotted the sword, the one Gates always claimed his great-great-grandfather had wielded at the Battle of Marston Moor. Well, it would give him good service now. He wrenched the weapon from its scabbard.

"Keep close," he told her. With those two men on the loose, he couldn't risk her making a run for it. He would have to take care of her. He needed to keep his wits about him. Protect her with his life, if need be.

This house was a mile from the main gates and the wall, but anyone could bring a horse in if he knew the different entrances.

Sure enough, the sound of galloping hooves on turf met his ears. He firmed his mouth. The ruffian would not get far, if Marcus had anything to do with it.

Viola might have a wild streak, but it did not usually tend to the stupid, especially in such circumstances. She jerked her head toward the stairs, indicating the way they should go.

They crept up a stair at a time, listening for any response. The house was deadly silent. Where were the servants?

At the top, they heard a groan. She would have pushed past him, but he held her back and headed toward the source of the sound.

In the main parlor, her father lay on the rucked-up and torn carpet, holding his head. He struggled as they entered, revealing his tied hands. They had not bothered to tie his feet. The thick bandage around his ankle would have made the task too difficult. The room was smashed, the furniture tipped over, the ornaments, the lamp on the table, and a shelf of books overturned and broken.

Viola rushed forward and dropped to her knees by her father's side.

Fear shaded his gray eyes. "You must go," he said, his voice barely above a whisper. "Get out of here."

"Is there someone else here?" she asked.

"How many people left?" He used a similar undertone when she spoke. "Two."

"Then they've gone." He made to sit up and retched.

Immediately she supported his head. "They hurt you, Papa." Her voice ached. "Was it thieves?"

Glass from the lamp crunched under Marcus's feet as he went to the window. "How badly is he hurt?" He could see nothing outside. Everything appeared perfectly normal.

"I'll recover. Help me to sit." Before he could go to them, Viola had her hand behind his back and was easing him up.

Marcus hurried to his side and helped, keeping his arm firmly behind Gates's back. "What happened? Can you tell us?" Already a bruise was forming on his temple.

"Not thieves. They wanted something particular." He turned his head and met his daughter's gaze. "They wanted you."

* * * *

Viola listened to her father, dull shock reverberating through her. "What would they want with me?"

"You are a prize, my dear. A treasure. It is no longer safe for you here." Her father stopped and closed his eyes. Had they broken his head? He opened his eyes once more. He gripped her arm. "Go to Scarborough."

The house? What was he talking about? "I can't leave you, Papa!"

"I heard them when they thought I was still unconscious. They were searching for the papers."

Marcus spoke to good effect. "Are they still there?"

She glanced up at the fireplace and nodded.

"Get them."

Casting him a wondering look, she got to her feet and crossed to the fireplace. In a matter of seconds, she had opened the panel, pressed the hidden spring, and opened the inner hidden place. Groping inside, she found the papers and drew them out. Three pieces of paper, all a little the worse for wear.

She gave them to Marcus. He glanced at them, nodded, and shoved them in his pocket. "You will have to show me where to go."

"You can't come!" How could he even think it?

"Yes, I can. Either that or you come to London with me. And once we're there, we will talk." He shook his head. "Why did you not tell me before? Did my father tell you of recent developments?"

"Yes. You must tell her." Her father had grasped the sleeve of Marcus's dark brown riding coat, his hand curved into a claw. "Do not let her out of your sight."

"I won't. Who else knows?"

"Of the house? Very few people."

"Wait here." Marcus strode to the door and left the room while Viola found some water to bathe her father's wound. She had cleaned it enough to satisfy herself he was not badly hurt when Marcus returned.

"They went through every room, but your bedroom is more or less intact. Let me carry you there."

Ignoring the older man's protests that he could get there himself, Marcus lifted him. He carefully carried him to his room, laying him on the bed still rumpled from the night before. A few items lay on the floor, but the ruffians had not had time to search too closely.

Although she was in control of herself, Viola's heart beat faster and tears pricked her eyes, more from shock than anything else. She sat on the bed while Marcus paced the room. "Where are your servants?"

"Only two live in. Cook has gone to market and McGregor went to the house to help with the guests. I gave him permission to remain there overnight if Mrs. Lancaster wished it." He closed his eyes. "My head is spinning."

Marcus touched her arm. "Come. I will send someone to you."

"What?" Bewildered, she turned her attention to him. "What are you talking about? I can't leave my father!"

"You must." Both men spoke at once.

Marcus took up the thread. "You heard your father. The men wanted you. I will take you to Scarborough today and I will stay there with you until we are certain you are safe." He appeared as if he would say something else, but he must have changed his mind. He closed his mouth with a snap.

"Papa, how can you think I would leave?"

Tears filmed his eyes. She had never seen him weep before. Never wanted to see it again. "My dear, it's the only way to keep both of us safe. They want you, and they will stop at nothing to get you. If you stay here, they will kill me to get to you."

"What?" She shook her head to get rid of the delusions pouring into her ears. "But what will that do for them?"

"The papers…" He coughed and then leaned back against the pillows.

"They're just fairy tales, a foolish story."

"They're not stories; they are real. Now do you understand?"

"I do," Marcus said.

She had never seen Marcus look like he did now. Every part of him was poised for action, the expression in his eyes hard and determined. Did she know him at all? "He is right, Viola. Come. We'll talk on the way. Can you run?"

She nodded.

"No," her father said. "It's not safe. Ride for the house. My horse is in the stable at the back. Take him."

Marcus did not argue. He came around the bed and held one hand to her.

Real? Those papers were real? Someone wanted her dead?

When she gazed into Marcus's face she saw trust there. She needed help, no doubt about it. With only a little hesitation, she took his hand.

Chapter 6

Back at the main house, Marcus curved his arm around Viola's waist and hustled her into the side hall. It seemed an age since they were last there. He had picked up her bag from where he'd dropped it outside, and they'd run all the way. Marcus had kept his body between her and the hedges, leading her away from the path and over the green parkland between her house and his. Protecting her.

"Watch her," he said to Tranmere. "Guard her with your life." Catching the footman's startled attention, he raised a finger. "Mark me, Tranmere. With your life."

"My lord," Tranmere said. His face was as grim as Viola had ever seen it.

When Marcus had gone, taking the stairs three at a time, Tranmere turned to her. "What have you done?" he said, his voice laced with wariness.

Viola slumped into the hard hall chair. "Nothing. I did nothing. Someone attacked my father, Tranmere. He's hurt, but not badly, or I'd have stayed with him. Marcus is taking me away." She looked up. "Will you go to him?"

Tranmere nodded. "As soon as I can. I won't let anything happen to him." Even without further explanation, he proved his worth.

Wearily she leaned forward, resting her elbows on her knees.

In a few moments, Marcus returned. "I've ordered two horses saddled. Do you have everything you need in that bag?"

"Yes." She looked up and met his clear gaze. "But no riding habit."

He glanced at her gown. "If I found one of my sisters' habits it would take you ten minutes to get it on, would it not?" She nodded. However fast she changed, she could not do it faster. All that unhooking and unpinning did not take too long. However, the rehooking and repinning, especially of an outfit she was not accustomed to, would easily take longer than ten minutes. "We'll take a gig," he said and disappeared again.

A gig? But he did not joke. Just as the clock was striking eight, the sound of rumbling wheels came from outside, and he yelled, "Come out and bring the bag!"

He was not driving a gig, but a fragile-seeming vehicle she doubted would last between here and Scarborough. He'd had two mismatched but good-looking horses put to, or he'd done it himself. She wouldn't put anything past him in his current mood. She had never known the man she considered as staid and careful behave this way.

Febrile excitement positively radiated from him as he put down a hand to help her up, while Tranmere gave her a boost from below. Anyone would think she was...royalty.

Tranmere threw her bag into the back, Marcus whipped up the horses, and they were off.

Viola did not speak until they reached the main road. Marcus glanced at her, and then briefly shot his attention to where she clutched the rail as hard as she could. Her nails were digging into her palm, but better that than have him jolt her from this thing.

"It's safe." He turned a corner so fast the vehicle nearly went on to two wheels. "It's my new phaeton. I had it brought up from town, thought I'd tool it around the countryside. It's made from the best materials, to be as light as possible. I ordered it in a moment of madness, and thank goodness I did. My brothers called me staid, so I thought I would outdo them in sporting vehicles. The horses are reliable and I can outstrip most vehicles on the road with it."

She still did not feel safe. "I see," she said faintly.

"Don't worry." He flashed one of his sudden smiles. "I won't let anything happen to you."

Events raced through her mind. "You know about all this?"

"What?" The horses had settled into a brisk trot. "The certificates? The letter?"

"Yes, that."

He jerked a nod. "Wait until we're past the village and I'll tell you. We are stopping for no one. If they try to hold us up, we're going to shoot them." He handed her a weapon, a hefty pistol, but he didn't ask her if she could use it. He already knew the answer.

Silence reigned until they had left the village of Haxby behind them. People stopped to stare at the vehicle that whipped past, but Marcus acknowledged none of them. Keeping her head down, Viola prayed none of them recognized her. Apart from any other consideration, she was sitting in a vehicle alone with a man she was not related to. Enough to ruin her if word got around.

Marcus did not seem in the least perturbed, although he'd complained to her about women trying to trap him. He'd put her in the situation where she could do precisely that. It might appear a small consideration, but not to someone who lived in the district.

Half a mile on, they were on the clear road to Scarborough. Marcus sighed and spoke for the first time. "The certificates are real. I have them in my pocket. But you, my dear, are the prize."

A sense of betrayal filled her. He knew? Had he known when he kissed her in the music room? "How long have you known?"

"A day." His mouth flattened. "Your father and mine decided the fewer people who knew, the better. That included me."

Relief replaced her previous mood. So he'd kissed her before he knew. "You believe it?"

"Of course." He glanced at her.

"Keep your eyes on the road."

With a ghost of a smile, he obeyed her. "In the last few months, my cousins and I have discovered the truth. There are others like you, my dear, and they are desperate to get hold of you."

"Why?" Her recalcitrant mind was still finding the concept difficult. What she'd imagined to be a fairy tale was real. Her father had told her the secret when she'd turned eighteen. So she knew she wasn't her father's biological daughter. It didn't make much difference to her. She was loved and secure in her family.

He flicked her another glance. She wished he wouldn't. This fragile vehicle made her nervous.

"Take my word for it. You look very much like your father. The same narrow face, dark eyes, and hair. Once they have you, they can do what they want."

"What will they do? And who are 'they?'"

"The Dankworths," he said, lines of strain around his mouth. "And they will probably force your marriage to one. They want the next Stuart heir."

That was the first time either of them had said the word "Stuart" aloud. The sound made reality from the tattered yellowed pieces of paper snugly tucked into Marcus's pocket.

"I'm a Stuart," she said dully.

"Tell me what you know. Then I'll tell you about the Dankworths."

The road was straight and true, and if he kept to the center, he avoided the worst of the ruts. By now Marcus had satisfied Viola he was an excellent whip, but she still kept a firm hold on the hand rail.

"My mother was Italian, but she was blond, not like me. My father fell in love with her when he accompanied your father on the Grand Tour. As far as I knew, I was born there, and they brought me home."

"Humph. And she died shortly thereafter."

"Yes. When I was barely a year old. She died in childbirth."

"Presumably Rome is where Maria gave the child to your parents." His voice tightened. "My father never told me until yesterday. Even recently, when—" He broke off and negotiated a tricky part of the road where someone in a heavy vehicle had driven deep ruts right across the surface.

Viola suspected that was merely an excuse, considering how well he drove.

"Let us start at the beginning. The Dankworths."

A lock of her hair came loose, but she merely shoved it behind her ear. Apparently distracted by her movement, he glanced at her, but turned his attention back to the road. "The Dankworths," he repeated. "That is the name of the family of the Duke of Northwich. Do you know of him?"

"I've heard of him," she said cautiously. "They are Jacobites." Realization followed hard on her words. Of course they would want her. "So they don't want me dead."

"No, they do not. But they will hurt as many people as they need to get to you." Sighing, he slowed the horses to a walk. "You need us. You need the Emperors to stand with you against the power of the Dankworths. They have found you out, and they will stop at very little to find you."

She waited. There was something else, she was sure of it. "You stopped. Carry on."

"On the other hand, the Young Pretender might want you. Now *he* wants you dead." As if the words poisoned him, Marcus whipped up the horses and sent them back into a trot. He stared at the road as if it had offended him.

Viola tried to absorb what he said. She was in line to the throne, albeit a displaced branch of the family. Another realization hit her like a brick. "I have brothers and sisters?"

"An unknown number, but we have found two so far, and a half-sister. The Old Pretender's wife, Maria Rubio, was persuaded to step aside for the wife he officially married, but the marriage did not last long. After it ended, when Maria Clementina left him and entered a nunnery, the Old Pretender's melancholy moods worsened. They brought Maria Rubio back. She died in a fire, with most of her records, in 1740."

She hadn't known that. "Poor lady."

"Indeed. Traduced, pushed aside and used. But not a helpless lady. She ensured her children were sent away, out of danger. Or she planned to use them as pawns later. We have no idea. We don't know a lot about her except the bare facts of her life. And that she was beautiful."

"Is there a portrait?" She would love to see a portrait of the woman who had borne her.

"There doesn't have to be. I just have to look at you."

Viola's head reeled. Cold seeped through her bones, although the day was fine. She didn't even have a cloak. For goodness' sake, she was out in public without a hat. "I'm bareheaded in public," she said dully.

"I have money. We'll buy what we need in Scarborough."

"My father bought the house for his retirement, but also as a house he could bring me to if he needed. Few people know it is ours." She was operating by rote now, too many new pieces of information revolving around her head for her to make sense of any of it. She left it to settle and concentrated on what she knew. "We don't have servants there, just someone who looks in once a month to make sure mice haven't eaten it or people haven't broken in."

"We may stay there for a while, if it is safe, and then return to Haxby. But you must stay in the main house once we return, so you may be guarded properly."

"Guarded?" she echoed in alarm, her voice rising.

"Until we discover who knows about you. Then we can ascertain how they found out. The Dankworths are the best outcome. They want to control you."

"And the Pretender's people want to kill me." That still had not sunk in. "Who in their right mind would kill a person for who she is?"

"Madmen," he snapped. "Fanatics. People who do not think in terms of people, but of causes and rights."

Weariness swept over her in a great wave, but she dared not sleep. She might tumble from this precarious vehicle. Despite the suspension, the comfort and the modernity of it, she could not feel happy sitting here. She clutched the armrest while Marcus bowled his horses along at a considerable pace. But they were still ten miles from their destination.

Her throat was parched, her stomach rumbled, but she would not stop until they had arrived at the Scarborough house. It was unlikely to have fresh food, but she could find something—salt beef, bacon, some provisions—that would do. An inn lay close to the house. She could go there—or rather, Marcus could, and buy food. "Do you intend for us to stay in the house unchaperoned? Without servants, even?"

"For a day or two, certainly. My valet will follow. I can trust his loyalty. To be safe, I did not tell him I was taking you to the house. He probably assumes I found a doxy, or a lover who does not want to be identified."

"Is that usual with you?" She hated to think of him with other women. Even though she had no claim on him, she did not want him with anyone else.

"No," he said calmly. "I do not make a habit of taking strange women to houses belonging to another person." He flicked a glance at her. "And in case you are wondering, yes, at times I have had a woman in keeping. I have needs, after all. But not one at the moment. And when I marry, I intend to make every effort to cleave to my wife."

"What if she detests…marital relations?"

"She does not," he said firmly.

What little she knew of the act of procreating a child was learned from Marcus. At least, the practical side. She had looked at books, but either the marquess did not approve of the more scurrilous works circulating in society or he hid them well, because she had never found anything that went into any detail. From her own tentative explorations, she knew a little about her own body, but not much about males. Except, thanks to the statues his lordship brought back from Italy, what they looked like naked.

"You said 'she does not,' not 'she will not.' Do you have anyone in mind?" she dared to ask.

"Yes."

After that one word, he fell silent, leaving her to speculate. The only words she spoke to him after that were to direct him to the house.

Scarborough spread out before them in the distance. The town sloped down toward the sea, which made its presence apparent by the brisk breezes that whipped past their cheeks and disordered Viola's hair. Impatiently, she shoved a strand behind her ear. "I really need to find a hat," she muttered.

He glanced at her. "I daresay we will find one."

Climbing down from the carriage, he tossed the reins over a nearby overhanging branch and came around to help her down. When he grasped her waist, she put her hands on his shoulders, his muscles flexing as he swung her to the ground. He did not linger, but released her as if she'd scalded him.

Before they left the carriage, he retrieved their bags. "We might as well take them in." He tossed the reins back in the vehicle. "As long as the horses are not disturbed, they'll be fine for five minutes. I want to ensure we're safe before we settle in."

The house, a tidy one of a similar size to the one on the Haxby estate, appeared closed up. The shutters were firmly bolted over the windows and the door was fastened tightly shut.

"Do you have a key?" he asked mildly.

"We keep a spare," she said.

For years, they had kept a key under a hollowed-out stone near the ash tree at the front of the house. With relief, she found it, although ingress was the least of their troubles. A small window at the back of the house led into the cook's pantry. In extremis, they could have broken it and slid in that way.

She unlocked the back door, a sense of relief filling her. She was safe. And once he had fetched the servants, Marcus could leave her and she would no longer be perturbed by his presence. Absence, she felt sure, would ease their connection. He had shown little sign of the passion he'd demonstrated the other day. That kiss was likely an aberration, something to pass to the annals of time.

It healed, they said. Time, that was.

The house smelled of disuse. No scents of burning wood from the kitchen fire drifted up to the main house, and no potpourri or burning lozenges sweetened the atmosphere. A touch of damp, too—she would have to investigate, but a house by the sea could expect some of that.

The banister on the wooden staircase bore a thin film of dust, but the floor was relatively clean. Viola determined to question the cleaner, who had obviously been skimping in her work.

A sound broke the silence. The whicker of a horse, but not from the front, where they'd stationed the phaeton. From the back of the house.

Before she had properly registered the implications, Marcus spun around, grabbed her arms, and propelled her out.

A shot hammered into the doorframe just above his head, showering them in splinters. Leaving the bags where they fell, Marcus seized her hand and raced away. "The bushes—quickly!"

The hedges around the garden were overgrown, the bases spindly. Vaguely Viola registered that she should have visited earlier and supervised the work herself, but at the moment, gratitude flooded her. Somehow she dragged her body through the hedge, ignoring the tearing sound of fabric. Another shot landed far too close, thumping into the ground. Her gown protected her from the inevitable scraping, but it did not save itself.

Marcus followed, without hooped petticoats hampering him. "Get rid of the damned hoop!"

"If I do that my skirts will drag and I won't be able to run. The gown is only ankle length as long as I have the hoops."

"Can you run?"

She was already running. Across the fields, getting away, not knowing where, until his voice, urgent, came from behind her. "Towards the town!"

She didn't need him to tell her twice.

Picking up her skirts, heedless of modesty and every consideration except saving their lives, she ran. The next hedge caused more of an obstacle, but she managed it. They found themselves on one of the streets leading into the town and eventually the harbor.

Where there were people. Where they couldn't be shot at without the danger of someone else getting hurt. Where there were witnesses.

A few people strolled down the street, but they continued, hurtling down the street until she tumbled over.

Marcus bent to help her up, and caught by the fever of the chase, she burst into laughter. "Do I look as bad as you?"

His face was smudged with dirt, his coat pockets torn. "Worse," he said. "But if we're taken up as vagrants, at least our enemies can't get to us in jail."

She cast him a disbelieving look. "What do we do now?"

"I have a plan." His eyes sparkled. How could he be excited at a time like this? But he was. Under the tension lay a reserve of challenge he was rising to.

She gave him a skeptical stare. "What plan?"

"I still have my purse. We will find somewhere that sells clothes and make ourselves respectable. Then we'll make our way to the nearest coaching inn and make our plans. We must stay in the vicinity of other people. You understand why?"

She nodded. "So the people chasing us won't shoot at us."

Their pursuers were nowhere in sight. Either they had retreated, or they had lost their quarry. Viola doubted it. The men were probably following.

"Take my hand."

"What?" That kind of intimacy, particularly in public, startled her.

"They may try to separate us. The shots might not have been for you, but for me. Then they will have you to themselves."

Realization dawned. "If they are Northwich's men, they want me but not you? What if they're from the Pretender?"

"Then they will want both of us dead. Nobody to tell tales."

Loath to argue, she took his proffered hand. He closed his fingers around her and led her farther down, into the town. With her hand in his, Viola had an absurd sense of safety.

Scarborough had grown in popularity since it had developed a spa where the fashionable of Yorkshire could gather. As well as the successful business of fishing and trade, it had drawn the local gentry, and people from farther afield, in droves. Today, a fine day in June, it was busy.

But knowing the town, Viola kept away from the more affluent parts, including the round classically designed spa building and pump room. While they wanted witnesses, they could do without gossip.

In a street populated by the respectable poor, they found what they were looking for—a shop, hung about with a variety of objects, including hooped petticoats and discarded clothes next to odd chairs and sticks of furniture. "How much do you have?" she asked him.

"About twenty guineas." A veritable fortune, a year's wages to many of the people moving around here. "Buy what you need to appear respectable."

"Are we returning to the house?"

"We'll talk about that in a while," was all the answer she received. "Get what you need."

He'd lost all pretense at politeness, but she could not blame him.

After touring the packed premises twice, she found what she needed. A riding habit. It needed no hoops, and it was the right length for her to walk in without tripping. True, it was in a particularly unappealing shade of olive green, but at this stage she was only pleased to find it clean and relatively fresh. Perhaps the original owner realized her mistake when she saw the color made up. To go with it, she chose a shirt and stock, and then picked up two shifts and two pairs of sturdy woolen stockings. A male-style cocked hat turned up, and a pair of gloves would at least have an appearance of respectability. In this get-up, she would look completely different to the way she had looked in the phaeton.

He appeared wearing a dark brown coat so old-fashioned and ill-fitting she nearly burst into laughter. Fresh breeches and hose, too, but he'd kept his shoes and his waistcoat. A new hat, much like hers, crowned his head.

Then she noticed his wig. He'd found a bob-wig, like the ones older men wore, and men who didn't want to concern themselves with the more elaborate queued kind. It made him look very different—older, less... noticeable. She hated it. He'd tucked all his natural hair underneath.

"That will get hot," she said.

"It will, but it serves its purpose."

He had lost the sparkle, and his mien appeared more like his public personality. She hated that, too.

Once he'd paid the ludicrously small amount the dealer wanted—she should shop second-hand more often—he led the way outside, into the brilliant sunshine. Only then did she notice that he'd added a worn leather bag to their purchases.

"What is that for?"

"We're buying some necessities. We might have to go from here."

She frowned. "What?"

"Do you know the main coaching inn here?"

That made sense. A coaching inn was where they would hear the best gossip and where people congregated all day. She took him to the Globe, by the docks, an inn that attracted the coaching trade and passengers from the ships.

The large building bustled with life. As they approached, a huge vehicle swept past them and through the arch into the inn, leaving only inches to spare. Viola stepped back, glad it hadn't rained for a few days, otherwise her new outfit would have been spattered with mud.

Marcus led the way into the main part of the inn. People rushed past, intent on some business known only to them. Ostlers hurried through to the yard outside, and the passengers from the stage coach raced into the main room, intent on getting food.

"We have a way out," Marcus said, deep satisfaction coloring his tones.

"What?"

Grabbing her hand, he towed her to the desk where a tattered waybill was tacked to the wall. A man stood by it, watching and counting the passengers. "Sir?"

Before she could protest, he'd bought them tickets to London. Bewildered, she watched precious coins leaving his hand.

Despite the safety of the crowded inn, she needed private conversation with him. She tugged him aside as soon as he'd stowed the tickets in his pocket. "We were lucky to get two inside seats," he said.

"What?"

The cacophony around them increased as servers hurried through from the kitchens, plates of steaming food piled on large trays. He tugged her aside, to a relatively quiet corner. "We do not have to travel all the way," he said, "But this gives us the choice. Normally I'd apply for passage on one of the ships in harbor, but the coach is leaving in half an hour. Besides, we don't have enough money for the ship. We have gained a march on our pursuers." He glanced at the way bill. "It goes through

Lincoln and Huntingdon. It will take four or five days in this weather, and it finishes in Ludgate Hill."

"We can't go to London!"

He regarded her seriously, his eyes grave. "I always meant to take you there."

"Why?"

"London holds people who can help us."

Not you but us. "Who?"

"My family, the Emperors." He took both her hands in his. "How brave are you, sweetheart?"

"I don't know," she said honestly. "I've never been tested this way."

"Trust me. I won't leave you, and I won't allow anyone to hurt you." The sparkle returned. "And we have an adventure ahead of us, do we not?"

A bell clanged and a man yelled, at the top of his voice. "The coach to London is departing in five minutes!"

The headlong rush almost swept them away. Outside in the cobbled yard the scene appeared completely without organization. Viola had never been this close to a stage coach before. If she'd been alone, the scene would have overwhelmed her.

As it was, she stayed close to Marcus and followed him into the body of the coach. Above them, heels drummed as the top passengers climbed up and settled themselves on the roof. Behind, thumps heralded the loading of luggage into the boot. This was not the first stage of the journey. That meant the coach contained pieces of clothing, discarded cloaks, and paraphernalia like personal bourdaloues, fans, and gloves. The interior passengers had left them behind in their headlong rush to find food. One of the bourdaloues, a pretty blue-and-white china example, had been used and its contents not dumped over the side of the coach, as was usual. Viola wrinkled her nose at the strong smell of urine.

For the first time in her adult life, Viola had only what she stood up in. "I don't even have a comb!" she murmured as someone pushed past her to take her place next to Marcus.

"Yes, you do. I bought a few things to weight the bag. My old coat is there, and your discarded gown."

"It's ruined. I can never rescue it."

"Then we'll replace it with something else," he said calmly.

How could he remain so stoic in the face of…this? He touched her hand. "I will take care of you. If we do not get to London this way, if you find the passage intolerable, we will stop and find someone to help us. I have an extensive circle of acquaintances, after all."

Some of the highest in the land. Viola would die rather than present herself to the exalted people Marcus must know in this state. Her hair was barely fastened, as she'd lost most of her hairpins in the struggle though the bushes. She had no fan or any of the accessories she was used to, not even a handkerchief.

With a deafening blast from the yard of tin, warning anyone ahead they were about to move, the coach set off. The six horses pulling the equipage were fresh and snorted as they swept through the inn yard, as precariously as the vehicle had sailed in. A few people stared as they passed, but with coaches arriving and leaving throughout the course of the day, most would be used to it.

Viola was not. The whole experience left her trembling with shock.

The harbor came into sight out of the left-hand window. It bristled with masts and rigging from the big ships. Gathered at one end, like a collection of children were the smaller vessels that plied the fishing trade. Seagulls shrieked and dipped, searching for the discards, as fishwives cleaned the catch and discarded the inevitable detritus. Sea air blew in through the open windows, making Viola clutch her hat for fear she would lose it.

She tried to concentrate on the outside scenery rather than the thoughts and fears whirling around in her head. Someone had tried to kill her, or Marcus. They wanted to capture her. She clutched his arm. "The papers!"

"I have them safe," was his calm reply, "But more importantly, I have you safe."

"Did you say we were brother and sister?" It would be acceptable for a brother to escort his sister with no maid or companion.

"Husband and wife," he replied tersely. "I told you, I do not want to let you out of my sight."

Yet more shocks reverberated through her. Could she take any more? "I don't have a ring," were her first bewildered words.

"That is easily remedied. Besides, not every wife wears a ring."

That was true enough, but in her confusion, Viola had seized upon the first excuse she could think of. Now she felt idiotic. Marcus clasped her hand tighter. "Sleep. That's the best cure."

Despite the relatively early hour of the day, to her surprise she found she could do as he said.

Chapter 7

Marcus and Viola were lucky to find a room available on the first overnight stop. Two would have been impossible and more than his limited budget could bear. Marcus had considered taking a gig to the estate of a friend who lived not thirty miles away. But once they had embarked on this reckless journey, he reconsidered.

In the presence of these people—chattering and gossiping, sleeping and staring silently from the windows—they went unremarked. In an open carriage or even a closed one, they were more vulnerable. If he could afford outriders and their weapons, Marcus might have considered the move. However he had no proof of who he was any more, so he could not travel on tick. He had not been carrying his card case. In any case, who would be fool enough to grant him credit on the strength of a visiting card?

The coach jolted over the uneven road, its suspension slack, if it had any at all. He gave one lingering thought to his phaeton and then forced his mind to move on. Such a sweetly balanced vehicle. He must buy another, because that one had gone. Their attackers would steal it or smash it. He'd never get another quite so fine.

Instead, he had the woman next to him. In her sleep Viola had slumped to one side, forcing him to curve his arm around her shoulders to hold her steady. He'd seen people numb with shock, and after what had happened to her and what she'd learned, he was not surprised she had slid into slumber. With any luck, she would accept her fate when she awoke.

Not that he had any intention of telling her everything. She knew too much already. Instead of feeding the information to her slowly, he'd given it to her in one big gulp. Unlike his father, Marcus believed she should know. She had a right, and she would need full knowledge to prepare her for what lay ahead.

Another jolt made him tighten his hold, but after a little moan of complaint, she settled back down. They were passing through a village, thatched cottages lining the main street. If it was like the villages he'd ventured into, behind those doors lay hovels. The family living there shared one room with the most precious of their livestock and a hole in the ceiling to act as a chimney. An inn at the end of the street gave them some respite from their daily labors. But at least they did not have people who wanted to kill them.

The attack at the Scarborough house had worried him deeply. The two shots were indiscriminate, aiming at whomever they could hit. The woman in his arms was precious to more people than he was. She was a valuable commodity. Married to one of the Duke of Northwich's sons, she'd give the Dankworth family a legitimate claim to the throne. They were dangerous enough without giving them extra ammunition.

The duke had escaped the bloodbath after Culloden, threatened with attainder but not brought to trial. Nothing had been proved against him, mainly because of his wealth and importance to the country. Lesser men had been swept up in the conflagration, but not Northwich. Where he was, plotting followed close behind, and sometimes even led. He would have taken care to send men to capture her and probably render him incapable of following her, but not dead. Death brought complications.

But the Pretender—that was different. Charles Edward Stuart was seriously challenged by the new developments. If anyone ever found the original certificate of marriage between the Old Pretender and Maria Rubio, the children would displace him in the succession. Except, of course, the Hanoverians had already displaced him. But they never gave up, the Jacobites. They'd be dead in the ground before they surrendered their claims to the throne.

He held her snugly, this royal child, the woman he had plans for. If she would accept them, he thought with a wry smile. Nothing was certain where Viola was concerned. She would fight anything she considered wrong, or interfered with what she wanted, or hurt those she loved.

He'd like to be one of the people she loved.

He glanced at his slumbering princess. A thread of a pulse throbbed in the delicate skin of her wrist. An urge took him to kiss her there, but he could not. Must not. He would guard her, a poor palace guard indeed, but he would do his best.

Marcus had found more than someone to protect. He would have this, this one thing for himself. He would have her. Together once more, after so many years watching each other from a distance—he would not let her go again. Friend or more, he would protect her and care for her and ensure she got everything she wanted or needed. Even if it meant returning to Haxby and living her life as the daughter of the estate manager. That had made her happy for the last twenty-six years. Right from the impulsive kiss in the music room, when his long-dormant desire for her had reignited, he had begun to dream.

She felt right snuggled next to him, heating his body more than she should in this confined space. Not just desirable, but right. Marcus had never considered himself an inarticulate person, but he found describing her and his feelings towards her difficult. So difficult he did not know how to begin. So it was probably as well she woke up when the coach hit a rut.

Viola squeezed her eyes tighter and then opened them wide. Tilting her head, she winced and then met his gaze. She tried to jerk away, but he held her firmly.

"Ease yourself back to consciousness," he murmured. He kissed her forehead, as much to demonstrate their masquerade as to ease his longing to touch or kiss her. In public, he would dare no more, nor would he put her in an invidious position. But he was posing as her husband. They were not exactly in the presence of the cream of society, who detested demonstrations of affection conducted in public. Bad manners and distinctly distasteful, they would have said.

"Why are you smiling?" She sounded petulant, but then, she had good reason to be. None of what had happened that day had been her fault, or even expected.

"We are safe, resting, and on our way to London. You said you wanted to see it. And so you shall."

"But I thought we were—" She bit her lip, obviously recalling where they were, and completed her sentence. "I thought we were visiting your relatives in Derbyshire."

"We're going to London," he said firmly. "It makes no sense to stop. We were fortunate to catch the coach when we did."

That gave them the advantage on any pursuers. He'd signed the tickets as Mr. and Mrs. Dunbar. He knew nobody by that name, so nobody would connect the neatly although shabbily dressed Dunbars with the illustrious Earl of Malton and his…friend.

"What time is it?"

"Barely noon," he said. "We have a way to go yet."

* * * *

Because of the good weather and healthy passengers, the coach made good time. Healthy passengers were important. They needed to scramble out, eat scalding hot food, and back on again by the time the ostlers had turned the coach and put fresh horses to the traces. Viola became adept at gulping hot coffee without burning her mouth. At the first stage where they paused, she forewent the meal. After begging a shilling from Marcus, she crossed the street to buy a novel from a bookshop there. Putting up with Marcus's good-natured teasing, she promised to lend it to him when they had done. "But it's the first part of a three-part story. The publisher says at the end the next installment will follow shortly, although I have no idea when that will be. He does not say. I was fortunate to find it reduced. Perhaps that is because the second and third parts were not forthcoming."

"It's unusual for a publisher to take the first part of a book without the others being ready," he said.

The read concerned a young woman whose conscience pushed her into far too many insane adventures, nearly losing her virtue in almost every chapter. Viola read on, absorbed, the jolting of the badly sprung vehicle hardly troubling her at all. At one point, the man of the cloth sitting opposite to them leaned his head out of the window and heaved. Clearly not everyone travelled well.

She continued with her book and had nearly completed it when they reached their destination for the night. Talk with Marcus had necessarily been short and stilted. They could hardly discuss their situation with the four other passengers, who were, in any case, more interested in their own situations than anyone else's.

A woman held a basket on her lap, which turned out to contain a cockerel—a breeder, she said, for her reluctant hens. "For with their current cock, they will not lay at all, and I need those eggs. Very good eggs they are too, just not enough of 'em." She was not travelling farther than a day with them, so either they could spread out more the next day, or they would have a new passenger. The boy in the corner was on his way to school in London and had someone meeting him at their destination. The lady sitting opposite, the one who was ostentatiously reading a book of sermons, was a governess on her way to a new position.

Viola learned about them all, through their chatter, and remained silent, reading her book. Marcus spent most of his time watching the scenery pass by, as if he expected trouble at every turn.

They passed through a number of pretty hamlets, and the day being fine, they appeared at their best. Even a larger town or two, but Viola had no idea where they were until dusk was falling and they reached their destination for the night.

The lady with the cockerel left with a large man, presumably her husband. The others trooped into the inn.

Viola tried to recall where they had been, but found herself getting drowsy once more. How she could, after falling asleep earlier in the day, she didn't know. When Marcus spoke to the landlord, she opened her eyes wide once more. "Yes, one room is sufficient," he said.

"Aye, well we're full with another coach that lost a wheel, but you're lucky. I have one room left," the landlord said. He didn't appear the least suspicious.

To the sound of the other passengers' complaints, Marcus went off with the key.

"Did you pay over the odds?" she asked.

He smiled, slowly, his eyelids drooping. "I may have done. We have sufficient, my dear. We can afford it."

"But one room?"

"Plenty of room for two," he said.

She didn't need his warning glance to tell her not to say too much. Instead, she tucked her hand in his arm and went into the main room of the inn. She was prepared, for once, to enjoy a meal taken at leisure.

Except her appetite seemed to have fled. The notion of sharing a room with Marcus disturbed her more than somewhat. How could she do that, when her feelings for him were far more than they should be?

After picking at her food, she declared she would go to bed. They had to be up at dawn to make the most of the light, the coachman informed them. Gone at six.

Marcus grabbed their bag, the only one they had, and took her upstairs to their room before anyone else could claim it, as he informed her on the way up. "You appear to have some experience with the stage coach," she commented as he unlocked the door.

"As a boy, and sometimes at Oxford," he admitted. "My father made me work to a specific allowance. He wasn't ungenerous, but sometimes I was too lavish, and at the end of the quarter I would find myself somewhat short of funds." He shot her a mischievous smile. "The stage isn't cheap, but it's much cheaper than keeping a horse stabled or hiring a private vehicle."

He opened the door and conversation ceased. Going inside, he glanced around and put down the bag. "I'll sleep in the tap room," he said abruptly.

His decision made her more than nervous. "But you promised not to leave my side."

He nodded. "I know. But this inn is a compact one and the room much smaller than I envisioned. I can find a spot where I can see everyone going up and down the stairs. There is only one door to this room."

She shook her head. "No." Fear clutched at her, unreasoning and foolish. She'd had enough for one day. "We are supposed to be married. Won't people think it strange?"

He closed the door, but stayed on her side of it. "What do we care what people think?" He spoke savagely, a vicious edge to his voice. Turning, he grasped her shoulders. "This room—I had counted on a chair, or even a stretch of floor."

Apart from a tiny washstand and bowl, the only piece of furniture in the room was a huge four-poster bed. The posts and headboard were elaborately carved, the wood nearly black with age but shiny from polishing. "How did they get it in here?" she asked.

"They would have taken it to pieces." He stared at the posts. "These old beds were often thrown out."

"You have one at Haxby." She recalled it in the attics, and yes, it was in pieces. But why crowd such a large bed into such a small room? That was anyone's guess. Certainly not hers. The sheets were fresh, and the landlord had promised them clean water. "I need to wash, and change, and—um—"

He nodded. "I will stay downstairs. You'll be safe; I swear it."

She didn't want to be safe; she wanted him. But she could not move him, and he left, promising her he would call her in the morning.

Viola finished her book before she climbed into bed. She washed the shift she had taken off and draped it over the washstand to dry. This whole situation was strange, totally unlike anything she had known before. How could she sleep?

In the end, she fell asleep listening to the almost constant noise from downstairs and outside. The inn appeared to be a popular drinking stage, as well as a coaching inn. Was Marcus carousing with them?

With questions revolving through her mind, she finally fell asleep.

A sharp rap on the door woke her from a restless slumber. "Water, missus!" someone shouted in an unfamiliar accent. Viola felt as if she'd barely slept for five minutes, but was keen to appear decent before Marcus appeared.

She was dressed in the skirt of her habit and the shirt by the time Marcus knocked on the door.

Disheveled was putting it politely. She had never seen Marcus less than well-turned out, but today was different. His clothes were crumpled and his eyes bleary. She had lit the candles in the branch, but they were not the best quality and they smoked. He blinked. "Did you sleep well?"

"Yes, thank you. Shall I leave while you dress?"

"No." He sounded determined. "Go over there and sit on the bed. Turn your back if you wish, but I won't strip. Only wash and shave."

"You have a razor?" She had not thought of that. Not being a male, she had little use for a razor.

"Yes, if you can call it that. And yes, I have shaved myself before. I do so on a regular basis."

"Oh." She had not thought a man would not be able to shave himself, but someone in his position would have a valet.

She did not look away as he dropped his coat to the floor, followed by his shirt.

Oh, my.

His back rippled with muscle, and when he lifted his arms, the flex made her mouth go dry. She had never, ever been this close to a half-naked man. If she moved closer, she could spread her hands over his back and soak up his warmth. She swallowed, and in silence, watched him.

Longing filled her, forbidden and wicked. That was why women were so carefully chaperoned, because for two pins she would give up all idea of propriety and fall on him. Warmth settled between her legs, and she'd never been so aware of her own body before. How could he remain so steady?

Watching him shaving was almost unbearably intimate. Few people would ever see him this way. He was a man of importance, surrounded by attendants in the normal way of things. Yet he was moving heaven and earth for her.

Her birth wasn't why Viola wanted him to escort her. That was only a legend she had only half believed until a few days ago. She wanted him to care for *her.*

Scraping the razor across his skin, he said, "If you carry on watching me like that, I'm in danger of slitting my throat from ear to ear."

"Oh!" Shocked, she stared at her hands instead. "I'm sorry. I didn't mean to embarrass you."

He laid the razor down carefully and turned around. "You can look at me now."

She didn't know if she wanted to, but his words were a command. Lifting her gaze, she met his eyes.

He burned. He flicked his gaze over her. "I want you, Viola," he said baldly. "I can't think of a better way to say it. I am at the edge of my control. You are lovely, intelligent, utterly desirable."

"To you?"

"To all men. The way that curate leered at you yesterday made me want to knock his teeth down his throat. Don't you know how utterly delectable you are?"

She opened her mouth, and closed it again.

In a minute he was across the room and he had her in his arms. He slammed his mouth down on hers, ravenously devouring.

She responded, circling her arms around him, and she had her wish. His warm flesh pulsed under her hands. The sheer power of his body made her feel deliciously weak and helpless, although she knew herself to be no such thing. She'd slept with the pistol he'd given her under her pillow, and she would have used it, had she felt the need.

She did not need it now.

He rolled on to the mattress, holding her close, bringing her over him, but he never stopped kissing her. When she dug her fingers into his back, he shuddered. He covered her breast with his hand. Despite the barriers of her shift, stays, and shirt, his touch made her arch towards him.

He tore his lips from hers. "No." His eyes were wild as he gazed at her. "This is why I slept downstairs, why I need to keep away from you. We cannot. Must not."

"No." Of course not.

"We need to dress and go downstairs." As if he'd done nothing at all, he turned away. He picked up his shirt from the bottom of the bed, throwing it over his head and thrusting his hands through the sleeves. His abrupt, ungraceful motions told her of his agitation. She said nothing. In truth, she didn't know if the power of speech had returned to her yet.

He felt so very good all she could think of was more. As she put on her stock and buttoned up her jacket, she could think of nothing else. They went downstairs in silence and ate at the big table with the rest of their fellow passengers. She did note that when they climbed aboard, Marcus ensured she was nowhere near the cleric.

The day passed, giving Viola an opportunity to come to terms with her new existence. She would return to her father and Yorkshire soon enough, but this was her chance to make this an adventure. Their pursuers had either given up the chase or could not find them. They were as safe as they could be, considering the circumstances. Now she could relax more and pay more attention to the experience of travel. Although she had travelled from Italy as a baby, Viola naturally had no remembrance of that time. This counted as the longest journey she had ever taken. Certainly the first on public transport.

The scenery passed, mile after mile of hedgerow, the occasional hamlet, and regular stops at inns to change the horses. Passengers did not alight at every stop, only for meals and to stretch their legs. If the coachman was ready, he would set off without a backward glance.

When she napped during the afternoon, Marcus did not hold her. However she found herself leaning against her corner of the coach with a cushion propped behind her head. So he was taking care of her.

In that position she could watch him. He had taken her book and was reading it in a desultory fashion, occasionally chuckling. Pointedly he did not look in her direction, and she did not disturb him, although she was fairly sure he knew she was not properly asleep.

Marcus was the most handsome man she had ever seen. She had never taken stock of him in this way. However, his appearance that morning, together with his out of control kiss, forced her into the realization this man meant much more to her than he should.

For years she had told herself simply that Marcus was too far above her for her even to dream about, but now that was not true. If anything, she was better born than he. But she felt no different. She was still Viola. Did he feel that way? That his titles were not a part of him, but separate? Was he lonely as a single man? Oh, yes, he'd had mistresses—he'd told her himself—but only to satisfy his physical needs, those needs he had so ably demonstrated that morning.

Towards three in the afternoon, Viola knew several things for sure. She wanted him. After their journey, they would probably separate once more. Even if his family sheltered her until the crisis had concluded, she would not spend such time alone with this man again. Soon Marcus would marry, and then his wife would spend time by his side. Even though the identity of his future wife was yet unknown, unreasoning jealousy seared its way through her heart. Nobody should have him but her.

Foolish thinking. But for this journey she was his wife, and she wanted all marriage brought, although their union would be instantly severed when they reached London. She didn't care. If unfortunate circumstances occurred, she would cope, somehow. Women often went away, bore their embarrassing child, and gave it away.

Just like her mother—her true mother. She had not wanted Viola enough to keep her, but regarded her as a political pawn. For what loving mother would choose to give her sweet baby to another with the prospect of never seeing her again?

Maria Rubio did not deserve the title of mother, Viola decided bitterly. She was merely the vessel that had borne her. Viola belonged to her father in Yorkshire, not the one in Rome. Her name was Viola Gates, not Viola Stuart.

What would their neighbors the Stewarts think of her alarming, not to say shocking, change in circumstances? Would they deride her or bow down to her? Viola would appreciate neither.

Marcus flicked over a page in the book, his attention apparently completely on the novel. But he glanced up, met her eyes, and smiled. Tentatively, she smiled back, and warmth spread through her. That was exactly how she'd seen the marquess connect with his wife without words.

For the next two days this man belonged to her. He was her husband and she would make him behave like one. He would not leave her again, even if the next bedroom was even tinier, with a narrow bed better suited to a maidservant than a fully grown man.

"The coachman says we are making good time," she said, knowing she could not feign sleep any longer.

"Indeed," he said, seemingly engrossed, but he flipped another page. He had not read that one. "We will be in London by Thursday night."

Tuesday, this was Tuesday. She would be a wife for another two days, that was all. Two days and two nights. Why could this not be a wagon, which would take a full week to reach London? But if she travelled in one of the hulking vehicles that carried passengers and cargo, she would probably sleep there, too. People who could not afford to travel any other way used the carts. Even the stage coach was a step up from that.

"I'd hire a carriage, but we are making good time, and you are not uncomfortable, are you, sweetheart?" he said then, sparing her another glance.

Sweetheart. Another treasure for her meager collection. "Not at all," she said. The lady with the cockerel had not been replaced by another passenger, although some of the travelers on the roof had agitated to be allowed inside. With vails not forthcoming, the coachman had refused them. "It ain't fair to the people who paid full fare," he'd said. "If you can't pay, you travel on top."

She could not imagine doing that, but if they ran out of money, she could find herself balancing precariously on top, open to all weather.

Chapter 8

The journey lulled her into a drowsy half-awake state of mind. She dreamed she was married to Marcus, who was, in truth, a simple country gentleman visiting his cousin in London. The cousin part might be right, but they were peers of the realm, not simple folk or the Cits he claimed when he spoke casually about them in the hearing of others. They would have their time in London, ogling the rich, attending the play, buying a few clothes, and conducting modest business. Then they would return home to their property, something like the house in Scarborough, comfortable but not spectacular.

Entertaining herself in this way, she was almost startled when dusk shaded the hedges and dulled the colors of the lush countryside passing by the window.

"We'll stop soon," the curate said. For he was traveling to a new parish, where he would do all the work while the rector collected the salary and hobnobbed with the gentry. Or so he'd told them. Not that she had conversed with him much. Now Marcus had mentioned it, she did catch the curate's attention on her too much for his greedy gaze to be coincidental. She was a respectable married woman. How dare he?

The smoother roads approaching the next town came as a relief after the bone-jarring roads outside. While the new turnpike roads were improving travel considerably, not all of the byways, even the biggest ones, had received the benefit of new surfaces and better maintenance.

They had reached Lincoln.

The center of the old city contained a hill so steep many people used the rails provided to climb it hand-over-hand. The coach avoided this peril. It took a side street, but the elevation the hill gave to the cathedral meant the passengers had a magnificent view as the vehicle did its usual breakneck turn into the inn yard.

Viola stared at it in wonder, her problems temporarily forgotten.

"Would you like to see it?" Marcus asked her. "We have time, if we have a late supper."

"Very much." And it would stop her sitting in the inn room wondering how she could seduce a man with so much more experience than she had. Perhaps something would occur to her, though surely not while in a sacred building. Perhaps the urge would pass, although since it had not yet shown any signs of doing so, she doubted it.

When the coach disgorged its passengers and the usual rush to the taproom had died down, they left at their leisure. A large coaching inn, it had plenty of room and Marcus had no problem bespeaking a room for each of them. Secretly, Viola hoped they would only use one, although her throat tightened at the prospect of what she meant to do.

He offered his arm, and after she had set the cocked hat on her head and pushed her hands into gloves, they set off. The balmy, warm evening cast a golden glow over their short walk. Viola set her mind to enjoying a rare moment of tranquility. Accompanied by a man who meant more to her than any other, even her father, she could feast her eyes on the vision of beauty that was Lincoln Cathedral and enjoy the fresh air. Despite the passengers keeping the windows open to freshen the atmosphere, the air in the coach had at times become stale and unpleasant.

"In London, you will become my mother's guest," Marcus said easily. "I want you to enjoy your time there. I'll find a likely footman to accompany you at all times, and then you may shop and see more of the sights."

"Will you take me?" She bit her tongue. She should not have asked that. It sounded too needy.

"To some of them." He smiled at her. "My father will command my presence for some tasks, and I have others to pursue."

She gripped his arm a little tighter. "If it concerns me, I want to know. Please, Marcus. I will not allow you to push me aside. It is my fate, and I wish to deal with it." As she must deal with everything in her life. She would learn to be strong, not to lean on anyone.

"Sometimes I may have to go to places you cannot come."

"And why not? I'm not your protected society miss. I have few expectations. Why should I not have a hand in my own fate?"

But he would only respond with a vague, "We'll see," and she could not push him any further. Marcus could be extremely stubborn when he put his mind to it. He was not perfect, she had always known, but he was the only man she wanted.

They had reached the cathedral. "It's so much larger close-up," she commented. The carved stone, blackened with the emissions of soot from the houses crowded around it, loomed up like something out of hell rather than heaven. But the figures set in the niches were of saints, gracefully carved, and the windows shone brightly in the light of the setting sun. The black was an illusion, a fault, that was all. Under it, the house of God remained serene and lovely.

"Would you like to go inside?" he asked. She nodded her assent and he led her forward.

The door was open. Had they just had Evensong? She had not attended church for nearly a week. Viola did not consider herself particularly religious. However, weekly attendance at the parish church at Haxby or the chapel in the house itself formed part of her regular routine. She missed it, the comforting rituals and the gossip afterward with the neighbors. She had not realized how much until now. Her whole life had shifted. Could she ever return home and resume her life? Did she even want to?

That notion came as a new one. She turned it over in her mind, unsure of the answer. The decision might well be made already. People knew about her, and her situation was perilous.

Despite the huge stained glass windows, she had to take a moment to accustom her sight to the relative dimness inside. The stone was paler here, less soot-encrusted, more the gray-tinged stone of the original cathedral.

Viola gazed up at the vaulting far above. "Men made this," she said in awe. "Could they do it today?"

"Many of the techniques are lost," he murmured. "However, they weren't perfect. This cathedral fell apart after an earthquake in the twelfth century and they had to completely rebuild it. This building was the tallest in Europe until the spire collapsed in the sixteenth century."

"How do you know so much?" she asked.

"I have friends who live just outside the city." He paused. "We used to come here for services on occasion. The cathedral petitions us regularly for funds."

He did not seem to think his last words were anything out of the ordinary, which gave her pause for thought. His family was wealthy, something she had forgotten in the last few days. To her he had become Marcus, not Marcus Aurelius Shaw, Earl of Malton. That title belonged to another man, a much better dressed, stately, imposing man. One she would be afraid of.

They strolled slowly around the space and stopped before the choir. "Can you see the imp?"

After glancing at his face, she followed the direction of his pointing finger. "Goodness, yes!"

"It's the symbol of the cathedral." A small carved figure, one leg crossed over the other, grinned at them from up above. "The masons often put little figures in the large churches. They may have a wonderful sense of humor, or it might have a meaning lost in the mists of time."

"Perhaps it has a magical quality," she murmured.

"Do you believe in magic?"

She opened her mouth to reply, but at that moment, someone said, "Good God, it's Malton!"

Her heart sinking, Viola tried to pull away, but he clamped his arm hard against his body, trapping her hand. "No you don't," he said, and turned to face the stranger.

A man dressed in fashionable, new clothes stared at her curiously. "It is you! What is that monstrosity you have on your head?"

Lifting his hand, Marcus touched the bob-wig. "You don't like it? I thought I'd give it a try."

"Why?" The man raised a dark brow. His wig was a fashionable white queued one, not the dismal grey of Marcus's. She had laughed at it when he first produced it, but she bridled now. Whatever his choices, he was entitled to them.

The stranger glanced at Viola and then lingered to pass an insolent gaze over her. From feet to the top of her head and back again, pausing at the place where her breasts pushed against the lawn of her shirt. But he said nothing. He would cut her unless Marcus introduced her, assuming she was a doxy. If he had accompanied a woman, they would have ignored him. That would have been for the best. Then maybe they would not have a closer look at her.

Marcus ignored the provocative remark about his wig and turned to her. "May I introduce my betrothed? Viola, my dear, this is Lord Frederick Howard. Freddie, this is Miss Viola Gates."

Freddie's brows went up even as he made his bow and murmured her name. She curtseyed, her mind temporarily numb. What had he done? And he'd said it loud enough for others to hear. *Betrothed?* She could not hope people would not gossip. Marcus was too important a personage for anyone standing by them not to chatter. Already they were attracting unwanted attention. The bystanders stared and murmured. Those murmurs would spread like ripples on a pond.

"Are you visiting hereabouts?"

"No, just passing through. While Miss Gates's duenna rests in their room, I offered to bring her to the cathedral."

"Thus gaining a few minutes alone, you dog!" Although he teased, Freddie's expression had undergone a change. He no longer surveyed her as if she were meat on a butcher's slab, but met her eyes and smiled affably. "I had not thought to see you married."

"Neither had I, before recently. Miss Gates is the daughter of our estate manager, who is a distant relation of the family."

"I see. So we have a love match?" Before Marcus could answer, he continued, addressing Viola for the first time. "You are on your way to London?"

"Yes, sir," she said faintly. Betrothed? He could not mean it. Ah, yes, he would claim they had called it off or she had jilted him. He could do that. Relief filled her. Not that she did not want for—long for—such an eventuality. But although he had kissed her, she could not allow him to sacrifice his freedom for her.

Thoughts chased each other through her head. The uppermost was regret she had allowed him to help her and thus embroiled himself in a situation he could not wish for.

"I shall look forward to your betrothal ball," Freddie said. He appeared amused more than any other reaction. Viola strongly suspected he did not believe Marcus. And well he might, because who would imagine he would marry the daughter of his estate manager? Love appeared the only explanation possible, yet…did she love him?

Facing her feelings for the first time before someone else she had to admit—probably. For she did not know what love meant or how she should feel. Women in love saw no fault in their beloved, and she certainly saw Marcus's faults as clearly as she had ever done. His careful consideration of all points in an argument drove her to screaming pitch, for instance.

Keeping the society smile pasted to her face, Viola fought with her emotions. She could show nobody, not even Marcus himself. His overdeveloped protective streak would have her married to him before she could think straight.

She did not like Freddie. His curiosity and his sly innuendo did not give her the best opinion of him.

"I still have to inform my parents of my success, so the ball may not take place until after the wedding," Marcus said smoothly.

How could he say that word—wedding—and not tremble? She was trembling enough for two, but she could not detect even a quaver in his voice. Or doubt when he gazed down at her and smiled. She forced a smile in return, but she was not sure it convinced him.

A small crease appeared between his brows. "You are tired," he said softly. "We should go back."

"No, truly I'm fine."

"Nevertheless, I think we should return before your duenna awakes and misses you. We don't want to upset her, do we?"

At last they took their leave.

He would not let them hurry, but paced in a stately way down the aisle with her. Her imagination rioted all on its own. The symbolism was not lost on her. How could they do this in reality? When she would have spoken, he touched a finger to his lips.

"Churches have ears," he said. "Also unexpected echoes."

So Freddie might overhear them.

Outside the church, she let out the breath she'd been holding. Without it, she wouldn't have walked so steadily, or she might have burst out with all her objections. "What was that for?" she demanded, and before he could answer, continued, "You could have said I was your mistress. Why did you not walk away?"

"Because Freddie, bless him, would have gossiped when he reached town. Unfortunately he has an excellent memory for faces, so he would doubtless have recognized you."

"You sound so calm! How can you?" She wanted to slap the smile off his face.

"What choice do we have? Why the fuss?"

"Oh, you foolish man! You have committed us to the most dreadful masquerade!"

He lost the smile then, just as if she had truly slapped him. "Indeed? Why is it dreadful? Do you fear a fate worse than death?"

She let out a breath and started to walk, abandoning the stately stroll for a full-bodied stride. "No, but you cannot marry me, so why say it? Oh, Marcus, I should never have allowed this to happen!"

The adventure, liberating and exciting up to this point, took on a shade of foolishness. "I should have returned to Haxby, to my father. We could have borrowed some footmen until—"

"Until when?" he demanded. "If we do not find who has done this to you, you aren't safe. I want you safe, Viola."

"But there would have been another way!"

"Not on that road." He brought her memories back to the house at Scarborough and her terror there. She'd thought them both dead. "Until we reached the house, I thought we were relatively safe. But two people attacked your father, and a different two waited at the house."

"How can you know that?"

"The horses," he said simply. "And the facts. They did not have time to get there and lie in wait. I drove you in the fastest vehicle in the Haxby stables with two of the freshest horses. They could not have left your father's house, reached Scarborough, broken in, and waited for you." He turned, taking her upper arms in his hands. "Even with the half hour it took us to prepare for our journey, even the time it took us to run from your house to the main house, they would not have had time. Their horses were not fresh, and they were riding. It's not possible, Viola. That means there are more men searching for you. Four at least. How could I leave you to that?"

"Easily, I'd have thought. Haxby has more than four footmen."

He clicked his tongue. "As if I would do that! Absolutely not, Viola. You are my responsibility. Mine."

Bewildered, she asked, "Why would you think it?"

"Because—"

She broke in. Although sure he had a ready answer waiting, she would not let him persuade her. "You take too much upon yourself, Marcus. You take charge and care for all your family and your dependents. And now me." How did her regard her? Family or dependent? She would never ask, fearful of hearing the answer. Either way held fraught challenges she was not yet ready to face.

"And now you," he said softly.

But she was ready to face one thing. She still wanted him. When he had introduced her as his betrothed, her first unthinking reaction had been pure joy. She could no longer deny that of all the men in the world, given the choice, she would have him.

"Oh, well, I can always jilt you." Putting up her chin in an imitation of jauntiness, she turned and continued their journey back to the inn.

"You can try," he said, but so softly she wasn't sure she'd heard him right.

They couldn't continue the argument because they had reached the inn.

Chapter 9

Marcus watched Viola all through supper. She had not eaten much. The shock of seeing Freddie had coalesced a few matters in his mind. When he'd said "betrothed," the word sounded like a perfect way to describe her.

He stuck his fork into an overdone potato, parsley sprinkled over it in a desultory fashion. The food on this journey had been uniformly dull and for the most part overcooked. The pie had black edges. The peas could have been spooned out in lumps. The carrots were of the consistency of mash. They would all go in his personal book of remembrance. With any luck, they would never be repeated in his life.

With this woman, he could find himself on another harebrained journey and forced to eat mashed carrots and lumpy, overcooked potato once more. He feared he would do it, too. He never knew where he was with her. He found her volatile moods and unpredictability fascinating. She had agreed with him only when he made it clear he would not give in, but she'd been ready to return home to her father. Her real father, the man who had brought her up from babyhood onward.

Why had he ever allowed his father to separate them? At the age of nine he had little say, but he could have contrived something. If his father had not made him so anxious to fulfill his role in life, perhaps he would have arranged to meet her clandestinely.

He would not allow anyone to separate them now. Whether they would end this adventure as friends or spouses he did not know—he, who organized and planned everything in his life. Who had condemned reckless behavior in his brothers and sisters. They would so enjoy teasing him now he allowed one small woman to lead him around.

Once he'd ensured nobody was following them, Marcus had relaxed considerably. That first night he'd spent in the taproom of the first inn, he had remained awake, watching and waiting for an attack. When none came, he was satisfied they had escaped the people who would have killed her—or him. That was why he'd decided to go to London. He would find out who was doing this, and he would stop them.

Now he leaned back and watched her trying to choke down the food, shooting glances at him when she thought he wasn't looking. She was planning something. He had not the faintest idea what it could be, but he would wait on events and keep watching her.

His announcement had unnerved her, but surely she would not be so idiotic as to try to escape him. He would find out, no doubt.

Giving up on his meal, he pushed his plate away. "This is by far the worst food in the whole journey. Let's hope the bedroom is in better heart."

Ah. Her glance certainly held apprehension. And something else— speculation. She having such dark eyes made interpreting her glances difficult, but he fancied he was improving in that respect. Two more days and they would be in London. Freddie wouldn't arrive until the beginning of next week, and he would probably not consider undue haste necessary. A betrothal, especially of a man not particularly known for excess, would not excite many gossips. Or so he hoped and prayed.

She forced a few more mouthfuls down before she sighed and leaned back against the hard settle. "You are right, and I'm not particularly hungry."

"Shall we go?"

"Very well."

She wouldn't look at him. He rose from his seat and came around the table to hers. She took his hand suspiciously meekly and allowed him to lead her to the stairs.

The inn appeared well kept, no collections of dust in the corners. Not something he usually looked for, but in this case, the food had made him suspicious. If that was bad, was the rest of the inn similarly ill-kept? Were the beds clean?

He opened the door to a bedroom with a reasonably sized bed and gleaming furniture and floors. Simple enough, with no extra furbelows, but adequate. They could find better inns in the city, but he had no mind to seek them out at this time of night. Without compunction, he dragged back the covers on the bed, but he saw nothing but clean white linen. No insects, or traces of them.

When he turned around to speak to her, she leaped at him.

Marcus barely caught her. As it was, she propelled him backward on to the mattress. The timbers creaked alarmingly under their combined weight but it held. She weighed nothing, and without her hoops, her body pressed against his all the way down.

Then she crushed her lips against his, and finally he knew what her plan was.

She would not have this all her own way.

* * * *

When Marcus kissed her back, Viola would have breathed a sigh of relief. Except his mouth was on hers, doing the most delicious things to her. When she opened her lips, he surged inside, exploring her with his tongue. Returning his caresses proved easy. He accepted her with a small groan.

He kissed her like a man denied sustenance, even though they had eaten well that evening. Unless he was hungry for something else. Oh, she hoped so, because she was. She'd tortured herself in the short journey back to the inn from the cathedral and then during the meal she didn't want. All the time her stomach rebelled against anything but him. Now she had him. On the bed, just where she wanted him.

What next? Should she touch him? Her hands had landed on his chest, and now he held her close she could not move them. His heart thundered in a rhythm that matched the pulse between her legs.

Perhaps she should just follow his lead. Except he still might reject her, as he had before. No, tonight she would discover what all the fuss was about. When he spread his hands over her back she squirmed, trying to make him move, but he needed no encouragement. He slid his hands up to her shoulders where he tugged at her jacket. He left her mouth long enough to mutter, "Take it off," before he returned to kiss her more.

She could not remove the jacket without breaking the kiss, so reluctantly, she pulled away.

Moving up enough to create a gap between their bodies, she kept his gaze. "I have to unfasten the buttons."

He did it for her, smoothing his hands around her, until he met the center fastenings. One by one he undid the row of small buttons, watching her reaction. So she smiled, and as he moved down her jacket, she leaned up, sitting astride him.

Keeping her attention on him, she slid her arms out of the sleeves. If she had been wearing a fashionable riding habit, she'd have found the task more difficult. But the sleeves did not fit as tightly as in a custom-made garment. With a little work she had the jacket off. Underneath she wore her shirt and stock. Lifting her hands to her neck, she unfastened the tiny buckles at the back of her neck and let the stock fall. He touched the hollow at the base of her throat, making her feel strangely vulnerable. But desirous. "I want you to touch me all over."

He smiled, slow and slumberous, his eyes warm. "I would like that. Will you do the same to me?"

She nodded. After undoing the buttons of her cuffs, she tugged the garment out of the skirt. Before she could lose her nerve, she pulled it up and over her head. And off.

"Lovely. You are lovely." He stroked her from her throat to her cleavage and back again. He traced the lines of her collarbones. Curving his hands over her shoulders, he cupped them. "Your skin feels like silk."

From his lips, the words did not sound like compliments. He made them sound like the truth. She waited as he explored the areas of skin she had exposed, her shoulders and her upper chest. He lifted his gaze to her face and undid the first hook on her stays. Although they fastened at the back, she had a row of hooks at the front, so she could get into her stays without help. He seemed to approve. He turned his attention to his work, and he finished the job with slow deliberation, as if committing every hook to memory.

Finding the hooks of her skirt, he undid them too. "How far dare you go?" he said with a smile.

"All the way," she said boldly. Otherwise, she could not see much point in this.

He lifted his hand and gestured like an emperor giving orders. "Continue."

His aristocratic attitude made Viola smile. She took off the skirt and lifted her foot on to the chair next to the bed to unbuckle her shoes, one after the other. "You should have leather riding boots," he said. "I will buy you a pair. Then you may wear them for me. And nothing else."

The thought of the leather caressing her all the time she rode caused shivers to break out, but delicious ones that increased her sensitivity. His eyes heated more as he watched her.

"Should you not undress?"

"How does the idea of you naked and me fully dressed strike you?" Rolling to his side and turning his body the right way, Marcus leaned up on his elbow. He even had his coat on, his neckcloth tied tidily around his throat.

"It's dangerous," she said. "I feel like a wanton."

"What's happening to your body?"

How could she tell him that? Her jaw dropped, and she paused, her hands on her petticoat drawstring.

"I will find out soon enough," he said, almost growling the words.

"I thought you'd make me stop." She swallowed. Confession was difficult, as was admitting her vulnerabilities.

"Did you? Why would I do that? When you want me and I want you?"

Doubt seized her, tightening her throat. "Are you daring me?"

"Do you dare, Viola?"

He was a different person. None of his grave sense of responsibility remained to taunt her. She put up her chin. If he left when she had revealed her body to him, she would never forgive him. But if she did not do it, she would never forgive herself. And she wanted to show herself, to let him know what he could have for the asking. Not even for the asking.

She stuck out her chin. "Yes, I dare."

Before she could change her mind or let her fears get the better of her, she stripped off her stockings. Then she let her petticoats slip to the floor and lifted her shift over her head. "There!"

He was still fully clothed. He gazed at her, taking his time, his eyes hot, caressing her body, raising goose bumps as if he touched her. "Show me your breasts," he said. "Hold them for me."

Her heart beat so fast she was afraid he would see its pounding. But she would do this. Raising her hands, she cupped her breasts and lifted them, displaying them proudly.

"Come here." His voice held a low command that utterly thrilled her.

She leaned over, releasing her breasts to rest her palms either side of him, letting them swing free.

He closed his eyes and drew in a sharp breath. "I can smell your arousal. It's sweet and spicy, spiked with sharp fruit. I want you badly, Viola."

Those simple words made her gasp. But she did not move away, instead crawled on to the mattress, straddling him. That meant she had to open her thighs. He could see anything he cared to. More than she could.

Grasping her waist in a sudden movement, he rolled her over so she lay where he'd been a moment before. The abruptness made her lose her breath. Would he leave her now? Was this just so he could judge her and find her wanting?

He climbed off the bed and stood where she had done a moment ago. "My turn," he said.

Viola opened her eyes.

He already had his waistcoat half undone when she dared to look at him and see him watching her with simmering heat. "Don't close your eyes again. If you do, you might find me gone. Keep watching, Viola. I want you to see what you are taking with me. I want to see your reaction, and I want to watch you. See me, not the titles or the wealth. Just me."

Yes, this was the man she wanted, the direct one, the man who was demanding parity from her now.

He stripped efficiently but without ceremony until he wore only his breeches and stockings. His chest was bare, his nipples crinkled into sharp points. Her mouth watered. Would he allow her to taste him? Or should she just take? What did he like? Would he like her?

Those questions and more rocketed through her as he unfastened the fall of his breeches and stripped them and his underwear off. When he stood, she saw everything.

His member was large, more than she'd imagined, stiff and pointing up. The head looked damp, and a bead of moisture seeped from the tip. Forbidden thoughts entered her mind—tasting, sucking, wrapping her lips around that juicy shaft and tasting him intimately.

"I fear I must be a wanton," she said. To emphasize the point, she touched her breasts again. Her nipples weren't soft any more, either.

"You want this?"

"Yes."

"For how long?"

A strange question, surely. "For as long as you will allow me here. With you, naked."

A slow smile curved his lips. "My answer to you is the same. As long as it lasts." His eyes promised more than she dared to dream. He'd said he wanted her to see him—the man—but his title and his standing in society were inseparable from that. Even the way he bore himself—proudly and without shame—spoke of it.

Tonight he belonged to her, and she to him. "Are we to stare at each other all night?"

"Perhaps." He propped his hands on his narrow hips. "What do you see?"

"A man. An earl."

He shook his head. "Only the man. I don't see an estate manager's daughter, only Viola."

She did not understand what he meant. She was Viola, a woman, and an estate manager's daughter in all but conception. But she would let him have his way, as long as he let her have her way. "Marcus. Marcus Aurelius Shaw." Stripped of his title, that was his name. A good one, named after a strong man. He could have made his own way in the world with no trouble at all, just bearing that name and no other.

He cupped his balls and stroked his shaft. "You want this?" A curious expression touched his features, the lines bracketing his mouth deepening fractionally. He had thought of something. She would let him guide her.

"Yes, I do."

"We shall see," he said, and at last, at long last, climbed into bed. He pulled her into his arms.

She sighed with sheer pleasure as her breasts grazed his chest. He glanced down and then back at her face.

"We shall see," he repeated before he kissed her.

He eased her on to her back and came over her, surrounding her as he had before. But he'd never done it naked. His shaft nudged her stomach, as if demanding entry. She knew what should happen next and she opened her legs, eager for him to take possession.

His kiss made her melt. He darted his tongue into her mouth in quick forays, teasing her, and then he finished the kiss and gazed into her eyes. "Remember to keep them open," he reminded her before dropping sweet, soft kisses on her cheek, her neck, and pausing to tease her throat.

When he nipped her, she yelped in surprise. He had sent a shot of pain around her body, a sharp contrast to the lush waves of pleasure consuming her. The difference sent her soaring.

He did not stop, but kissed further down. Viola held her breath as he pulled a nipple into his mouth and sucked.

"Oh!"

His dark hair, unencumbered by his wig but still tied back, tickled her when it swept forward. As he ran his tongue around her nipple, she moaned and squirmed. He covered the other breast with his hand, teasing and plucking until the other peak was stiff and hard. She had not realized her breasts could be so sensitive.

He released the nipple and kissed it lightly. "Such a pretty color. Dusky pink. I shall find a rose that color and dedicate it to you."

Lavishing her with kisses, he gave the other nipple a similar treatment before moving down once more. He could not be—but she had thought of it, so why should he not think something similar? Dipping his tongue into her navel, he showed her how he could make tingles spread over her torso. They travelled down her arms and legs, so she clenched her fists to keep the sensation.

Down even more. He drew a breath, noisily. "I can't wait to taste you," he murmured.

Yes, he was. He was touching her with his tongue. The little peak of flesh at the front of her cleft rose as if to meet him, and then he had it in his mouth. She could say nothing, only gasp and fight to keep her body still. At first warmth spread through her, the peak becoming the center of her body, everything she had to give. He sucked harder and then brought his hand into play. He touched her opening, pressed a finger against it. Would he take her virginity that way? Viola cursed her innocence and wished she knew how she was supposed to respond.

Thoughts fled when her arousal rose to swamp her reasoning, overwhelming her with sheer sensation. As if it had a will of its own, her body jerked up, arched into him. His only response was to hum against her and suck harder.

When he flicked his tongue across the tip, she was lost. Grasping his head, she cried out, heedless of anyone who might hear her, before she crammed her fist into her mouth and bit on the knuckles. If she had not done so, the whole establishment would have heard her screams when she tightened and bucked against him. Ripples turned into a veritable torrent. Viola could not have restrained herself, even had she wanted to.

She was outside herself, a strange experience. Part of her observed the proceedings and condemned them as immoral. That was the part that had always stood outside her, the rational part had warned her and kept her safe.

But tonight she did not want safe. She wanted the man doing wicked, lascivious things to her.

A dreamy lassitude settled over her as Marcus came back to her and eased her into his arms, holding her close. She would have snuggled in and drifted off to sleep, but something made its presence apparent, and guilt rose to swamp her. "But you have not—"

"And will not," he said softly. "Believe me, what you allowed me to do gave me happiness enough."

"I want it. I want you." She did, more than anything.

"Then touch me."

Grasping her hand, he guided it down to where his shaft still rose hard and hot. She closed her hand around it as much as she could, for it was large enough to give her pause. Then she let him show her what to do. He seemed to want her to move her hand up and down. When she tried to ease her hold, he tightened his hold on hers, so she gripped him more tightly.

"Yes, just like that," he murmured, his breath hot against the rim of her ear.

When she lifted her chin to see how her actions affected him, he smiled down at her and kissed her. His tongue moved in her mouth in lush praise that went further than words.

She continued the up and down rhythm, hardly noticing when he moved his hand away and laid it on her breast. He kissed her repeatedly, his eyes closed as she worked him.

He paused, completely still, before he rolled on to his back, and covered his eyes with his forearm. He let out groans as he shuddered. Every part of him responded, as she had done in her turn. His shaft pulsed, emitting its seed, which splashed in a hot stream on to his stomach.

His chest heaved as the breath sawed in and out of him. He lay supine, affording her a view that awed and excited her. Naked, Marcus was all man. Hair skimmed his chest, concentrating in a line as it descended to the bush surrounding his member. A shade darker than that on his head, but still with a reddish sheen. He had long, strong legs, sculpted with powerful muscles.

A fine figure of a man, and for tonight at least, all hers.

Tilting his head to one side, he let his arm fall and met her gaze. "What are you looking at?"

"You."

"Not just my cock?"

Oh, that word, used by country folk. She had not known a word could contain so much power, but when he said it, it did.

He took a corner of the sheet and roughly cleaned himself before swinging off the bed and going to the washstand to do it more thoroughly. That action gave her a fine view of his back—the rounded buttocks she had a sudden urge to feel under her hands and the long, strong muscles either side of his spine and framing his shoulders.

Glancing at her over his shoulder, he smiled. "Do you need anything?"

"Only you."

"Now those are words every man longs to hear." He strolled back to her. Although she had pulled the sheet over herself, she felt vulnerable, and she loved it. He could do whatever he wanted to her. She had put herself in his power, and she could not wait for more.

He settled next to her and pulled her into his arms. "We should get some sleep before we leave. We have to be up early, don't forget."

Even Viola in her inexperience knew the night was incomplete. "But you haven't…" How to say it?

Luckily, he got her gist. "We will not. Not tonight." He gave her a soft kiss, passion temporarily gone. "I do not want to limit your choices,

Viola. If you choose me, it will be because you want to, not because I have forced you into it. But I do have one request."

"What's that?" His reasoning came from the heart and because of that, Viola could accept it. Reluctantly. She had done her job as far as she could. Falling on him as soon as they had entered the room was the only way she could have shown him she wanted him. While disappointed he had not taken her, she had to accept his reasons.

"We arrive in London as a betrothed couple and we remain that way until we have tracked down who wants you and why."

"Will the task be easy?"

"We shall see." His voice gained a grim tone. "I will discover it, though. Never fear that. When it's over, you may break the engagement, if you will."

Jilt him. Not that anyone would mourn her loss. Marcus was too good a catch. Once society knew he was looking for a bride, young ladies would flock around him.

She didn't want to do that, especially now. But she might have to, in the interests of fairness.

When he pulled her into his arms, Viola had no difficulty sliding into slumber. With his scent surrounding her, their bodies pressed close together, she slept better than she had ever in her life before. For now, she forgot her troubles. Tomorrow was time enough.

Chapter 10

Dressing seemed wonderfully intimate. He helped her with her stays and petticoats, and she fastened his stock for him. Not without a few kisses punctuating the process of making themselves decent. Viola almost hated leaving the shabby little room.

Another day of weary travel later, after jolting through Northampton, they stopped for the night at Huntingdon. The coachman told them they would reach London the next day. However, Viola was not a little surprised to discover Marcus had bespoken two rooms for them at the inn. They ate in the main inn-room. The food was considerably better than at Lincoln. They lingered over their repast of an excellent mutton stew and oysters, accompanied by apple pie with local cheese. That was when Marcus told Viola he had been fortunate to obtain them a room each.

The other passengers, who had come to view the young couple as their own private romance, frowned.

Marcus continued smoothly, "We must be well rested for our arrival tomorrow. My cousin will have planned several entertainments for us. And you know you sleep better on your own."

She knew no such thing, and so she told him indignantly when he escorted her upstairs. The night before as dusk was falling they had been engaged in activity so pleasurable she had not noticed anything but him. But tonight, she was to retire with dignity.

Her spirits rose when he went into her room with her. Even more when she saw the neat arrangement of the furniture and the larger size.

As if driven to do it, he pulled her roughly into his arms and kissed her. She arched her back so his hand fit comfortably into the hollow and curled her arm around his neck, the hated bob wig tickling her wrist and fingers. She would have pulled it off, but he drew away. His eyes had that dark, wild look she adored.

"If I spend another night in your bed I will take what I am not entitled to have," he said.

"My virginity? It is not so precious." She no longer considered that puny piece of skin of any importance. Not when he could give her so much pleasure removing it.

"Consequences could happen. I will not remove the choice from you."

"What if I don't want the choice? What if I give it to you freely?"

He groaned and set his forehead against hers. "I feel it in my bones, Viola. It's not right to do this to you. Not in an inn room, not hurriedly or furtively. You deserve better. Although I doubt I would hold off for long if you insisted. Please don't. Not until we know exactly what is happening and who is chasing you. Marriage is for life. It should not be rushed into."

And so the thoughtful, rational Earl of Malton returned, the man she'd known for so long. He thought every decision through and that, it appeared, included this one.

"But someone has seen us," she felt compelled to point out.

"Lord Frederick believes we have a duenna with us. He would also believe we are traveling in a chaise or a private carriage. Not on a stage coach, unchaperoned, with the riff-raff of the country drumming a tattoo on the roof."

The top passengers had not been silent, that was true, but Viola had put it down to the whole experience of her first long-distance journey. She would probably return home in style, but when she thought of it, her heart plummeted to her shoes. Because she might be traveling alone.

Once he spoke, she knew he was right. If he was not willing, and it appeared he was not, it would be unfair to seduce him into marriage. If he took her completely, broke her maidenhead and made her his, he would marry her come what may. She could not do that to him any more than he could compel her.

She slept badly.

* * * *

The next day the coach rumbled on, but as they approached the city, traffic grew more dense and the coachman's curses more colorful. The horses slowed even more than they had during the rest of the journey, when they had rarely gone above a walk. They had to wait for other drivers to pass or for a comfortable collection of vehicles to gather so they could cross the more dangerous areas close to London in a group. "Highwaymen love it here," Marcus commented. "There are rich pickings, if they are not caught."

"They are almost always caught," the curate remarked.

"Who knows?" Marcus answered. "The authorities like to claim so, but we have no way of knowing."

True enough. Although her part of the country was not devoid of highway robbery, either. Viola shivered when she recollected the road between Haxby and Scarborough and what could have happened to them there. Any attack on them could have been put down to a random robbery, if nobody was left alive to gainsay the claim.

They crossed the dangerous Heath in a group with some private vehicles and another stage coach. Marcus shaded his face with his hat, appearing so sinister Viola was forced to laugh at him, but he did not join in.

An hour later, she watched, fascinated, as London passed by the windows. Like her own private panorama, scenes rolled past, small dramas she would never know the end of. A pickpocket snatched a handkerchief from the pocket of a man who immediately cried out and ran after the boy. Would the pickpocket get away, or would the man apprehend him? What would happen to the handkerchief? Sold in a shop, like the one where she and Marcus had obtained their clothes?

Clothes she was now heartily sick of. She would never wear the scratchy, ugly riding habit again.

Ladies gathered around a print shop window, laughing at something inside. What was it? A caricature of the royal family? It came as a shock to realize the subjects could be Marcus's family. The Emperors were powerful and numerous, notorious and famous for the extent of their reach. They had members in the City and county, in court and the law courts.

The coach made its way to Ludgate Hill, the massive dome of St. Paul's dominating the top of the peak. Viola stared at it in wonder. "How does it hold together? Why does it not just fall down?"

"Engineering," Marcus answered. "Should you like to visit?"

"Very much." While Lincoln Cathedral was a marvel of the Middle Ages, St. Paul's was less than sixty years old, belonging to the modern era. Its air of serene immortality was deceiving.

The coach swung into another inn yard, and relief flooded through her, together with a tinge of regret. Their journey was ending.

They clambered out once the roof passengers had climbed down. Marcus linked her arm through his and went to the back of the coach to collect their bag. The measly single leather bag that had managed to collect a few more scuffs on their journey looked paltry next to the huge trunks some had travelled with. Nobody took any notice of them. The yard was crowded, but she could see no stables at the side. "What do they do with the horses?"

"Underground," he said briefly. "The stables are under the yard. Property is too valuable in the city for them to waste it on stables."

"Goodness!" she said faintly. She had expected they kept the horses some distance away. "What an ingenious solution."

He cast her an amused glance. "I suppose it is. Seeing London through your eyes promises to be very interesting. You will show me things I took for granted before, will you not?"

"I shall try," she said primly, and received a shout of laughter as her reward.

Outside the inn, people rushed hither and thither. They were intent on business that must be the most important in the world, from the way they refused to slacken their pace. Buildings lined Ludgate Hill, narrow at the front but stretching up to four stories and more, as if some giant had squashed them between his great hands. Two men ran by, a sedan chair between them, the poles in their hands.

Everything was soot-stained, and despite the warm weather, chimneys smoked, adding to the miasma that hung over the great city.

A lady wearing a preposterously large hoop pushed past, cursing under her breath. Marcus shocked her by emitting a sharp whistle.

"What did you do that for?" she demanded.

A cab with faded, cracked paint halted. The poor beast drawing it drooped his head, his blinkers denying him of everything except the road ahead. Marcus opened the door for her and shouted an address to the man, tossing him a shilling. The bright silver turned over in the air before the man deftly snatched and pocketed it. He wore a mishmash of clothes, the bright green of his coat warring with the blue waistcoat for attention.

He tipped his cocked hat. "Right y'are, sir," he said.

She climbed aboard and made room for Marcus. They were going to Mayfair. She had never imagined visiting Marcus's exalted family like this, in a shabby riding habit, drawn by an equally shabby cab.

The carriage rocked its way through the streets, passing the raucous and animated city to the quieter Thames-side mansions. Awestruck, Viola gazed over the broad expanse of the river. "I didn't realize it was so big."

"It matches the city," he said, his voice revealing warmth. "It will be my pleasure to show you some of it."

"After I make myself decent."

"After that." Warmth changed to amusement. "I'm sure my sisters will help you."

The gracious squares and streets of Mayfair were a recent addition to London. They reached as far as Hyde Park, which Marcus referred to casually as "The Park." Even the newer establishments were soot-blackened, but not as badly. Soot-shrouded might be a better description. These streets had pavements, broad areas lifted an inch or more from the level of the road. Watchmen's boxes, like upturned coffins with hoods punctuated the corners, and brackets outside the shiny black front doors revealed where torches would be mounted after nightfall.

Many of the doors were without knockers, a sign the residents were not at home. That sent relief washing through her, the knowledge London was not crowded with the great of society. Fewer people to witness the jilting of Marcus Aurelius.

She did not want to hurt him, especially after the way he had cared for her. He deserved better, so much better than her.

The carriage drew up outside an imposing residence, the knocker still firmly in place. Marcus leaped down and held out his hand to help her. She took it without hesitation, remarking how easy that simple act had become. Yet still she thrilled to his touch. Two nights ago she had spent the night curled into his embrace, the safest she had ever felt in her life.

They did not have to ply the knocker or pull the bell mounted beside the door. As they climbed the shallow steps, the door opened, revealing a footman clad in familiar silver-and-blue. Showing no surprise at Marcus's dress, even the terrible wig, he bowed. "Welcome home, my lord."

"Thank you. Have hot water prepared, will you? Enough for two baths."

Oh, yes. She would love a bath. The thought made her sigh with pleasure.

"Is anyone in?"

"His lordship is in the bookroom and her ladyship is entertaining in the drawing room."

The marchioness would not appreciate a vagabond such as Viola appeared. She felt out of place in this marble hall, the staircase rising in a graceful arch to a landing above. The wrought-iron balustrade was gleaming with polishing. Viola felt grubby. She *was* grubby. She had not managed her customary all-over wash since she had left Haxby, the inns not providing the privacy or the hot water she required.

After her bath, she would have to scramble back into the hated riding habit. That did not fill her with pleasure.

"Send a maid to Miss Gates, will you? Her maid was taken ill on the journey and we were forced to send her back to Haxby."

The footman deigned to cast a jaded look on to Viola. "Indeed, sir." He was a London servant, so Viola did not know him.

Lynne Connolly

"My sisters will be pleased to see their old playfellow. Are they available?"

"I will inform Lady Drusilla and Lady Livia you have arrived."

"Put her in the bedroom at the back. The one with the blue drapery." Marcus smiled at her and lifted her hand, brushing his lips across her knuckles. "I will see you at dinner, if not before," he said.

His gaze spoke of the intimacy they had shared. She had to fight against blushing.

A maid appeared as if from nowhere. The stairs to the basement, the servants' domain, were not obvious in this style of house. When Viola visited her aunt in York, she stayed in a vastly different style of establishment, built two hundred years before this one. The layout was completely different.

"If you will come this way, ma'am, I will show you to your bedroom." The maid all but sniffed.

Viola followed her meekly up the stairs and past a pair of closed double doors, where feminine laughter and murmurs sounded softly. They climbed another flight to the bedroom level. "His lordship has requested we put you in here," the maid said, and opened the door.

The bedroom that met her gaze was utterly lovely, the kind of place she would have designed for herself if she'd had the opportunity. Blue sprigged silk hung from the bed canopy, the same fabric covering the daybed and the chair by the window. Just the place to sit and read a book.

Crossing the room, Viola looked at the garden. A swath of greenery sprinkled with rose bushes and flowerbeds met her eyes. She would hardly believe she was in the city, apart from the distant sound of passing traffic in the street.

Someone knocked at the door, and another maid entered, followed by another, both carrying huge cans of hot water. A footman followed with a large bath and towels.

Viola gave herself up to the attention of the maids. Two of them stripped her and helped her to climb in the bath, washing her with efficiency, including her hair. They dropped fragrant flower petals on to the surface of the water. The water felt heavenly. Then they left her to lean back and rest her head on the edge of the bath.

Viola dreamed of a life spent bathing and loving, attending the highest in society and being feted as a great beauty. Well, she could dream. And at the center of her life, Marcus would remain.

She sat up hurriedly as the door opened, admitting Marcus's sisters, Livia and Drusilla. Except they were the Ladies Livia and Drusilla, of course.

They demonstrated no such attention to their state. They tossed a pile of fabric on to the bed and joined her, where the bath was set before the fire.

"Marcus says he has proposed to you!" Drusilla was all smiles. They had played together, and while Marcus's friendship with her was curtailed, the family had allowed her to remain friendly with the girls.

"Yes, he did," she said, but she could hardly be more forthcoming with the maids still bustling around the room. No doubt London servants gossiped as much as their country counterparts. While the Shaw family travelled with its closest servants, they had a different establishment in town. The butler, not present today, and the ladies' maids and valets were familiar faces, but not the housemaids and most of the footmen.

"We could not be happier," Livia said. "Since Claudia left, we've had a gap at the dining table."

Livia and Claudia were twins, and Livia probably missed her sister more than the rest of the family did. Claudia had recently married—a blissful match, by all accounts—leaving her sisters to find their own happiness.

They would find it soon. That was a given truth. They were rich, pretty, and well connected. How could they fail?

On the other hand, Viola would watch the man she had given her heart to marry a well-connected, beautiful lady of fashion. Why would he have her, when he could have someone like his sisters?

Determined not to repine, she signaled the maids she was done, and they helped her out of the tub. The water was decidedly murky, but better there than on her. Roads were dusty, and when they weren't dusty they were muddy. The maids wrapped her in thick towels and wrapped another around her hair.

"I feel more like me again," Viola said.

"We brought you clothes," Drusilla said. She was a lively maiden of twenty-six, the same age as Viola.

Her sister was two years younger. Now Claudia was gone, they were pushed together. Although Drusilla, as the single child between two sets of twins, had not always felt completely comfortable in the family group. She and Viola had played their imaginary games and learned to sew together. Viola had shared Drusilla's lessons, and for a time they had been as close as sisters. But Viola had made the break between them. Although Dru had offered to ask her mother if Viola could accompany them to London and come out with her, Viola had seen the foolishness of the plan. She gently refused. How could she do that when she had no dowry to offer, nor was she unbelievably good looking? Either of which would have secured her a place in society. Or even better, both. Dru had both. Viola was constantly surprised Dru had not received an offer. Perhaps she had and decided against the gentleman.

"Thank you for the clothes. I will return them in perfect condition."

"No you will not," Dru said. "We chose clothes that would suit you on condition you accompany us to the mantua-maker to select new ones."

"So I am the excuse for a shopping expedition?" she asked, amused despite her intentions to return the garments.

"Indeed you are. That green silk becomes me not at all. I knew when I tried it on it was a mistake. You may keep your maid busy for a time, adjusting them to the latest mode. Some have lingered at the bottom of the clothes press for years."

Viola rolled her eyes. "So long!" But she was glad she would not have to appear at dinner wearing the riding habit. Rather than that, she would have taken her meal in her room.

"You may refashion the pink," Livia said. "I do believe any color becomes you."

"You have never seen me in dark brown," she said. "Or olive green," she added, recalling the riding habit.

Dru glanced at the maid. "The rose pink would probably be best for dinner tonight."

Goodness. They had even thought of stays. A pair of Dru's would do until she could bespeak her own. Hers were so well-worn as to be useless. She had left all her good clothes at home.

Dru and Livia would not leave until the last minute, declaring they would scramble into their gowns in no time at all, which meant half an hour before the family was due to collect in the drawing room. At least, according to Drusilla, they were not expecting guests tonight.

When she walked into the drawing room, becomingly attired for a change, her hair dressed into a pretty style with the curls she had longed for brushing her shoulders, she was surprised to find Julius, Earl of Winterton there. Or more precisely, Julius Caesar, Earl of Winterton, heir to the Duke of Kirkburton, cousin to the Shaw siblings.

Also a man who intimidated with a look. His effortless air of command seemed inborn and terrifying. He had defied his even more terrifying father more than once.

He greeted her like an equal, bowing to her curtsey and taking her fingers with a smile. His lips did not touch her hand, but remained a polite inch above it. His brilliant blue eyes gazed into hers. "Congratulations, my dear. I hope you are both very happy. I claim the privilege of taking

Miss Gates in to dinner. Precedence demands it." He was magnificent. It was a wonder people had not called him *Il Magnifico*, but someone else had claimed that epithet before him. He was dressed perfectly, his pure white wig set on his head, his buttons glittering with brilliants. Either that or diamonds.

"But Lord Malton is an earl too," she protested.

"He is the heir to a marquess. I'm the heir to a duke. It is a near thing, but I scrape through." He offered his arm and glanced back at Marcus.

Marcus grimaced at him.

Lady Strenshall nodded. "Shall we go in?"

The footman flung open the door, and Lord Winterton led her into the dining room. He seated her himself. "I beg your pardon if I upset your numbers," he said to his hostess.

Lady Strenshall waved her fan. "Don't consider it for a minute. We are *en famille*. Let us be as informal as we usually are."

In informal terms, Lord and Lady Strenshall, who she could never call anything else, topped and tailed the long table. Between sat Dru, Livia, the twins Valentinian and Darius, and of course Marcus. All Emperors, except, strictly speaking, Lord and Lady Strenshall and her. The lady was the sister of the Duke of Kirkburton, Lord Winterton's father, so they were first cousins.

Together they made a formidable bunch. Viola was sitting at table with some of the most influential people in the land. She was betrothed to one, however temporarily.

She had met them all before and knew them with various degrees of familiarity. Dru best—no, of course not. She had never lain naked in bed with Dru, her arms around her all night. Marcus, then. When she glanced at him, he smiled reassuringly.

"You look delightful this evening, my dear," he said to her across the table.

"Thank you. You're not too shabby yourself."

The family laughed, but she meant he looked wonderful. He wore a dark blue coat that gleamed in the summer sunlight steaming through the windows. His waistcoat was embroidered with tiny flowers down the front opening and around the plackets of each pocket. He had on his finger the signet ring he often wore, but had not on the day of their escape. He must have more than one. And that awful wig had gone, for good she hoped.

"I'm flattered you should think so," he said. He gave her far too much attention, considering Winterton was attending to her needs most solicitously.

At one point, when she'd thanked him shyly for helping her to a dish, he said, as he was replacing the porcelain on the table, "Since we are only family, as my aunt would say, I would count it a pleasure if you addressed me as Julius."

She opened her eyes wider. "Not 'Winterton?'"

"Our parents were so good as to bestow such interesting names on us. It would be a shame if we did not use them, would it not?"

Interesting was one way of putting it.

They ate, chatted, and then Julius asked Marcus what his plans were. He smiled and glanced at her. "We have decided to take things as they come."

"That doesn't sound at all like you, Marcus," his mother said. She picked up her white wine and took a sip. Beads of condensation frosted her glass.

"Viola has reformed me and shown me what joys lie in impulsivity." He toasted Viola.

She managed a smile. "I try to curtail the more outrageous."

"Oh, this will be an interesting union," Julius said, leaning back. "I predict fireworks."

"You may live to be disappointed," Marcus said.

"Nobody has ever managed to eke an impulsive action from Marcus except Viola," Valentinian, commonly known as Val, declared. "When we were children, I saw him take dares from her he would never have taken from anyone else."

"Marcus's pet," Val's twin, Darius, put in. "But I think we are about to see a reversal. Will Marcus become Viola's pet?"

"My only concern is for her," Marcus said, just like a lover should.

Except he was not her lover, not in truth. Their betrothal was one of convenience. That was all. Marcus had said he was fond of her, but that made her sound like his pet again. Not his equal, his lover, or even his beloved. If she did not remind herself, she might forget it, with disastrous results.

She lowered her gaze and got on with her meal. Although it was better cooked and better served than anything she had consumed for the last four days, it turned to ashes in her mouth. It might already be too late. She might already love him.

After the meal, Lady Strenshall led the way to the drawing room, but the men were on their heels. Tea was served and port brought in.

Julius waited until the last servant had left the room. Until then, he had conversed easily on society gossip, keeping the topics light, but after the domestics had left, his expression turned severe. "I did not come by accident," he said. "We had news yesterday." He glanced at Lord Strenshall. "Your man brought the news, so you might wish to announce it."

Lord Strenshall's face showed signs of strain. His mouth turned down at the corners, and his eyes were grave. "It is no better coming from me than it is from you."

Julius took her hands in his. This was so unlike his behavior she turned her attention to him immediately. She had not grown up with him as she had his cousins, and such familiarity shocked her.

"My dear, riders travelled ahead of you. We have been waiting for you to arrive." He sucked in a deep breath, the buttons on his waistcoat glittering in response. "Unfortunately the people who attacked your father in his home returned. He is dead, Viola."

She swallowed. The words meant nothing at first, but they returned with the impact of a bullet. Her father—the man who had championed her, cared for her, and never treated her as anything but his own. "I will never see him again?" were her first words, followed immediately by, "Are you sure?"

Hands touched her shoulders from behind, hands that trembled. "I did not know either," Marcus said. "You should have told us earlier, Julius."

"You both needed sustenance," Julius said calmly. "And I did not want the servants to suspect anything. I wanted to discuss the matter with you and your family first. This is the first opportunity we have had to be alone."

"I have no family."

The grip on her shoulders tightened. "Yes, you do."

The others fell silent, but they had known her father, too. They stared at her, obviously shocked. Not as shocked as she was. "Why did you not want anyone to know? Is the news so secret?" she asked.

"We received the tidings from a man I can trust not to speak. Tranmere, your footman. He fought the intruders, but they shot your father before he could reach him. Tranmere is currently resting at my house, but he is your servant. I will send him to you tomorrow. While your district is in an uproar by now, no doubt, nobody else in London knows of this. Yet."

That didn't precisely answer her question. Numb with shock, she let him talk.

"The house was set alight, but they extinguished the flames before they had properly caught hold," Julius continued. "I believe they were trying to cover their tracks. They had searched the house. Did they find what they were looking for?"

"No." Marcus rounded the sofa.

Julius released her hands and got to his feet, making room for his cousin.

Heedless of convention, he put his arm around her shoulders. She leaned against him with a sigh.

"I have the papers safe," he said. "More importantly, I have Viola safe. I knew getting the stage was the right decision. Keeping people with us at all times."

"Except at night," Julius said, straight-lipped.

"I slept in the tap room, where I could keep an eye on the comings and goings," Marcus said. Thank goodness for that one night he had done so. That meant he wouldn't have to lie to his cousin. Uncomfortably, Viola suspected Julius could spot a lie the moment it was told.

When Julius turned his attention on her, she found his concentration unnerving.

Marcus spoke next. "I considered Gates safe once I'd taken their quarry away. I should have known better." He shook his head regretfully. "I'm sorry, sweetheart."

She barely noticed the endearment this time. Tears pricked her eyes and finally had their way. She dropped her fan to take the large white handkerchief Marcus pressed into her hand. Turning her into his body, he held her close while she wept for the man she considered her father. He would always be her father.

Marcus spoke quietly to Julius and the others. "I took her to the house Gates had bought in Scarborough, but there were people waiting for us there. I have no idea how they discovered the existence of the house, since Gates took care to make the purchase quietly. He knew who Viola was, naturally, and he took precautions with her care."

Viola dried her eyes, ignoring the tears that still escaped. But the first torrent was gone now, and her mind started to work again. "The estate office," she said, her voice quavering. "He kept a copy of the bill of sale in the estate office."

"People come in and out all quarter day," the marquess said somberly.

"So they discovered the existence of the house and bided their time. When Marcus took more than usual interest in Viola, they struck," Julius said. "How long have you been courting her?"

Marcus paused, so Viola answered for him. "Not at all. He declared we were betrothed so he could care for me and keep me with him."

Julius nodded, but before he could speak again, Marcus interrupted. "I have been courting Viola for a long time. We wrote and slowly we fell in love. That is what I want society to know when I marry her. Which will happen tomorrow or the day after."

Shock fell on shock. Viola jerked away, shoving the handkerchief back at him. "There is no need." The ultimate sacrifice. She could not allow him to make it.

With his whole family watching, he took her hands. "Look at me, Viola."

She lifted her watery gaze to his. Nothing but sincerity lay in his dark gaze.

"We cannot marry once we hear the news of your father's demise. Or rather, when society knows. We can officially hear the news the day after we marry. But marry we will."

"No!"

An odd smile twisted his mouth. "Yes. I want to. Would you like me to demonstrate how much? In front of my whole family?"

He would do that? She caught her breath, everything else temporarily forgotten. His offer was so unlike the usually staid Marcus her mouth dropped open and her tears dried up. "No," she managed to say. Clearly the man was deranged.

Marcus was chivalrous in the extreme. She could not accept his offer, naturally, but she appreciated his making it. "I'll be safe here."

"Possibly." That was Julius again. "You would be better closer to one of us."

"Who would do this?"

"I explained," Marcus said. "Either the Young Pretender's people or Northwich's want her and their ambitions are different."

Julius nodded briskly. None of the louche leader of fashion remained in his sharp, precise tone. "Indeed. So if you marry Marcus, that puts him in danger too. Except killing the heir to the Marquess of Strenshall, and an Emperor, would give even Northwich pause."

"But not his sons," Darius remarked. He sat on the sofa opposite to the one Viola and Marcus occupied. He crossed one leg over the other at the knee. His diamond shoe buckles flashed in the light. "They are reckless. At least, we know one of them is."

"Maybe all of them," Julius said. "He is ruthless but cautious. His sons are cut from different cloth." He paced, three steps one way, tracking the pattern on the carpet, and then returned. "They would kill to obtain information."

"Northwich would disown them in a minute if they were found out," Marcus observed. "When William was nearly caught out by Tony, he sent him abroad for a time. But he will not repeat that if one of his sons is caught in wrongdoing. He has more than an heir and a spare, after all."

They called their cousin Antoninus Tony. Viola didn't know him very well. He'd joined the army and returned from service only recently. But he had married recently and become an earl, when the Crown granted him the title his wife's family had borne.

Had he performed a special service to the Crown to earn the title?

She would not put Marcus in danger. But he obviously had other ideas.

Chapter 11

Marcus watched his mother take Viola away with a sense of foreboding. He knew her better than she imagined. She would do her best to break the connection with him. "She needs us," he said.

"Yes, she does," Julius said. "Are the documents the same as the others?"

Marcus nodded. "A copy of the marriage certificate, a birth certificate, and a letter. Very short and to the point. She obviously didn't have much time. Placing Viola with Gates and his wife gave the child all the protection she needed." He turned his attention to his father. "What happened?"

Lord Strenshall studied his son. "We were in Rome, and a lady approached us. She carried a letter of recommendation. This was not Maria herself, but one of her servants, who said she needed parents for a motherless child. Gates jumped at the chance. We could not take her, obviously. That was all. When I read the papers later, I wanted to return her to her parents. I advised Gates to have nothing to do with the whole sorry business, but he had fallen in love with the mother and the child by that point. As, I recollect, you are in the process of doing. The daughter, at any rate."

Marcus considered denying the accusation, but not for long. He chose to shrug and let them make their own conclusions. What he felt for Viola was private, mostly because he was not sure himself. She confused him and intrigued him to such an extent he suspected he would never discover everything about her. That appealed to his rational mind. And taking recent events out of the picture, he'd enjoyed their race to London more than he should have. Protecting her gave him a sense of belonging, of having a worthwhile task.

No, he did not want Viola out of his life.

"I have some very safe, very secluded places I can hide her," Julius said. "Nobody knows of them. I have been very careful not to keep the associated papers anywhere they could be discovered." Unlike Gates, whose passion for order had led him to keep the bill of sale for the Scarborough house with his other official papers.

"I was so anxious to get Viola safe I left him to face the wolves. He was hurt in the previous attack, but not seriously. Do you think the accident in the park that broke Gates's ankle was a deliberate action?"

Julius nodded and took another turn about the carpet. At this rate he would carve a track into it. "I wondered when you'd come to that. I believe it was. Easy to rig a trip line in his way. We can no doubt discover for sure, but at this time there is not much point. The man did not die easily."

"You will not tell Viola," Marcus said. He would not have her hurt any more than she was already.

"I did not, did I?" Julius turned an accusatory stare on to Marcus, but he met his cousin's gaze without flinching. "Neither will I."

"Instead, we fled to the town and took the stage," Marcus said. "They could not have done anything had they caught us in such a public arena." He paused. He knew one way of getting his family on his side, but that would mean embarrassing Viola. He could tell them they slept together.

"I introduced Freddie Howard to Viola, calling her my betrothed. I had little choice."

"Do you want her, Marcus?" Typical of Livia to get to the point and ask the question that mattered. The only one that mattered.

Marcus could protect her just as easily if they continued with their fake betrothal. But when he'd seen her face tonight when Julius had told her about her father, he'd changed his mind.

He wanted her, and he wanted to be the only person to take care of her. He wanted that right. Even now, the thought of her going to bed alone, sleeping alone, tore him apart. She needed someone to hold her, to comfort her.

It would be him. "I will persuade her to marry me." He got to his feet and faced his parents, who were sitting together by the cold fireplace. "I'm sorry if it isn't what you wanted for me, but I want to marry Viola."

His mother sighed. "I knew it. Until you were nine years old, she followed you around like a puppy. We could see it happening. We knew who she was. I did not want that for my son. Had she been the daughter of our estate manager, we might have allowed the friendship and see where it led, but we could not. Where she went, danger followed."

His father added, "We would do anything except that. Except give up our son."

Marcus spun around to walk away but then turned back to them. "Yet it has happened. And it will."

Certain now, he returned to his seat and tried to appear as he always did, concerned but in control. But he was not. He would put his hands around the next person to hurt her and throttle the life out of him. He was very much afraid he would enjoy doing so. "Do you have a plan?"

Julius nodded. "Of sorts. It is clear we must discover who is responsible for this attack. Once we know, we may behave accordingly. The Dankworths' interest will end when you marry Viola, since she will be of no further use to them. Either that, or they will try to kill you and free her once more."

Even that prospect did not daunt Marcus. He would stand between Viola and any number of bullets. He nodded. "Go on."

"The Young Pretender will want to kill her, and that is all. Just wipe her out of existence. When he met Claudia's husband, Dominic made sure he had insurance. The Young Pretender couldn't rid himself of him with impunity. We could do that for Viola. If she is killed, we will ensure certain facts are made public. St. Just did not care; he only wanted them to leave him alone. He would have released the documents to the press. We have longer-term issues. Politically, that could be a disastrous move and push the country into the civil war we are doing our best to avoid."

Marcus had a thought. "If St. Just is a son, he takes precedence over Viola in any claim to the throne."

"He does indeed," Julius answered, "But she can bear children who will be a threat. And if the children gather together, they can show the government they are more responsible, younger, and fitter than the current claimants. It is still possible Prince George will not inherit the throne, if his grandfather does not live a little longer. Bute as Regent would split the country."

Lord Bute, reputedly the lover of the widowed Princess of Wales, Prince George's mother, was a political agitator. He had the Princess and her family firmly under his thumb. In the eyes of many people, the man had no scruples and no principles. If the King died while Prince George was still a minor, Bute would become far too powerful. In that case, prominent politicians could well look elsewhere for a less troublesome heir, one with strong Whig principles. Like Viscount St. Just, the only legitimate son of the Old Pretender they had yet discovered.

Dear God, this was complicated! Marcus had never enjoyed playing politics. He was not about to do so now. "I will marry Viola, but not to bend her to my will. She must do as she sees fit and act as her conscience dictates."

Julius glared at him, but nodded. "As long as you take all the factors into consideration. This country will hurtle back into war before too long. Everyone knows that—everyone in power, at any rate. Weakening the country will only feed into that danger."

Too much for Marcus to consider. "Then we will pray for guidance." He meant it. Sometimes in the dead of night, with his mind at rest, an answer would come to him of a problem that had been troubling him for some time. Such as that night with Viola. He watched her sleeping and came to the realization he wanted her, whoever she was and whatever she represented. He had protected her against the teasing of his siblings when he was a boy. Perhaps the strong desire to protect her had started then. Whenever it had begun, it wasn't going to go away now.

"You deal with the politics, but know my first consideration is Viola and her safety. Nothing else."

Julius nodded. "Fair enough."

His father sighed. "You always were a stubborn boy."

Dru sighed too. "I wish I could find someone like you for my own, Marcus."

"I'm your brother. I will always care for you and protect you."

"Out of duty," Livia said. "Not from love. The kind of love a man has for a woman, not a brother for a sister."

Marcus opened his mouth to deny the accusation, but thought better of it. He would allow them to believe he married Viola out of love. He would not tell them he did not love her.

At least he thought he did not love her.

* * * *

Viola could not sleep. She'd churned the crisp white sheets into a mass of creases and lumps as she'd tossed and turned. At first she'd cried, unable to stop, and then she'd risen and bathed her face, taking a clean handkerchief back to bed. She considered lighting the candles in the sconces above her head, the ones built into the headboard, and then changed her mind. She might fall asleep with them burning and wake up to singed sheets or worse.

So much had happened. She would be tired, but her change of circumstance had confused and distressed her. If she had been the daughter of the estate manager in truth, she'd have expected to move to Scarborough and make way for the new employee. She'd have a small income. It would be enough to keep her and a small staff and to form a dowry, should she meet a gentleman desirous of her hand.

She doubted Marcus could arrange a marriage between them as fast as he supposed. Perhaps he was thinking of a time before the Hardwicke

Act, when marriages were more of an impulsive affair. It took time these days, at least three weeks.

Her father would have liked to see her married. All those evenings sitting with him in their parlor, him reading, her stitching or reading the latest novel to come her way, they would chat about life. In many ways her father had been her best friend. Perhaps it was best to think of him that way.

Someone had killed him to get to her. He had given his life for her.

The tears came again, pouring anew. She didn't seem to be able to control them.

Without warning, her door opened. She did not look up. Perhaps Dru or Livia had come to comfort her.

But that deep voice didn't belong to either of them. He spoke her name and she turned her head to look at him, tears blurring her eyes. Then, with a curse, he dragged back the sheets and climbed into bed with her, pulling her into his arms.

Too unhappy to protest, she sobbed against his chest. He murmured to her, soothing words that meant little but sent rumbles of sound through his chest. She tried to stop, but only cried harder, and as he had done downstairs, he pushed a handkerchief into her hand.

She mopped her eyes and blew her nose. "I'm sorry. I must look a mess."

"I don't care what you look like. You're not driving me away. Try to sleep, sweetheart."

She loved it when he called her that. "You should not be here."

"I couldn't stay away. You need someone with you. Me."

When she felt better, she would send him away. Surrendering to the warmth he always brought to her, she allowed herself to relax into his arms.

Much to her shock, he was still there when she awoke. Light filtered through the gap in the curtains, a bright shaft of it falling across the bed. He was still holding her, and he was snoring, not at all gently.

The masculine sound made her smile when she thought she would not smile again for a long time.

When she moved, he woke up. Blinking the sleep away, he smiled down at her. "Good morning."

"You should not be here," she said. "The maid will be in soon."

He lifted himself on one arm and glanced across the room. "She has already been in. She left a tray."

She followed his gaze. Steam rose from a silver pot. The maid had brought tea. It all felt so natural that she was deceived, but only for a moment. "Scandal?"

He touched his lips to her forehead. "No. We are marrying as soon as I can contrive it."

"But that won't be for three weeks!"

"Today or tomorrow. No later."

Shocked, she stared up at him. "We cannot marry for three weeks, surely?"

"I will set out for Doctor's Commons this morning, to obtain a special license. Then we may marry when and where we like. Officially we may not marry for twenty-four hours after the license is issued, but I will do my best to counter that."

Now he had truly shocked her. "You cannot want this." She wanted no sacrifice.

He hugged her closer to his hard—aroused—body. "Can you really doubt it? I can wait no longer to have you in my bed. You will make an excellent countess, and you have plenty of time to learn how to be a good marchioness."

Not her.

"You are marrying down," he reminded her.

"Not in the eyes of society."

With an impatience she marked as not at all customary, he said, "Hang society! You are far more important. What gossip there might be we will live down or ignore. You will be an Emperor and under our protection."

She felt particularly protected at the moment and could not resist snuggling into his strength. Sometimes she would need it, and today she did. "Can we not wait?"

"No."

She had expected a discussion, but he refused to give her one.

"You said yes, and I want you with me as soon as possible. Now kiss me, and I'll fetch the tea."

Not at all shy, she reached up as he dipped his head and their mouths met. After a kiss of greeting, he drew away.

He climbed out of bed, his nightshirt rumpled. Sometime in the night she'd lost her nightcap, but she didn't waste time hunting for it. Since her nighttime braids were also loose, she suspected the man who had shared her bed had a lot to do with that.

He brought the tea, but climbed back into bed and settled himself, his back against the padded headboard before he passed her a cup. "Now drink up, and then I'll leave you to dress."

"I should wear black." Not being a saint, she thought wistfully of the pretty clothes the sisters had brought yesterday. She would have to put them aside.

"A black armband will suffice," he said. "We will have blacks made for you for public appearances, but you will not be going into public much."

"No." She could not, because of her father. She had no desire to do so.

"And not today or tomorrow," he reminded her. "We will officially hear the sad news the day after tomorrow. Julius only heard this early because Tranmere rode *ventre à terre* to bring him the news. Even though the stage was slower than private transport, the coachman made good time, so we can expect the news to arrive more slowly. We will marry first, before we go into mourning."

"We?"

"Gates was a distant relative, brought closer by our union," he said firmly. He took a sip of his tea. "But I will have you close, so put your mind at rest about that. The decision is out of your hands."

Her grief had ameliorated to a dull sadness today. Only when she thought of it—she would never see her father again, sit with him in the evenings, or discuss the affairs of the estate—did a sharp pain bring tears. Not being a person who enjoyed torturing herself, she would avoid that until she could think of those happy memories without weeping.

Her father would be pleased for her, and she would do her best to do him justice.

Not that she would not miss him. Sudden recollections of him would not bring the tears for some time, but she had to face what lay ahead with as whole a heart as possible.

Marcus was as good as his word. Once he had drunk his tea—telling that two tea-dishes were on the tray the maid had brought in—he kissed her and left her. When she would have prolonged the embrace, he gently disengaged.

"I meant to bring you comfort, nothing else," he told her.

But she had felt his erection beneath his nightshirt and knew he still desired her. He had refrained for her sake, and he was right. They should not make love fully in the wake of such sad news. She did not want her first experience of full lovemaking to be comforting rather than passionate.

She spent the morning trying on the new clothes, standing still while her new maid stuck pins into the fabric and occasionally into her. Then Drusilla surprised her by bouncing into the room and asking her how soon she could be ready.

"We have ordered a visit from the mantua-makers," she said firmly. "You need so many new things. We would go out, but Marcus has ordered you stay indoors."

A pang of regret struck Viola when she realized she might have no clothes at all, except what lay here. The thieves had destroyed their belongings, which probably included her wardrobe. Her life as she had known it had emphatically ended.

So Marcus had ordered, had he? "Is he always so autocratic?"

"Sometimes." Dru tucked her bottom lip between her teeth. "But not as firmly as I heard him this morning. He was most emphatic."

Of course, she could not venture outdoors, not without a veritable phalanx of footmen to protect her. Someone wanted her dead. Or captured. They were still no closer discovering what the consequences of their wedding might be, and she suspected Marcus of planning a busy day for her.

The mantua-maker brought bolts of cloth, lace, and trimmings, and quite turned Viola's head. She was so busy deciding what she would have and which trim should adorn which fabric she had little time left to think of her current problems. But think she must. Not until the cobbler had come and measured her feet, and then a milliner arrived to fit her for new hats. "We may order underwear and stockings without fittings," she said, although even that gave her pause. It appeared that a lot of effort went into being a lady. Also, a great deal of money. Not that she was allowed to think about that. Even when she demanded the cost of an item, the mantua-maker was extremely reticent to disclose the answer, discussing discounts and patronage as reasons.

Just before dinner, when she was sitting quietly with a dish of tea and a book, Marcus came to her. "I have been all day at Doctor's Commons," he said. "At least it feels like it. I sat and waited. I made it perfectly clear I was going nowhere. People walked past me and stared, and others joined me on the hard seats. It's an old building and the floor and walls are stone. The chill struck right through to my bones."

"Should I send for a hot water bottle?" Her solicitous air carried humor, because the day outside was still fine.

"No, indeed, I am not so old as to need artificial warming. Although I'm sure a kiss would help."

Giving a long-suffering sigh, she put down her book, rose, and crossed the rug to his sofa. He pulled her down, folded her in his arms, and kissed her. She enjoyed the kiss so much she almost forgot the import of his errand. Nestled in his arms, she said, "I collect you had no luck?"

DILEMMA IN YELLOW SILK

"I had a great deal," he said. "I have the license, handily dated to the beginning of today, so we may marry tomorrow."

Viola caught her breath. It was real. He meant to marry her. "Do you need to make the sacrifice to ensure I'm safe?"

"No," he said, and kissed her again.

His negative made her feel better. It implied all kinds of things, but mostly he wanted to marry her for herself and not just to protect her.

"While I appreciate your concern, I want you to get something from the bargain."

"I will." He smiled down at her. When he did so, creases appeared beside his mouth and his eyes warmed, just as when they were in company and he laughed without moving his mouth. "I will get parents who are not constantly reminding me they want to see my heir before they are completely in their dotage. I get someone to warm my old bones in bed, and I get a...friend."

That sounded far too lukewarm for her taste. She would have responded, but he touched a finger to her nose and followed it with another kiss.

"Friendship is too often disparaged. Good friends, constant friends, are one of life's joys. When we Emperors were children, we banded together. Our outrageous names at first made us constant targets for others, and we fought them and decided to bear our names proudly. Even without the current troubles, we would be friends. But outside the family, I have few. I don't seem to have the knack of making friends."

"I was your friend."

"For a brief time when we were children. But you had an indelible effect on me. You made me believe friendship was possible, that I could talk to people as if they were human beings and not objects of terror."

The confession sounded odd, until she realized what he was telling her. He was an earl, heir to a great title, something that could prove a burden to a boy of natural reticence. He was a clever boy, she remembered. The teasing he received from his siblings when he preferred to read a book than go outside and play. She would sit by his side, enjoying the tranquility, before going off to get into yet another scrape with Livia or Claudia. Dru had always been quiet, like her brother.

She had thought him pompous and pedantic. He was not. He was only shy.

To have to face people when inside he was burning to run away took a great deal of courage, yet Marcus did it every day. Or had. The social mask he had perfected even fooled her. She had assumed he had grown into a man who took dignity for granted. Until recently, that was. Their race to London had taught her a great deal about him, some things she was only beginning to realize. He was potently male, powerfully built and…shy. His good breeding drove him to cover it up with formality.

A man of power needed to take the reins and do everything equally well. Marcus had accepted the challenge, leaving his siblings free to take their own courses in life.

Of course she knew Darius's secret, but it was one that might have dire consequences. Darius was not drawn to the fairer sex. He would probably never marry, become what society termed "a confirmed bachelor." So Marcus had protected Darius, too. If he had given way, his brothers might have taken that part. Doing so would have put Darius in even more peril. To love a person of one's own sex, to love him physically, was punishable by death.

Now Marcus wanted to put all that protection her way, to put her above all others as the marriage service required.

The urge to curl into him, to let him take control and shield her, overwhelmed Viola, but she resisted it with everything she had. She would not do that. She would not become another burden for him to bear.

"Perhaps we should wait to marry," she said.

"No. If you are not married, you are in even more danger. Northwich will take you and force your union to one of his sons. He is searching for the girls for that reason. If I marry you, that renders you useless in his eyes."

"Forced marriages are not legal," she pointed out. The same law that had compelled him to seek a license before their marriage had declared abduction and forced marriage illegal. They could be annulled. Very little could be annulled, but the law laid out the rare circumstances, and that was one of them.

"If they discover it." He touched her cheek. "Northwich's sons are handsome, they are wealthy, and they could make such a marriage palatable."

Marcus was always fair. She was discovering that, too. "But marrying me would put you in danger. If he has you murdered, I would be a widow." Tears filled her eyes at the reminder of her father's end and what might happen to Marcus. "I want to meet this man, or I will make a demon out of a human being."

"When we are married," he said firmly. "After we have discovered who wants you, who is sending men to find you."

"Could it be both?" she asked.

"It could," he admitted. "Northwich is a supporter of the Young Pretender. But he is firstly for himself. If he can benefit his own ambitions, he will, over everyone else."

What a world this was!

After dinner, his lordship had asked her into the study. She had never entered the room before—a dark place, redolent of port and maleness. His man of business was there, someone Viola knew slightly because of his visits to Haxby. "I know you have no man of business, my dear, but we have been as fair as we can."

With no dowry, Viola had assumed she would not sign a contract to marry. She had very few belongings, and after the attack on the Scarborough house, no idea of their condition. She stared at the small print, honor bound to read it all.

"Allow me, ma'am." Mr. Gordon outlined the conditions. Viola listened in horror. Her pin money amounted to what appeared to her to be a fortune. "I cannot take that amount out of the estate," she protested.

"His lordship wants to give you more," Mr. Gordon said, his mouth tightening into an almost invisible line.

"No!"

From behind her, Marcus put his hand on her shoulder. "You need clothes, trinkets, carriages, horses, and any number of personal items we do not want charged to the estate. Don't argue, sweetheart."

Oh. He had called her the name in public now, well, in front of his father and his man of business.

Mr. Gordon explained where she would live if her husband died early and what her daughters could expect in the way of dowries.

The more he outlined, the more she wanted to sink into the ground. "I will cost you too much!" she protested. She had not thought this far, to imagine what a drain on the estate a bride without a dowry would be. "I can't do this!"

"You may still change your mind," Lord Strenshall said quietly. Their eyes met, and for the first time she recognized his reluctant acceptance of his son's choice.

"Sign it," Marcus said. He sounded strained.

If she did not marry him, the contract would not be valid. And she could economize, not spend so much. Pay the estate back.

"You're stressed," Marcus said this time. "Please, just sign."

The "please" did it. She signed where the lawyer told her to and then demurely excused herself.

Chapter 12

When the lawyer had gathered up his papers and left, Marcus faced his father. "I would like to know what you are about, sir. I had no intention of making Viola sign a contract."

"She must. Every bride in our family needs to sign one. We need to make it clear what her role is to be." Lord Strenshall shook his head. "I have remained silent through this. I suggest that if you wish me to remain so, you leave the room now."

"No." Marcus wanted this discussion now. "She has very little of material value; you know that. It is not as if we cannot afford to support a woman with nothing. You have made it clear to her how little she brings to the estate, and now she feels worse than ever."

Lord Strenshall stared back at his son, unmoved. "I like Miss Gates. She proved an excellent helpmeet to her father when she came of age. But she is trouble, Marcus, whether she wants to be or not. Bringing her into the family is taking protection too far. Were you aware I was in negotiations with the Earl of Spenlove about his daughter for you?"

"Yes," he said shortly. "The discussions were in their infancy, with nothing decided or agreed. I am sorry for Lady Myra, but if she had any hopes, I will have to disappoint her." Myra was an insipid, though pretty, miss. She would have bored him in a week. Lord knew why he imagined he could ever be happy with her. But before Viola had re-entered his life, happiness was not one of his considerations for marriage.

It was now.

"I have sent a note to tell him the impossible has happened and my son has fallen in love. How else to explain your sudden start? This is most unlike you, Marcus."

"Perhaps not," Marcus said. Since his father had begun, he took the seat Viola had just vacated. It was still warm from her body. The thought of having her in his bed all the time sent a shot of heat to his groin.

"Tell me, Marcus. Do you love her? Is this the reason for your sudden decision?"

"She is in danger," he reminded his father. He did not want to think about the question. Brought up to discard the idea of love as a necessary part of marriage, he had not factored it into his decision. Or tried not to. "I can protect her more efficiently by marrying her. If she is married, she is less of an interest to the Dankworths. And I can stay close."

Lord Strenshall snorted. "If that were your concern, we could have married her off to a more suitable candidate and protected them both. We are not short of houses to send her, or we could purchase one. With a ring of servants between her and the outside world, we could protect her flawlessly. You do not have to become involved. We will not abandon her. Of course that would be out of the question. We could hand her to Julius. He has even more ways of protecting an innocent threatened by the Dankworths." He said the word as if it were poison on his tongue. "It is not too late. The contract is only in force if you marry her. And you have not signed it yet."

No, he had not. Still simmering with anger, he seized the quill from the pot, ensured it was charged with sufficient ink, and scrawled his signature on the document. He threw the quill down when he'd done. "Then that is one consideration dispensed with. I will not abandon her now."

"But what kind of marchioness will she make?"

"A damned good one," Marcus growled. "She's lovely, she's intelligent, and she's—" *Mine*. He left the word unsaid. Appalled, he wondered when he had turned into a troglodyte. But he would not back down. The notion of marrying Lady Myra, or anyone else for that matter, left him feeling hollow and unsatisfied.

Was that love? But love was supposed to bring happiness, was it not? "Did you love Mama when you married?"

His father shocked him by saying "No." The devotion between his parents was evident for everyone to see. The children had grown up in an atmosphere of love, knowing their parents were together in all things. He held his tongue while his father spoke. "I imagined myself in love with a girl who would have made a very unsuitable marchioness. She was the daughter of—never mind, that is not the point."

But oh, it was. Marcus longed to discover who the paragon who had taken his father's heart was.

"Tell me of her," he said. "What made her unsuitable?"

"She was pretty, sweet, and charming. On the face of it, a perfect marchioness. But the responsibilities would have killed her. When my parents informed me I was to marry Frederica, I will tell you I was appalled. I refused outright. I wanted Amabel." He closed his eyes briefly. The only Amabel Marcus knew was the daughter of a local businessman in Haxby. She was sweet, but she had put on weight over the years. She was also the contented wife of a prominent member of the Chamber of Commerce. Her? Surely not!

"But if it is the lady I am thinking of, her understanding is a little less than average." And she could gossip for hours. That would surely give his father a headache. She must have been pretty indeed.

"The point is I nearly sacrificed the marquisate for a whim. I soon fell out of love with her and learned to love Frederica. It could not have been a lasting affection, if I was so easily persuaded into a different connection." Lord Strenshall sat up, facing his son.

This was always his way, to reason Marcus out of any rare start he might have. He would continue until he won, once he had the bit between his teeth. His tenacity had worn down many an opponent. But not this time. He would not best his son.

The notion of anyone else taking personal care of Viola made Marcus feel ill. And marrying her off for protection? No. Except that was what he had planned for himself. He gripped the arms of the chair, dug in his nails, and tried to make himself return to the utterly perfect reasoning that had brought him to this point.

It was no good. The thought of having her in his bed had taken hold. Already the predictable result had begun, heating his groin. "I am more rational where Viola is concerned. Good God, sir, she is a daughter of the Stuarts. Her grandfather was an anointed king!" Taking that into consideration she deserved better, not worse.

"But to all intents, she is the daughter of our estate manager. She has lived in the country, controlling a limited household, regarding herself as a servant."

"Not a servant!"

"Before this affair erupted out of control, I had plans for Viola. She was in training to become a housekeeper, if she did but know it. I would have given her control over the household after Mrs. Lancaster retired. It is no mean thing, housekeeper at Haxby Hall."

"Instead of which she will be the mistress of it," Marcus said firmly. "And of the other places we own." He would remain with her, give her strength and support.

"Do you not think London will go to her head?"

His Viola? "No. Why, is that the reason for the contract?"

"One of them."

Anger simmered low in his gut, but if he got up and stormed out, his father would account his leaving a victory. He had done that before and lost the argument. Even if he married tomorrow, his father would always be ready to say, "I told you so," the minute they fell out.

Marcus was not a fool. He knew he and Viola would not always agree, but the prospect of the hammer falling every time added to the pressure on his shoulders. He would not stand for that. So he had to remain and argue the matter out. He wanted Viola, and deep in his heart he knew she would make a good marchioness. But also, he did not care. He wanted her.

His father loved him, so he would appeal to that part of him. "Most people would consider my position a privileged one," he said, and as he spoke he recognized his speech was long overdue. "But as the years have passed, you have put more and more responsibilities on my shoulders. I know what the conditions are like down a mine because you compelled me to visit one. I know how to scythe a field of barley and gather corn into stooks. I can keep a complex series of account books and manage a portfolio of investments. I know which cargo to invest in and where our ships are at any time. Do I not deserve something for that? I am claiming Viola. She is my reward. You know from your experience running an estate such as ours is not always easy. I want a helpmeet by my side, someone I can talk to and share with. Not a pretty miss with not a brain in her head. I want Viola."

"I see." The buttons on Lord Strenshall's waistcoat glittered as he heaved a deep breath. "There is no moving you?"

"None."

"So you have won your prize." Lord Strenshall nodded and drew the contract towards him. "So be it. Then the consequences are yours. Make her happy, Marcus." He wafted his hand twice, as though shooing a fly.

Marcus laughed. He had won. His father's petulant response told him as much as his words.

* * * *

Before dinner, Viola received a message from Lady Strenshall, civilly asking her if she would stop by her room before she went down to the drawing room. Arrayed in her new splendor, a light blue with white petticoat embroidered with forget-me-nots, she tapped on the door of the marchioness's private boudoir. Her maid answered it, and opened the door wider to let her in.

Lady Strenshall was dressed for dinner already. Even her jewelry was in place. "You may go, Horrocks."

The maid bobbed a curtsey and left.

"Now, my dear, come and sit."

Viola did as she was bid, sitting on a chair by the marchioness, who would tomorrow become her mother-in-law.

"We are on our own. You may speak freely," the lady said. "I will not repeat anything, neither will I take offense at anything you say. Unless of course, you intend to make offense." She smiled, such a sweet expression.

Viola smiled back, unsure what the lady meant.

The marchioness folded her hands in her lap. "My husband told me that you have signed the marriage contract. I have no idea why he made you sign one, except for one reason." She met Viola's eyes. "He wanted you to think, really think, about the step you are about to take. He will tell you that we can protect you in other ways."

"He did." She trusted Lady Strenshall. Perhaps she was too naïve, but she would not close herself off to people she instinctively liked.

"And what do you think?"

"If Marcus wishes me to withdraw, I will. But he does not."

"He wants you," her ladyship said. "I have seen him grow up, and I know how deeply he feels things, although he has learned not to display it so blatantly. He cares for you. It is true, we can care for you without marriage. There is no reason for you to marry him. You do not have to do it if you don't wish to."

She leaned back, watching.

Viola wanted to. A realization like a jolt of lightning hit her. She had to fight not to gasp. "He—I care for him too." Loved him. She always had, but not as much as in the last week. He'd shown him herself, shared her perils with humor and bravery, and been the best companion she could have wished for. "I will do everything I can to help him. To become the wife he wants."

"Oh, don't do that!" Lady Strenshall clapped her hand to her chest. "That is the last thing you ought to do. Do not indulge him. He needs a person who will tell him the truth, whatever that happens to be. He needs a true helpmeet. That is the wife he needs."

Viola swallowed. "I have a lot to learn."

Lady Strenshall shook her head. "Not as much as you think. Oh, I know it is easy for me to say, but you can do it. Let me tell you about the way I came to be the marchioness."

Her gaze, at first alarming, became sympathetic. Viola nodded and folded her hands over her fan.

"As you know, my father was a duke. My brother is a duke now, so I grew up knowing powerful people and becoming accustomed to them. I will not insult your intelligence by telling you they are all the same under the skin. Or a duke could become a ploughboy with no trouble, and vice versa. It is possible, of course, but learning is difficult. So are expectations. However, when my father approached me and told me I was to marry John, I was concerned. Worried, if you like. The Strenshall title is a great one and the marquesses have a long tradition of public service. They were allies, my brother and John, so the match appeared natural. But John wanted someone else." She paused. "I will not tell you who it was, because you might have met the lady. But she was not intelligent, and she was pretty instead of beautiful, and she had no fortune. You need at least one of these to succeed as a public figure."

Viola listened in astonishment. The Strenshalls appeared so perfectly matched, she could not imagine them with anyone else. And their love for each other was undeniable. They showed it in the way they read each other's thoughts and acted in such harmony.

Lady Strenshall continued, "The lady would not have been happy. At the time I loved John. I always loved him, since the day I first met him, but I refused to allow him his own way in everything. The opposition was good for him. He could have so easily become too autocratic, I fear. He came to love me, but we had a fraught few years when we were first wed."

"But ma'am, mine is a different case. I bring nothing to the marriage." The marriage contract had humiliated her, and she suspected it was meant to. To scare her into backing away.

"You bring everything my son needs," she answered calmly. "He does not need wealth, nor does he need land or political power. We have all those. Any more and I would be concerned for him. You bring him the salt he needs. You are the only woman I have ever seen to out-reason him, and not because he allows it. You are his match, my dear, and that is precisely why I support this marriage."

Viola caught her breath. True, she had never allowed Marcus to intimidate her, but she had assumed the reason was because she had known him as a child. Perhaps not so, because of her stubbornness and her determination never to allow anyone to overwhelm her. That was why she chafed at the idea of him marrying her to protect her. And the necessity. If she had intelligence, as Lady Strenshall believed, she had used it to suppress her natural repudiation. She was entering a new world, with or without Marcus. She would much rather she did it with him. "I will do my best. But we could create fireworks. Marcus is a stubborn man."

Lady Strenshall smiled slowly, wonderful to see. Knowledge shone from her eyes. "His father was ever the same. Still is. All I can demand is your best. But now, I wanted to give you an early wedding gift." She picked up a black leather box from her dressing table. "You should have something to wear on your wedding day, rather than a lace ruffle around your neck. I do not know what gown you will wear, but I chose jewels that will become anything."

Pearls. Beautiful, round, perfectly matched pearls—a single string and matching earrings. "These are lovely." Viola touched them with one finger, their cool beauty reflected in the silky texture. "Thank you." She smiled and finally decided which gown of the half-dozen she now owned she would wear for her wedding. "I'm wearing yellow."

* * * *

Rather to her disappointment, Viola slept alone that night. However this time she did sleep, although she woke early as dawn crept through the house and the maids began the day's work. At Haxby the house would be bustling, but Haxby was a much larger establishment, and the staff started early.

Downstairs in the kitchen, the cook would be preparing for the day, especially since Lady Strenshall had performed a miracle and arranged a wedding breakfast. "We cannot have people thinking you have married hugger-mugger," she told them over dinner last night. "This is the heir to the title marrying after all."

"If you can manage, my dear…" His lordship did not appear surprised.

Could she do that? Viola had no idea, but she would have to try, which meant extending her acquaintances. She would have to learn to cultivate people who would prove useful to the title. That was part of her new position.

This was about more than protection or secrets. This would mark the way the rest of her life went. Wrapping a sheet around her body, she went to the window and pulled back the curtains. Gardens were so beautiful at this time of the morning. Dew beaded on the petals, and the morning mist still skimmed the greenery, adding a veiled mystery to the loveliness.

Searching her conscience, Viola found no gaps in it. Lady Strenshall's reassurance had strengthened her resolve. She would make a good wife to Marcus if it killed her. That she loved him she would keep to herself for now, not use it as a weapon to brandish at him and make him guilty he did not love her. He was fond of her, he liked her, and he wanted her in bed. That would have to be enough.

The maid found her asleep in the chair by the window at seven. She bustled in with the gown Viola had chosen, and from then on her morning was filled with preparations. Mostly of her. She had even agreed to have her hair powdered, a procedure she disliked. But after the maid had performed the task, filling the air with rice powder and creating the most appalling mess in the little powder room, Viola changed her mind. She had all the powder washed out. Her hair was so dark, the powder had to be caked on. It felt bad and she did not look like herself. She would have to suffer it on her court presentation. That was another ordeal she had done her best to put out of her mind, but otherwise she disdained powder.

The yellow looked much better with her dark, shining hair as a foil. This was a pretty watered silk, in the butter yellow shade that she loved. Under it she had a white petticoat embroidered with spring flowers. Ruffled robings adorned the front, emphasizing her small waist. A row of white silk bows covered the front of her stomacher.

The maid draped the pearls around her throat. Viola's hand came up to touch them. Already they were warming from the heat of her body. The earrings dangled from her lobes, pear-shaped drops that drew the attention to the pale skin of her neck.

Triple ruffles of Mechelin lace frothed from the cuffs at her elbow. She had never looked so fine. Appropriate for her wedding day.

When she went downstairs she discovered her betrothed had already left. His mother had sent him off, warning him to go straight to the church once he had collected his cousin Julius. After a light repast, they too set off on the most momentous journey of her life.

Nerves made Viola tremble, but happiness suffused her when Lady Strenshall put her gloved hand over hers and squeezed gently. "You look lovely," she murmured. The carriage bearing them, together with Dru and Livia, jolted over the cobbles on the short journey to the church.

People waited outside, and Viola had to swallow down her fear. If someone wanted to kill her, he could be lurking here. Even knowing she refused to give them the satisfaction of seeing her afraid, but her stomach tightened all the same.

But the carriage did not stop outside the church. It carried on around the corner to another door, much less frequented.

Outside stood Tranmere, the footman from Haxby.

Viola was so glad to see him, she could have flung her arms around his neck, and probably shocked him silly. Instead, she smiled at him.

The big man touched his forehead. "I'm so sorry about your father, Miss Gates." He could be the last person to call her that.

Reminded of her father's death, she swallowed back her tears of sorrow and went into the church. She would have loved him here today, to see her married. She would have had someone to talk to and laugh with before the wedding, someone she could utterly trust.

He was gone. She would never see him again. But this was her wedding day and she would not shed a tear. Not one, unless happiness overwhelmed her. Her father would not have wished to mar this day for her, and she would not allow their enemies to win by letting it happen.

The church was not full, but everyone who mattered to her had attended, and a few more for good measure—all the Emperors who were resident in London, their spouses if they had any, and their parents. She came out of the side door but walked down to the closed front door for the traditional walk up the aisle.

Marcus was waiting for her. He had glanced her way when she appeared, but then looked away. He waited with his back to her, his brother Darius by his side. The vicar, a man renowned for short sermons, which helped to explain the popularity of this small unprepossessing church, stood smiling encouragingly at her.

With her father…absent, Julius was walking her to her new husband. He was, as always, immaculately attired. Although she knew Julius from his visits to Haxby, she had never seen him in full town splendor before, and the sight gave her pause. Viola looked at his perfectly coiffed wig with not a little envy. If only she could leave her hair to be dressed in her absence, she could add half an hour to every day. And that was without evening activities. He wore a dark blue coat with monstrous gold-laced cuffs and a waistcoat that blinded the onlooker when the sun struck it. Obviously he did not care if he outshone the bride. Which he effectively did.

Viola forgot her astonishment when he smiled into her eyes, his expression warm and understanding. He patted her hand when she laid it on his sleeve and murmured, "All over soon," without moving his lips. An impressive feat, since she heard every word.

Their progress up the aisle was stately. She would have taken it at a run, if only to get it over with. But Julius held her back, like a strong hand on a skittish horse.

At the top of the aisle, Marcus took over. He gazed at her, but he did not smile. Instead, he smiled with his eyes.

Twenty minutes later, they were man and wife. Viola had tried, she truly had, to listen to everything the cleric said and concentrate on her vows, but her mind kept scampering off in odd directions.

She made the responses well enough and heard his sonorous tones as Marcus made his oaths. When he touched her, she blinked, startled, before she hurriedly dragged off her glove and gave him her hand. He pushed a ring—gold, with tiny diamonds that caught the light and sparkled—on the third finger.

The ring made the whole ceremony real for her. Blinking, she lifted her gaze and met his eyes. They blazed into hers. He was not just smiling. He was laughing.

Chapter 13

Lightness filled his being as Marcus took his bride back down to the entrance. Someone flung open the doors, and they stood blinking at the sun. This day marked the beginning of a new phase of his life, one he had waited for a long time to begin. No doubt marked his emotions, but certainty filled him as a weight lifted from his mind. She was his now. Nothing short of death would take her from him, and neither of them would die today. He had determined that.

Outside, he and Julius had made their arrangements. The crowd stood at a distance, about thirty people by his reckoning, drawn by who knew what. Footmen dressed in ordinary clothes stood by. While Julius had pointed out one stray shot could cause his undoing, Marcus refused to skulk out of his own wedding like a thief in the night.

The carriage stood outside, the door open and the steps down. He led Viola to the steps and waited for her to climb in. Then he joined her. The footman in his best livery smartly let up the steps and they were off.

"So, Lady Malton, do you approve of your new husband?" He could smile properly now, and he did so.

She nodded. "The ring is lovely."

"And yours. It is not an heirloom. It has no history, except that which we will give it."

The carriage turned a corner, and she lost her balance. Taking his chance, he pulled her the rest of the way towards him and kissed her, cupping her cheek to hold her steady.

She tasted like heaven, like everything he had ever wanted. The toffee apples he'd craved as a child, desire, a summer day—he tasted all those in her kiss. He delighted in the way she responded, careless of the stares of passersby or any considerations of propriety.

The kiss lasted, on and off, all the way back to the house. He only stopped kissing her when the carriage slowed to a halt.

Breathless and laughing, she pulled away. "Goodness, Marcus, you will give us a reputation."

"What for?"

"Wanton behavior in public. I will lose all my dignity, and people will be...very jealous."

As the footman let the steps down, he kissed her again. If he could not kiss his bride on their wedding day, what hope was left for him?"

He was not so far gone he failed to check for anyone unusual loitering in the street. Only then did he hand her out of the carriage. But he did not go into the house immediately. Instead, he put his hands on her shoulders and turned her. "That is yours."

The footman closed the door, revealing the crest freshly painted on the shiny black panel.

"Oh!"

He loved she was lost for words. "But we shall leave it to another day to travel. Today we will enjoy our wedding breakfast, and then leave the company to its own devices."

"Oh."

That sounded more apprehensive than he liked. He would not stop, though. Last night he had longed to go to her, but she was not as grief-stricken or she had it under control. If he had gone to her, he would have anticipated the wedding. He had not waited this long to break his word to himself now. He would give her a proper wedding night. Wedding afternoon, if he could contrive it.

Taking her hand, he led her indoors and upstairs to the drawing room, where they were to receive the felicitations of their friends and family.

* * * *

Viola blinked, exhaustion sweeping over her. Her early morning combined with more wine than she was used to had spread weariness through her. But as the wedding breakfast wound on and on, she lost track of time, and almost place. She could be anywhere, and the people gathered for any other meeting.

The Emperors were a rowdy group, taken as a whole. Lord Ripley and his wife had sent their apologies. Connie was pregnant and sickly, so Alex had taken her into the country. She had met Alexander only a few times and did not know him as well as some of the others. Maximilian and his wife were there, her hair almost as dark as Viola's own. Lord Augustus Vernon, Julius's brother, was still abroad. He had gone on the Grand Tour and now only came back to England for short periods. He'd been a scholarly boy, with the face of an angel, but she had not seen him for some years. Perhaps he had changed in the intervening period. She certainly had.

The ladies found plenty to discuss, their arguments as rational as the men's. They put Viola's meager knowledge of certain topics to shame. She would have to read more of the Greek poets if she wanted to keep up with them. In translation, although Livia could quote the original, and did, once or twice.

For once Viola was glad of the hours she'd spent with Drusilla, ploughing through the books the governess had made them study.

And all the time Marcus sat next to her, accepting toasts, ensuring she had enough to eat, and watching her. Every time she looked at him, he was looking back at her. Had he taken his attention from her once?

He leaned over to murmur to her, ignoring the, "Oho! Love talk!" that came from several directions.

"When my mother leads the way to the drawing room, go upstairs instead. Wait for me. I will not be long."

She opened her eyes wider. "Why?"

"It's either that or a public bedding. I heard my brothers plotting."

So this was it. A public bedding would be humiliating. They'd put the bride and groom to bed, so they could make a sham of their first joining. These days they did not actually do the deed, but a great deal of raucous jesting would go on.

Relief and apprehension mixed in her while she considered what could have been—and what would be.

Did he mean his room or hers? How long would he be? Should she send for her maid?

When Lady Strenshall got to her feet and indicated the ladies should leave, all the gentlemen stood. Marcus kissed Viola's hand and glanced at her meaningfully. She nodded, lingered until nearly all the ladies had left, and then glided out in their wake. Instead of following them to the drawing room, she slipped up the stairs and into her room.

She was alone. Her maid was not there, but the room was in perfect order. She drifted across to the window. A gardener was just visible in the distance, making himself busy among the bushes at the end of the garden. A back door next to him led to the mews at the back of the house. For two pins she'd run down there and find a horse to take her away from all this.

Viola was terrified. She had lain with him before, but not as his wife. It was not so much the prospect of that, but the ordeal she had just gone through. She hated being the center of attention. The bawdy jokes from some quarters had worried her. Where had this streak of cowardice come from? She stamped her foot, annoyed with herself. She had faced so much so far. Surely this would be easy?

Would she prove a disappointment to him?

Oh, how weak of her! He would have to take her as he found her.

She would prepare. Going to the dressing table set before one of the two windows, she stepped on the dais and reached behind her neck to unfasten the pearl necklace.

"No, leave it on. I have an idea."

"Goodness!" Too intent on her thoughts, she had not heard him come in. But here he was in his wedding finery, walking across the room to her. Viola froze, her hands still on the clasp.

He closed his fingers over hers and guided her hands away, circling her waist and lacing their fingers together. He bent his head to kiss the bare skin at the base of her throat. His mouth lingered there, warm and firm. He lifted his head. "You looked utterly lovely today," he said. Over the top of her head, he gazed at their reflection in the mirror. "I will never forget it. And you remembered the yellow."

"It's not the same shade as the other gown, but it's much better quality."

"It looks the same to me."

Was he teasing? Indignantly she began to outline why this gown was superior to the other, but he stopped her by the simple expedient of kissing her throat again. "They are both lovely because you are in them," he said.

That compliment stopped her completely. "I'm not a society beauty."

"Yes, you are. Everyone will say so. You are the only woman I could see today." He lifted his head.

Once she saw his eyes, she could not doubt his sincerity. He burned for her.

"I could take you to bed and deflower you with all decorum and modesty, or I could show you another way."

She swallowed. "What?"

"I want this marriage to be of equals, in the bedroom as everywhere else. I have always wanted a partner, just like my parents."

He slid his hands up to the top of her bodice, shaping her curves as he went. "Lovely though this gown is, I want it off." He unfastened the first hook. Her gown unhooked on both sides, and slowly he undid each one, her gown loosening as he went.

She watched their reflections in the mirror. After every hook he glanced up and met her gaze, as if reassuring her.

The gown fell undone. Stepping back, off the dais the dressing table stood on, he drew the gorgeous yellow silk off her and tossed it over a nearby chair. It sighed its surrender, as did she.

He unfastened her stomacher next, pulling the tapes that fastened it around her body. Gently, he drew the panel of white bows off her, and it joined the gown. Then he removed his heavy blue coat. It thumped on top of the silk. His casual discarding of the garments betrayed his excitement as much as the heat in his eyes. Marcus was an orderly man, taking care with his garments. Now he tossed them aside as if they were of no value to him.

Her petticoat came next. Once he'd loosened the drawstring, it slid down the silk under-petticoat to land in a flowing river of silk around her. He bent. "Lift your feet, sweetheart."

She did so. He supported her ankles and removed the petticoat, not even looking as he shoved it aside. "I have missed you," he said, standing. He made himself busy with her under-petticoat and hooped skirt.

"I thought of calling my maid."

"I'm glad you did not. This is delicious torture." Quickly he undid the gleaming buttons fastening his waistcoat from throat to thigh. His neckcloth and stock followed.

Torture it was indeed. With every garment, part of her was stripped away. "You know how to deal with women's garments," she said, keeping her voice low to stop it trembling.

"Watch," he said. "They're like the outer petals of a flower. All I'm doing is revealing the true beauty beneath."

He undid the laces on her stays, the swish of the tapes through the eyelets the only sound in the room. She held her breath. He pulled it away and she was left in her shift, stockings, and shoes. And the jewelry. Bending once more, he undid the buckles and helped her to step out of her shoes. When he unknotted her garters, his fingers brushed her thigh. Viola gasped.

"Soft," he murmured, his voice a whisper above a breath.

But he did not venture further. Instead, he straightened, bringing her final garment with him, pulling it up over her head.

She was naked but for her stockings and jewelry. She could see down to her hips in the mirror.

"Take a step back."

That brought her to the edge of the dais, where her maid would stand to do her hair. She saw all of her torso now, from the top of her head down to her thighs and everything in between. Her nipples were furled, the tips rosy and prominent.

He gazed at her without touching. "Stay there." His voice was tight. He finished undressing, tossing everything aside hurriedly, and then stood behind her and circled her waist. The step brought her up to his brows, so he was only just taller than she was in this position. "Another time I'll take you here," he said. He kissed her throat, while bringing up his hands to cup her breasts, teasing them into high, blatant prominence. When he brushed his thumbs across her sensitive nipples she caught her breath. Her head went back against his shoulder and she closed her eyes.

"No, Viola. Watch." His voice gained a stern tone of command that sent shivers through her. When he pulled her back against the heat of his body, she did as he told her.

They were pressed together, his bigger body surrounding hers. His hands cupped her breasts, caressing them, tugging gently at her nipples. "That looks so good. It feels even better," he murmured against her throat. The heat of his breath feathered across her skin.

Watching them in the mirror added a new dimension to an experience she had expected to be embarrassing, but which had proved nothing of the kind. The sensations pouring through her body increased when he caressed her. He slid his big male hands over her skin and into the cluster of curls at the top of her legs. Watching what he was doing made her deeply conscious of their intimacy, and when he pushed one finger through her crease, she whimpered in reaction.

"You are wonderfully sensitive," he said. "Trust me now. Just watch."

He had not even kissed her mouth. But here they were, naked, just a string of pearls between them. He kissed down her spine and moved his finger deeper, touching that part of her he would enter before too long.

Here, time slowed down. He kept his movements deliberate, taking his time, but he murmured to her, praising her. "You are so wet, sweetheart. That will ease my way and make it better for you. Do you remember that time at the inn? When I did this?" He tweaked the hard knot of flesh at the front of her crease.

She saw it in the mirror, a small pink pearl nestled between her legs. Opening her delicately, he continued to caress her, sliding his fingers in her wetness. When he stood, he brought one hand back up to stroke her left breast as he worked her. His cock pressed against her back, hot and fleshy, the head leaving a spot of dampness when he shifted his position.

He watched his movements as she did, the way he stroked and aroused, each touch bringing her closer to the peak she had experienced once before. Sharp edges of sensation ran along every part of her body, forming her, defining her.

"That's it. Enjoy. Don't think of anything but this. But us."

His voice thrummed along her veins, stirring her senses. The sound of what he was doing between her legs came to her, illicit and infinitely arousing. Soft and wet and altogether wicked.

When he slid his fingers from that place, she murmured in protest, but he put his hands on her waist and urged her to turn towards him. When his eyes met hers, he smiled. "That's better."

Bending, he lifted her, one arm under her knees, the other around her shoulders, and carried her to the bed. Laying her down, he came after her, inserting his knees between hers, opening her up.

She put her hands on his shoulders, his muscles tensing under her touch. He was magnificent, powerful, his hair tightly drawn back, leaving his features in sharp relief. "Lift your knees, my darling."

She did so, hugging his narrow hips between her thighs. Watching her eyes all the time, he took his cock in his hand and guided it to her. It slid down her crease as easily as his fingers had a moment earlier, until he reached her opening. He pushed.

Shards of pain shot through her, and an unbearable tension, as if he were probing a part of her that fought back. Her back arched, and her face contorted.

"Keep looking at me," he commanded, his voice harsher now.

She obeyed him. His eyes were dark with passion, but reassuring. This would be over in a moment, and she knew it would never hurt this much again. He pushed again. More pain.

"No." Closing his eyes, he climbed off her and rolled on his back by her side. "That's too much."

"Are we not to do this, then?" Bewildered, she turned her head and gazed at him.

He cupped her face, and despite the pain of a moment ago, she nuzzled into his palm. "Not like that, sweetheart. I can't hurt you." Drawing closer to her, he planted a kiss on her lips, sweetly soothing.

Was she to retain her virginity? How were they to get past this without a little pain? "It didn't hurt too much, truly."

"Yes, it did." He stroked her cheek with his thumb. "Don't lie to me, Viola. Never do that." He sighed, his breath warm on her cheek. "Some women find more difficulty than others."

"How do you know?" she demanded indignantly.

He smiled. "Gossip at White's."

She neatly fell into his trap. "They gossip at a men's club?"

Leaning back, he hooted with laughter. "Where else? Although that kind of gossip is more likely at the House of Lords." Still grinning, he turned back to her. "Sorry, sweetheart, I couldn't resist. I just know, all right? Take it from me. I have never deflowered a virgin before, but I did do a little reading."

Her eyes rounded. "There are books?"

"Pamphlets and books, yes."

He studied the subject before he tried it. The knowledge melted her heart. "Won't you come back?"

"I have a better idea," he said. "You come here. Come, sit."

He stayed on his back. She stared at him, not knowing what he meant. "I am here."

"Have you ever ridden a horse astride?"

Heat rushed to her skin when she finally understood.

He grazed her face gently with the knuckle of his first finger. "Your skin is so beautifully soft. Sit astride me. You can take me at your pace and the angle that is best for you."

Yes. But he would see everything—everything she had. The prospect of such intimacy cowed her, made her think. But this was Marcus, lying next to her stark naked and aroused. He would do it. So could she.

Holding her bottom lip between her teeth, Viola rose and mounted him. That was what she would have called it. She'd ridden astride as a child, before learning to do it side-saddle. These days she could do anything side-saddle she could do astride. Except this.

She pressed against him, her…private parts against his stomach. When he tensed, he nudged the knot of flesh. Daring, she touched it. "Is there a name for this?"

"Clitoris," he said immediately, and touched her hand where she touched herself. His eyes burned. "You look beautiful doing that. Do you remember what I did for you at the inn?"

He touched it, sent pleasure rocketing through her. "Yes."

"Let me do it again. Move your hand. Not only will it give you pleasure, it will make you wetter. You can take me easier then."

When she slid her hand out from her clitoris, he took over. He had a sure touch, confident as hers was tentative.

"Put me inside you, Viola."

"Yes." She licked her lips before rising up on her knees. That brought her opening close to his member. His cock. She had to support it with her hand, so with him touching her, their hands nudged each other, their touches deeply intimate.

He felt hard, hot, but essentially human, the skin delicate, especially over the head. His cock was slick, the liquid clear. She moved over it, feeling the rounded head nudge her. When she pressed, the pressure began again. She leaned back a little, and the pressure eased.

"That's it," he whispered. "Keep going."

She pushed a bit more and found she could take more. His sharp "Oh!" told her she had worked him farther inside.

He moved his hand. He was watching. "I'll keep still. You do it," he said in a tight voice.

She pushed in farther and waited until the stretching had ameliorated somewhat. Then a little more. She took him a tiny bit at a time. Stopping to rest, she smiled down at him, trying to show him she wanted it. "I'm not boring you?"

His laugh shook his whole body, including the part inside her. She must have gained an inch from that alone. Still laughing, she bore down more, and more. Until suddenly he was fully embedded inside her.

The ball sack was under her, touching a part of her she had not realized was so sensitive. She felt every wiry hair as it brushed against her skin. "I'm full."

"So you are. Full of me." Reaching forward, he grasped her hips and moved her a little.

She liked that, liked it a lot. A new experience, but not exactly unexpected. It was just knowing about it, seeing the animals in the fields and occasionally a villager taking his pleasure with his woman out of doors. Seeing that and knowing it were so different she had no words to properly describe it. Only part words. Intimate, certainly. Strange, yes, that too.

Wonderful. It was wonderful.

She wasn't aware she'd said the word aloud until he answered her. "It is rather wonderful, isn't it? How do you feel now?"

"Better." More used to it.

She dared to move and found the response good. So good she did it again.

He urged her to lift up. "Up and down. I'll take care of the rest. Just tell me when it feels particularly good."

Doing as he told her, she lifted up so the bottom part of his cock left her body.

He pushed her back down. "More."

She did it again. Some liquid seeped out of her, easing her passage. She tried again. Easier this time. And again. Until she realized she was riding him, and his analogy made sense. A laugh surprised her, escaping to echo around the room.

As she pushed down, he thrust up. She gasped, but did not stop. Repeating the motion felt so good.

She was sitting upright, not as much as when she rode a horse, but not leaning forward, as a jockey did. Her breasts shook as he moved. When she leaned back even more, his cock nudged a spot inside her. Intense quivers rocked her, so much that her vision went out of focus, and she cried out.

"A small orgasm," he said. When she frowned he said, "The climax of passion, when every part of you peaks. You will have more, sweetheart, if you want them."

"Oh, yes, yes I do."

"Then *move*."

Not needing to be told twice, she kept working, riding him, moving from an easy trot to a canter, faster. He met her plunges, forcing his shaft deep inside her, more powerful with every stroke. Her body slammed down on to his. When he put one finger down there, where her clitoris hit it every time, he urged more intense responses from her. Sweat broke out on her body, but she ignored it. This was too good to stop now.

Deeper, harder, her reactions rose, the piercing pleasure rocketing through her, taking her to a point she had never known. He grunted, an essentially male sound as his groin tensed and became hard.

Everything in her coalesced, peaked, and exploded, like a shower of fire, spreading the warmth right to her fingertips. He cried her name, froze, and his cock pulsed deeply inside her.

She watched in wonder, saw a powerful man come completely within her orbit. He hid nothing, showed her his response to her lovemaking, gasping. The pulse in his throat throbbed, speeding up.

He pulled her down and gave her an open-mouthed, luscious kiss. He thrust his tongue into her, imitating their play below, supporting her when she collapsed against him.

They kissed until the pleasure ebbed, leaving contentment in its wake.

"So that was it," she said, when they finally broke apart.

"Some of it," he replied shakily. "We have a long way to go, though. Many avenues to explore together. You were wonderful, sweetheart. That was perfect."

As a learning experience, she could not disagree.

Chapter 14

They practiced a great deal over the next week. With the news of her father spreading, Viola took to wearing a black armband and subdued colors. She felt right doing that, although black would not be appropriate for a new bride. When she thought of her father's fate, such happiness seemed wrong, but Marcus listened to her, held her, and let her weep when she needed to. Then he made love to her.

He brought her a deep joy she had not known possible.

"You should go out a little," his mother said after he first week when they were sitting at dinner. "Not to dance, of course, but the theater, the opera, and dinner with friends is entirely allowable. Did you not say you wanted to see more of the city?"

"No," Marcus said firmly. "Viola is in danger, and we are no nearer discovering who did it than we were before."

"I should be safe in company," she responded. "You said so yourself."

He had. Nobody would shoot at her in a crowded place, surely. They could hit any number of innocents. She had fired weapons more than once herself and knew how inaccurate they could be. "If nobody can get close enough to stab me, or I'm with people you trust, surely I'm fine."

"I don't like it." He took her hand as if to assure himself of her safety.

"Marcus, this house is beautiful, and the garden too, but…"

His mother continued when Viola's voice trailed off. She had not seen the look of helplessness in Marcus's eyes. Or if she had, she chose to ignore it. "She will run mad if she stays here much longer. Marcus, Viola is a country girl. She is used to roaming free."

He turned his attention to her as if nobody else sat around the dining table, giving her his complete attention. "Is this true? Are you unhappy?"

"No, of course not," she said, but his mother's exasperated sound told another story.

"Take her out," Lady Strenshall said. "Show her some of the city. And for heaven's sake, let her meet our friends. Not just the family. People will begin to believe something is wrong."

"Nothing is wrong!" Viola said.

Marcus lifted her hand to his lips. "Yes, it is. Mama is right. Would you like to go to the opera tomorrow night?"

Instead of preparing for a night at home, Viola had her maid dress her in a brand new lavender silk. Then she tied the black band around her upper arm. She wore black gloves, too, but excitement simmered low in her belly. She had never been to the opera before. Plays, of course. Her aunt in York adored going to the theater, but she had an aversion to opera, so on opera nights they'd stayed at home.

Viola liked singing, doing it and listening, although her voice was not above average. She could play, though, and she enjoyed music.

What she did not feel was fear. Marcus would take care of her, and just in case of danger, she had a small knife secreted in her pocket, sheathed in soft leather. Small, but enough to do serious damage should she wish it. She would not hesitate if anyone attacked her.

The opera held a danger if she sat in the Strenshall family box. Isolated in that way she could form a target. So Marcus took her to a more public seat on the balcony. A footman sat behind her, not in livery. Tranmere made Viola feel much safer. She suspected Marcus had employed others, but when they had taken their seats, he leaned to her and murmured, "Julius knows we are here. He has put men in the audience."

She almost laughed. Who was she to draw such attention? She still felt like Viola Gates, the unimportant daughter of an estate manager, a woman who could not expect her appearance to attract undue interest.

She had not changed.

People stared at her. They would not know the secret of her parentage, so they were staring at her because she was a new bride. She had unexpectedly taken one of the most eligible bachelors in the country off the market. They wanted to assess. Maybe the ladies who were freer with their favors wanted to see exactly how devoted Marcus was as a husband.

He gave her most flattering attention. He took her fan from her and wafted cool air over her face when she exclaimed it was hot in the theater. A chandelier blazed above them, the a hundred burning candles heating the air.

Despite those distractions, plus the constant chattering of the audience, Viola thoroughly enjoyed the opera. At a particularly poignant moment when the soprano was giving her all, a tear escaped from the corner of her eye. It slipped down the side of her cheek.

Marcus gave her his handkerchief, which she took with a grateful smile, dabbing at the tear before she returned it to him. "Music affects me very much," she explained.

His smile held warmth, but the corners of his lips were tilted. "I remember."

Ah, yes, that time when he'd caught her playing a bawdy song on the best harpsichord. "That was different." But although she lifted her chin and tried for her best haughty expression, she glanced at him and gave him a reluctant smile.

Then she returned her attention to the stage. The performers were excellent, and the music superb. Handel, she assumed, from the stately pace and the tragic nature of the opera. A king returned from exile to find a wife and children unfairly persecuted. Of course, after expressing a number of admirable sentiments at length and musically, they perished horribly.

Viola thoroughly enjoyed it. She especially enjoyed the part where the king sang for a good five minutes, although he was poisoned and pierced through with half a dozen swords before finally succumbing.

The whole experience drained her. Although the evening held more entertainments, a ballet and a farce, Viola had all she wanted from the opera.

"You're tired, sweetheart?" Marcus asked.

When she said yes, he set about ordering the carriage to take them home.

Seeing the moonlit piazza of Covent Garden before them, Viola would have dearly loved to walk back and see more of this tantalizing city. The glimpses she'd had of it were not nearly enough.

They stood in the portico of the opera house, breathing in the cool night air, when someone approached. Marcus stiffened, and then relaxed. "Lord Dorsetshire," he said.

His lordship, a man of around fifty, and his wife, who needed a considerable amount of pink satin to swath her form, smiled and bowed.

The lady watched Viola through narrowed eyes. "I wondered who was lovely enough to draw Lord Malton's attention away from our Elizabeth," she said. "Now I see you for myself, I perfectly understand why he could not resist you."

Just as if she'd seduced Marcus into marrying her. For two pins she would have told her ladyship so, but with a rare moment of discretion, Viola controlled her tongue. "We have known each other for a long time," she said.

"Ah, yes, your father was...his estate manager?" A note of disbelief crept into her voice.

"And a distant relation to the family." She hated making that claim, as if that made everything all right, made her eligible.

Marcus drew her closer. She had her hand tucked into the crook of his arm. The soft fabric of his coat rubbed her fingers. "Viola has her own charms," he said.

Viola could have groaned. He'd made matters worse. Could he not see the lady was looking for a reason for him to have spurned her daughter in favor of someone who was no better than a servant? She kept the smile on her face, but it had become a rictus.

"And such haste!" The lady's gaze deliberately swept Viola from head to toe, lingering on her stomach.

Ah, yes, she could be pregnant. After the way they had spent the last week, the likelihood had increased. That would give the society matrons—jealous cats!—reason to chatter. Lady Malton had trapped his lordship into marriage. Not because he wanted to keep her close to protect her from enemies who would stop at nothing to see her dead. Oh, no, that would not matter in the least.

"My lady, a woman may attract a man without trying." She did her best.

Marcus lifted Viola's hand and pressed a kiss to the knuckles. Even though she wore gloves, he affected her, and she could barely resist the sensual way her eyelids drooped when he used such tactics. He knew it, too.

A wicked smile deepened the creases at the corners of his mouth. "A woman may indeed do that," he said. "I could scarcely believe I was so blind when I met her recently after a few years' absence. I had nearly missed all that loveliness."

"Your father approves?" Lord Dorsetshire said. He looked at Viola too, but his gaze lingered on her breasts.

Viola wanted to cover up. He made her feel unclean, the way his lips loosened even more, revealing a very wet underbite.

"Naturally," Marcus said in a tight voice.

He was not pleased. Why the Dorsetshires could not detect his displeasure Viola didn't know, because to her it was unmistakable.

"But had my father opposed it, I still would have gone ahead. I would not willingly let Viola go to any other man."

He sounded like a man in love. Which was wrong, because he had married her for different reasons.

Her carriage drew up, the crest gleaming in the golden light of the flambeaux flaming in their sconces, making it easy for everyone to see them.

Relieved, Viola allowed Marcus to hand her into the vehicle before following her himself. At once he reached for her, drew her face to his, and kissed her. Although he did not make the embrace an overly passionate one, it was nevertheless a potent exhibition of what their marriage meant. Not a meeting of great fortunes or political alliances, but a meeting of bodies.

Viola would have liked a meeting of minds, but she would take whatever came her way.

What did come her way was passion. Marcus kept her hand in his on the short journey home. As soon as the carriage rumbled away over the cobbles, he let out a sigh of relief. "I cannot tell you how glad I am that ordeal is over!"

"Did you not enjoy the opera?" she asked, disappointed.

"Not that. Our first appearance in public as a married couple. I detest being the center of attention, and I fear we were. People gossiped about us, and I daresay we will feature strongly in the scandal sheets tomorrow."

"I wasn't aware you read them."

"Papa reads everything. We all do, if we have time. Those rags tell us what public opinion is tending towards as much as any serious piece. Nobody admits to reading them, yet they sell hundreds of copies every day. They can't all be to coffee houses and the lower orders."

"You did not like people talking about us. Neither did I, but they will do it whether we are there or not."

"I will find some select musicales to take you to. Whatever got into my head, taking you to a public place? I must be going insane," Marcus said with feeling. "I could not rest for looking about me, wondering where the next attack would come from."

"It will not do, Marcus," she said decidedly. "We cannot go about our lives worrying. The people who—" She broke off, finding it difficult to articulate the next part, took a breath, and continued. "The people who killed my father to get to me may never be found."

"Oh, we will find them," Marcus said, a grim line to his mouth. "Never fear. And we will do it soon, because I want you to enjoy next season."

"I'm enjoying this one."

"It's hardly a season. They will close the playhouses and opera houses soon for the summer. We will either stay quietly in town or go into the country. In any case, we should return to Haxby next month for the shooting party."

She shuddered. A week or more of sudden retorts and dozens of birds thumping to the ground. They would be eating pheasant for a week, and so would the villagers. "I will do my best."

They rolled through the smoother streets of the West End, towards home. "You don't need to do your best," he said. "You only have to be yourself."

As well for him to say. He did not have to endure the insolent stares of people trying to assess why she had trapped him.

When they arrived home, he hustled her upstairs and into her room, startling her maid, who was preparing the place for her. Her night rail lay across the embroidered bedcover and the dressing table was laid out neatly with freshly cleaned brushes.

At their entry, the maid took one look at them, bobbed a curtsey, and scuttled away through the jib-door.

Viola doubted very much Marcus had noticed. The gleam in his eyes demonstrated intent clearly enough for her. Her heart beat harder, and her breath came in short gasps. "Marcus…"

He seized her by the waist and pushed her against the wall by the door. Half crushed by the weight of their bodies, her hoops belled out at the sides, ominous cracking sounds coming from the whalebone. Marcus ignored her protests and took her mouth in a savage kiss.

Viola responded. When he dragged handfuls of her skirts up, she pressed against the wall. She pushed her body towards his, wetness dewing the apex between her legs. He shoved his hand between her thighs, roughly urging her legs apart. Then he lifted her, dragging her up with one hand while he fumbled at the fall of his breeches with the other.

With clumsy haste, he freed his shaft and pushed it into her. Swaths of lilac silk fell between them, but he pulled them free and kissed her again before pausing.

"What you do to me, Viola. I could not bear the danger. I have no idea what was happening on stage. I took no notice of it." He thrust deeply into her over and over. "I will not lose you. I will *not*."

Gasping, she said his name. That only impelled him to further efforts to nail her to the wall. He hammered into her, her body thudding against the paneling, the dado rail digging into her back with every hard, punishing stroke. He drove her higher, and when her fall came, he growled like an animal claiming its mate.

Thrills coursed up her spine. They exploded in her head, forcing her up and up, until she exploded in a series of what felt like jagged sparks.

The conflagration burned out of control. He continued to thrust inside her. Her passage clenched, tightened around his cock, until he gave one sharp cry and pulsed his seed deep inside her. Continuing to thrust, he pressed his forehead against hers and whispered her name, so intimately she melted all over again.

The sound of their breath sawing in and out of their lungs mingled with the clop of horses and carriage outside, the occasional shout from someone in the street. But that was another world, not the one that occupied them now.

"All I could think of was your safety," he said between hard pants. "Any minute I expected to hear a shot or feel cold steel in my back. I'm going insane, Viola. Stop me doing this."

She laughed shakily, rejoicing that she should matter so much to him. He had gone beyond duty, whether he realized it or not. "Marcus, I will be safe, I promise. I won't let anyone hurt me."

"Now that is a foolish answer." He sounded more normal as he drew away and let her feet slide to the floor.

She had lost a shoe in their encounter and landed awkwardly, but compensated by standing on tiptoe. "I do believe you cracked my new petticoat." She tried to sound stern, but she could not.

"So I am reduced to the status of lady's maid again tonight?"

"Certainly not. I will ring for her, and you may return in half an hour." It would take that long to unwind all the silk and find the pins he'd dislodged. Her hair was half down, and not from design, and her stomacher had twisted. She must present an exceedingly bedraggled figure.

"Spoken like a true countess." He stepped away and found her shoe when he nearly stumbled over it. He picked it up and handed it to her with a bow. "And perhaps a Cinderella."

She had read the quaint tales of Perrault in a book in the library at Haxby. Perhaps he had read the same book. "I will not prove the point by sleeping in the ashes."

He caught her hand and lifted it to his mouth, but this time he pressed a kiss into the center of her palm. He folded her fingers over it. "Keep that for me. I will return. I will not apologize for what I did to you just now, Viola. I wanted to possess you, God help me."

"Did I demand an apology? I would rather you did it again. It was"— she paused, searching for the right words—"deeply thrilling."

She received another kiss for that before he left to prepare himself for bed.

He left the room through the door connecting with his. He appeared just as disheveled, half his waistcoat buttons undone or torn away and his breeches only fastened with the two buttons at the top. She'd rammed her fingers into his hair, and it was as tousled as hers must be.

But that encounter had shown her how much he wanted her. Dared she assume he cared for her more deeply than protection or duty would suggest?

Chapter 15

Town gossiped. It had gossiped when Marcus and Viola had kept to the house. Now they appeared in public, it gossiped even more. Finally Viola decided to take her fate into her own hands.

Tired of staying in, receiving only the guests Marcus and his cousins approved of, after another week, she came to a few conclusions. However, when she tried to discuss her situation with him, Marcus kissed her into submission and made love to her instead of engaging in rational argument.

The problem was not resolving as quickly as Marcus would have liked. It could go on for years, the thought of which gave Viola a terror of being overprotected for a long time to come

Accordingly, once Marcus had left the house for his club, she called her maid and Tranmere and announced her intention of going shopping.

As she might have predicted, one of her sisters-in-law, Drusilla, arrived in her bedroom to remonstrate with her. "Marcus will be deeply displeased," she said, sitting in the chair provided for her.

Viola, sitting before her mirror while Dubois curled her hair, spared her a glance. "If I do not go out from time to time, I will run mad. I cannot stay here any longer. If you try to stop me, I will resist."

She stood while Dubois helped her into her hat and a light shawl against the inclement weather. Even the rain would not deter her. She felt so good to be wearing sturdy shoes again and a gown that only went as far as her ankles, instead of slippers and a loose sacque. "I take it the household discovered my plans when I sent for my carriage?" She had to risk someone finding Marcus before she had time to reach the house. But she would do this. "You may accompany me if you wish. I will do a little shopping and then return home. That way I may prove to my stubborn husband I will not be murdered the moment I leave the house."

Dru frowned. "I will accompany you. Please, give me twenty minutes."

"Ten," she said, and even that concerned her. Marcus had told her he was headed for a coffee house in the city, so she felt reasonably secure giving Dru that time. Marcus would not hear of her jaunt and to return to the house anytime soon.

She still worried, her stomach tied in a tense knot. When the ten minutes were up, she stood in the hall, tapping her foot, and spun around just as Dru scurried down the stairs.

"I'm ready," she said breathlessly.

Viola was relieved not to see the whole family. That eventuality had only occurred to her after she'd extended the invitation to Drusilla. She did not want to put the whole of the family in possible jeopardy, nor did she wish to discover herself surrounded by protectors.

She was fortunate Dru had told nobody of her intentions. They went outside and climbed into the carriage. As well as Tranmere, Viola had asked for one more footman, the burliest the house had to offer, which was saying something. To appearances, she had two well-dressed prizefighters with her. She was not at all sure the carriage would hold them if they both swung up behind her.

Tranmere travelled with them, and the other footman, one Hanson, trotted by the side of it. Since their progress to Bond Street was stately, to say the least, that solution served and was not so unusual.

They reached the bottom of Bond Street, and Viola and Dru climbed out, going into the nearest shop.

Viola had begun her expedition in defiance, not as a genuine shopping expedition. But she had missed this exercise in feminine companionship. Having the owners bringing goods to the house did not compare with going to the shops and browsing, before selecting items for herself.

The toyshop before her offered some delectable wares in the broad, curved bay windows. Several fans, patch boxes, and *necessaires* met her gaze. She should certainly buy more fans. "Do you not find they are extremely delicate?" she asked Dru as she entered the shop.

The proprietor approached, rubbing his hands together at the prospect of wealthy customers. Several people were already sitting or standing at the three counters framing the interior. Most favored her with curious stares. One nodded, a lady she had seen at dinner last week.

Viola and Dru spent a delightful half hour perusing the wares and choosing several. Especially fans. One had a saucy scene on one side and a depiction of people decorously bowing to each other on the reverse. The scenes were labeled "Before" and "After." "After what?" Viola asked.

"Several bottles of wine, I assume," Dru said dryly. She bent to examine "After." "Brandy, more like."

Viola would not leave the fan for someone else to buy. It could prove quite a talking point. Better than a caricature from a print shop, because it had a practical use.

Bond Street was a haunt of the fashionable. Even at this time of year, when most of the fashionable world had left town, it contained a good number of people dressed as finely as she. Of course, Viola was one of them now, a fact she occasionally forgot. At home with the family, forgetting had proved easier. People stared as they walked past, but they did not acknowledge others more than a polite nod or two.

She could not resist a milliner's shop. Viola had always had a weakness for hats and trimmings.

As she entered the shop, the faint scents of fresh size and fabric wafting around, she realized how much she had missed this. She had never considered her appearance as paramount in her concerns, but that did not mean she disregarded it altogether.

Probably recognizing the livery on her footmen rather than Viola, the proprietress swept forward, all smiles, and dropped a curtsey.

"Show me what you have that is new," Viola said. Then she introduced herself and watched the deep curtsey with admiration. She could have never managed one quite so perfect. Considering her clientele, the lady probably performed such *obeisances* several times a day.

A moment later, she and Dru were sitting in chairs before mirrors. The lady unpinned her relatively plain hat. She handed it to an assistant and produced a plain *bergère*, but one in an excellent quality, better than any Viola had owned before. She'd have been perfectly happy with that and some new ribbons.

But what was good enough for Miss Gates was nowhere near good enough for Lady Malton.

Admiration filled her when the milliner proceeded to pin flowers, ribbons, and feathers to the hat in a seemingly haphazard way. But when she had done, the result was charming. It was worth the price just to see her do that.

Recalling her new riding habit, which she had not yet had an opportunity to wear, she ordered a cocked hat to accompany it. She promised to send some of the trim the dressmaker had used on the jacket. Then it seemed natural to order a few new caps, little more than frills of lace, but very pretty lace. Very expensive lace, Viola guessed, but she didn't ask the price.

The door to the shop burst open, admitting sound and fresh air. And also the deep male voice that, regardless of the other patrons in the establishment, bellowed, "What are you doing here?"

Viola did not need to turn to see him. His appearance in the mirror told her all she needed to know.

Her wrath rising like a red tide, she turned slowly, forcing control on her senses. "What does it look like? Do you like the hat, or do you have some kind of unnatural objection to headgear?"

"You know what I'm talking about!"

Beside her, Dru fell silent, her face white.

Viola felt no such restraint. "No, I do not. Do tell. Did I forget my ball and chain?" She lifted her skirts and viewed both ankles. "Oh, dear, it appears I did. Should I return home immediately to find them? Indeed I don't feel properly dressed without them." How dare he make a scene? Did he assume she would weep or slink away like a woman caught in adultery?

Dear Lord, no. She rose to her feet, her skirts responding with a satisfactory shush of silk. "My lord, if I had known you wished me tethered hand and foot, I would have reconsidered your generous proposal." Recalling the wicked scene on the fan she had just bought, she added, "Or perhaps you approve of such activities for other reasons?" She put her finger to her chin in an exaggerated attitude of thought. "Sir, I am all ears. Do tell."

Marcus's jaw dropped. Behind him, one of the two footmen he'd brought, presumably to swell the ranks she already had with her, coughed and covered his mouth with his hand.

Marcus recovered quickly. "Madam, you know the reasons for my decision. I cannot consider your safety if you constantly defy me."

"This is the first time in two weeks! After our visit to the opera, I thought you had come to terms with"—however agitated, she would not repeat the deep-seated reason for his protective attitude—"our problems. I cannot live in the house all the time. I can barely exist that way."

"So your answer is defiance?"

"You know how often over the last week I have asked you? And you... distract me." With lovemaking and kisses. His tactic had worked very well until today; she had to give him that. "My lord, I cannot allow this situation to go on. I am perfectly capable of taking care of myself."

"Indeed?" He curled his lip. "So you can shoot straight. How will that help you when you are faced with a man with a sword or dagger? Will you have time to draw it out, prime it, and cock it?"

"I would face him with my sword."

He raised a brow. Clearly he did not believe her.

"Why so surprised? Ladies take fencing lessons. They do in my world."

A few of the ladies, their ears flapping, murmured in agreement, but none raised their voice to join in the conversation.

At the moment, Viola cared little for any gossip they might spread. Let them pour the information over the whole of London, if they chose. She cared nothing for what they might say. Only her husband did not ride roughshod over any declaration of independence she cared to make. She would answer him.

"You can fence?" he said incredulously.

"Naturally. Why are you shocked?"

"Because ladies' fencing lessons are meant to teach them deportment and grace."

Showing all the grace she could muster, she glided across the shop to stand right under his nose. "Try me," she said. "I challenge you." Grabbing up a glove from a nearby table, she struck him with it.

Although a blow from a kid glove must have been as painful as a brush with a feather whip, he flinched. The symbolism of the challenge was what mattered. Snatching the glove from her hand, he tossed it aside furiously. Although he left his hand by his side, he clenched his fist. "You would not dare." Spoken in low tones, his words were thrillingly arousing.

Or maybe her anger was changing.

He was doing it again, damn him! Angrily she shoved his chest. Shocked, he took a step back, but recovered himself quickly.

"I would dare!" she answered him. "If I had known you intended this when we married, I would never have agreed."

"And for the rest?" he said silkily. He regained the step he had lost.

But she knew what he was at this time. She would not succumb to his devastating sensual appeal. "Will you answer my challenge? If I win, I choose where I go and when. You trust me, Marcus. If it is difficult for you, you must learn to do so."

"And if I win?"

"I will agree to do as you wish. For another month. After that, another challenge."

He nodded briskly, all business, except a residue of desire remained in his eyes, lurking there ready to trap her. "You accept that as your husband, I can dictate your actions?"

She would not. "You can try." And she would not allow it. He would not behave as cruel and unnaturally as to lock her away, she knew that.

He must know it too. The only way to persuade her to accept his will was by winning the challenge.

"Then I accept."

"Swords, then?"

He bit his lip. Would he impose his will? Or trick her and insist on a lesser challenge?

He did neither. "Swords. Now."

Before she could move away, he'd seized her hand and dragged her from the shop. He strode across the street, not waiting for the crossing-sweeper to clear their way. She had to skip over two particularly generous clumps of horse dung to keep up with him. He tromped through a patch, not even noticing.

Across the road lay an establishment marked only by a paneled wooden door covered with cracked green paint and a brass plaque. In contrast to the door, the plaque gleamed with polishing, to the point of obliteration.

The legendary Domenici's Fencing Academy looked like nothing from the street. Set above a row of fashionable establishments, mostly dedicated to the male aficionado, the stairs leading up gave no indication of what lay in store.

Two rooms were made one, the walls decorated with crossed swords, paintings of swordfights, and prints depicting classical positions. Although Domenici did not forbid women his establishment, he did allow them in for only one day a week. And today, Wednesday, was not it.

Men were in various states of undress. The ones who had stripped off their shirts to mop themselves down shouted when they saw Viola. "Hey, get out!" and other such charming sentiments.

She ignored them.

Her husband strode across the space to where padded vests hung on pegs. He selected one for himself and then threw a couple down before he yelled, "Where are the boys' vests?"

Stunned, one of the patrons waved to a place near where he stood. Marcus strode across, grabbed one, and tossed it across the space at her. "You want this?" he shouted. He was still furious. His eyes blazed.

Men shouted, but now their names were bandied about. In his right mind, Marcus would have fought not to have her here, so it was just as well he was not in his right mind. Finally Viola felt alive, in touch with reality again.

This she understood. This she could handle, even the men's bawdy comments, before someone said suddenly, "By God, sir, it's Lady

Malton!" thus driving the assembled crowd to a frenzy of speculation and then, in the next breath, to betting. The odds were long on her.

They cleared the floor, forming a ring outside it. Chairs were dragged into place, men sitting astride with their arms draped over the back, others standing, all avidly watching. She doubted Marcus saw any of them.

She didn't reply to her husband's question. She only tucked her lace ruffles up her sleeves so they would not get in her way. Then she threw the shapeless, brown garment over her head, before fastening the tapes at the sides. She took her time, which gave her a chance to breathe deeply a couple of times. She pulled air into her lungs and forced calm on her body.

Marcus was in a fine temper. So much so he tossed a small sword to her, albeit handle first. She caught it deftly. His eyebrows went up.

"You still want this?" he repeated.

"Why would I not? I set the challenge. What would you call someone who backed down?"

His upper lip curved up. "You are certainly not a coward." Bringing his sword up, he saluted her with it, the blade whipping through the air as it swished down. The unbuttoned blade.

That gave her pause. She'd always practiced with blunt-tipped blades. What if she forgot? She bit her lip. She would not; that was all.

She copied his salute and took a pose, thanking the lord for the fashion in shorter skirts.

Their blades met in a clash of metal.

The cacophony stilled, as shouts of "Be quiet!" and shushing noises echoed around the big room.

Speech did not completely cease, but it settled into a quiet murmur when the proprietor, an Italian of imposing height whom Viola recognized from the prints of him, strode into the main room, followed by another man. The man's attention flicked from one to the other, Marcus to Viola, and then back again.

Viola only noticed him because she faced him, holding her sword in a defensive position.

Marcus circled his weapon, tracing elaborate patterns in the air. He was trying to distract her, making her wonder how he would come at her. She did not watch the tip of his sword. She watched his eyes.

A fraction before he struck, she saw the spark, the instant he made the decision. She countered, and then looked for an attacking position of her own, but she did not find one.

Not that time.

They went back to circling, their shod feet scraping the bare floor, sliding on the polished floorboards. She faced Domenici again. His face was impassive, but the moment she flicked her attention to the fencing-master, Marcus went in.

When she swung to one side, his blade grazed the padded waistcoat.

She would not be doing that again in a hurry. But his determination gave her an opening, and she lunged, touched his side. Hit the vest and drew back swiftly. "Touché!" someone called.

"One to the lady!" someone else announced. "One more and the day is yours!"

Viola was gratified to hear the odds shortened on herself.

Someone remarked, "Fighting his wife, how can he win?" and the odds shortened even more.

He skipped to the side and showed his teeth in a grin as he lunged forward and caught her on her blind side. He slapped the sword on the jacket, a symbol he could do more if he wished.

Bringing her sword down, she knocked his blade away, and they went back to circling. He held up his hand in the prescribed posture, a way of countering his balance when he was circling. She didn't bother.

She went for the groin.

He cried out, and she was afraid she'd misjudged her lunge, but no. The tip of his blade touched her chest. "You may have my manhood," he said, "But I have your heart."

He did, and in more ways than he knew.

She lifted her hands, and her blade clanged to the floor.

A round of applause broke out as, white-faced, Marcus cast his sword aside and dragged her into his arms.

After a fraught moment, he started to laugh, his reaction as much shock as genuine amusement. After a moment he caught his breath on a gasp. "You witch! How could you drive me to this?"

"I could always do that," she murmured for his ears only.

The applause continued, but Marcus ignored it. With his arm around her waist, he led her out of the place. It wasn't until he had her in the carriage she realized they still wore the hideous vests.

"So I believe I have ruined my reputation in society," she said as calmly as she could muster, unfastening the ties at her waist.

"You probably have." He sounded regretful.

Before she could speak again, he rapped on the roof of the carriage and stuck his head out of the window. "Home!" he commanded. "Then return for Lady Drusilla."

To her shame, Viola had forgotten Dru.

* * * *

Julius stood to greet them when they entered his drawing room. Like Marcus, he was in shirt sleeves, but at their entrance, he picked up the heavy coat he'd thrown over a chair. "I beg your pardon," he said.

Viola waved his apology aside. "I won," she said to Marcus. "What is a man without his manhood?"

"A eunuch," Marcus said promptly. "Or a castrato. An alive one. I had your heart."

"Only if I drove in. Otherwise I could have fallen back and saved myself."

Marcus put his hand on his heart and bowed. "Then shall we call it a draw?"

She could live with that. But not a loss. "I won't stay immured in the house forever, Marcus. I would have waited, but it's clear this isn't going away as quickly as we'd like." She turned her head and met Julius's blue gaze. "Is it?"

"Possibly," he said cautiously.

"If I stay behind heavily guarded doors, how long will it take before you discover who killed my father? Or will the killer go to ground?"

Julius grimaced. "That, unfortunately, is likely. He has probably done so already."

Viola nodded. "I expected as much. You have lost the initiative."

"You're a perspicacious woman," Julius said, indicating a sofa.

She deigned to take a seat. Marcus sat next to her and took her hand. She glanced at their joining. "Is this the start of a new, informal Marcus?"

"I'm just ensuring that you don't get the idea to leave and go—where next, Viola?"

"I did not go to Domenici's. You took me."

Marcus released her hand and used it to cover his face. He groaned. "What megrim got into my head?"

"I suspect your wife did," Julius said, studying Viola anew. "What did you do?"

"Fought. I won," she said.

"A draw," Marcus corrected her from behind his hands. He drew a deep breath as he dropped them and regained his hold on her hand once more.

"Very well," she conceded grudgingly. "I merely went shopping."

"How on earth…?" Marcus shook his head. "I have never, ever lost my temper like that before. Not in public."

"I saw you do so when we were children." She remembered several occasions when she'd driven him to a frenzy of fury. But he'd never touched her in anger, and he had never intimidated her. Always he had apologized, whether it was his fault or not.

A rumble came from the chair Julius occupied. It developed into a full-scale laugh. He threw back his head, and roared his delight. "Oh, I wish I had been there!" he cried when he could.

Marcus exchanged a meaningful look with Viola and raised her hand to his lips. "I was, and I still don't understand how she rouses me in that way."

"I think I do," Julius said. He was still smiling but his gravity was restored. "I will leave it to you to discover the reason." Crossing his legs, he rested his hands on his thighs, over his pristine white small clothes. "Viola is right. You cannot keep her locked away indefinitely. Or rather, if you do, how could you prevent her going mad?"

"I grew up in the country," she said. "I'm not used to staying indoors all the time."

Marcus sighed. "I cannot bear the thought of losing you," he said, meeting her gaze. His eyes no longer held that febrile look, but gazed at hers with warmth, a little heat lurking there. As, she realized, it always did. They opened wider for a second, as he watched her. What was he saying to her?

"You will have to accustom yourself to the idea," Julius said soberly.

"Oh, Julius," she said softly. She knew his history. Julius had fallen madly in love with his wife, only to lose her. She had the deserved reputation for wildness, and it had killed her. He had a beautiful daughter to show from it, but he had never remarried.

He shook his head. "I remember too many times when I wanted to throttle her." From the urbane, smooth Julius the words sounded incongruous. "She would go off on another mad adventure, and society would shake its heads and say it would all end in tears." He shrugged. "Which it did. But the last thing Caroline would want was for society to call her "Poor Caro." Which of course, it did."

Yes, it did, when one prank too many had killed her. But Viola was not in the least like Poor Caro. Or was she? Was her impatience a result of a wild streak? People had called her "madcap" before now. Not recently, and since she'd arrived in London she'd done her best to conform to society's expectations.

"I cannot be a conformable wife," she said sadly. "I cannot do everything I'm told or behave in the way expected of me."

Julius nodded. "I understand. Caro tried her best in the early years of our marriage, and I think that was one of the problems plaguing us after Caroline was born. Caro loved her to distraction." He paused. "As do I. But it was not enough, and the baby made Caro feel trapped in a way neither of us understood. I still don't understand it completely, but if I had allowed her more…freedom, I might have kept her for longer."

Marcus glanced at her, then snagged his cousin's attention. "Are you telling me to let Viola do whatever she pleases?"

Julius's mouth flattened. "No, I am not. Nor am I telling you to restrict her movements. I'm asking you to treat her as a trusted partner. Discuss with her what we're doing and why." He turned his attention to Viola. "I know something of you, Viola. I've watched you on my visits to Haxby Hall." Julius watched everybody. "You're reckless, but not without reasoning the chances first. I don't know if you realize you are doing it, but you calculate as you go."

No, she had not realized she was taking those steps, but now he mentioned it, she understood. She would not ride a skittish horse without observing it carefully first and wearing protective clothing if still unsure. That must be what he meant. "Today I took the two burliest footmen in the house with us, and I went where there were many others. But not so many I would be jostled."

Julius spread his hands in a graceful gesture. "You see?"

Marcus gazed at her, studying her. His eyes were grave, but something deep inside lifted.

"I swear I will never take unnecessary risks."

"You don't have to tell me that," he said. "I know. I should have trusted you more."

After a fraught moment, he nodded and turned his attention back to his cousin. "So what now? Have you found anything new?"

The expression on Julius's face surprised her. He was a rational man, a handsome man, and rabidly sought by every matchmaking mama in society. He was wealthy in his own right and heir to the dukedom of Kirkburton. In time he would become a powerful man who even kings would listen to with respect. If he wanted that.

For the first time she wondered what it must be like to have that kind of expectation. From birth, Julius and Marcus had their lives mapped out for them. They had to grow into the kind of people who could bear such responsibilities and control the power. No wonder not every duke or marquess turned out good for the estate.

She had been brought up the moderately well-off daughter of a man with a settled career and some standing in local society. She could make of her life what she would. So why did Julius look so vulnerable?

"You two are trapped, are you not?" she said impulsively.

"I prefer to look on my inheritance as opening opportunity," Marcus said, "But yes, sometimes it feels like that."

"And you and the rest of the Emperors are at the center of society's attention. Your appearance in the gossip sheets is taken for granted, and if you do something unusual, you are watched. How do you keep the secret from everyone's ears?" The secret of her birth, of her origins.

"Like this. We only discuss it with certain people. If it comes out, we will decry it and denigrate it. We have already agreed to that." Julius smiled, without humor. "We will say things like, 'what are the chances of that happening?' Someone would have discovered the documents long before. And without documents, we have no proof."

"So we get the documents, and we destroy them?"

Julius shook his head. "We lock them away. We have not yet decided what to do about them. Perhaps this is part of history better kept hidden. But what do we know about future events? We may need your line one day."

Ever the politician. She shifted uncomfortably. "I want no part of it." Except Marcus had married her because of it. He had married her to protect her from people who would have married her forcibly to someone else. He had put himself in danger.

Her guilt about that had kept her toeing the line for the last two weeks, but no more. This had to end. She did not know what they would have left once they had brought this sorry matter to an end. But she wanted a life of her own, not as a political pawn. "I want to meet the Duke of Northwich."

Chapter 16

"My goodness, what a fuss!" Lady Strenshall put the paper down and laid her lorgnette on top of it. The pretty bejeweled spectacles caught the light, the brilliants twinkling merrily. In the cheerful parlor facing the garden, the table was set for breakfast, and the whole family, apart from the honeymooning Claudia, sat around it. Val, the next brother in age to Marcus, wore a soft satin robe over his shirt, breeches, and waistcoat. His rheumy eyes told their own story.

"Another gaming hell, Val?" Marcus enquired, letting censure color his voice.

"One has to try them out," Val said. "And one hears the best gossip there."

"Then do tell us," his mother said. "The papers are full of the match between Marcus and his bride. Tempestuous, they are calling it. I call it reckless." She heaved a deep sigh. "Whatever have I done to deserve such a fate? You children give me gray hairs every time I step outdoors."

"Surely not, my dear!" Lord Strenshall gazed at his wife, a half smile curling the corner of his mouth. "I can recall a time when you decided you would ride in the park unchaperoned. Your mother nearly had a fit."

"But I had a reason," she said softly.

"I daresay Val had a reason," his lordship answered her. He lifted the taller of the two china pots on the table. "Coffee?"

"You know I never drink coffee in the mornings," she snapped, but rosy color tinged her cheekbones. Some kind of private message was going on between them, but nobody else sitting at the table knew what it was. Just that she had probably met his lordship clandestinely before they were married and somehow coffee was involved.

A romantic tryst of some kind. And they had kept their secrets, so why couldn't she?

"In the full glare of everyone in Bond Street," her ladyship said, returning to the subject in hand. There was a gleam in her eyes, not a censorious one.

Marcus had taken a seat next to his wife this morning, unwilling to leave her side. He still wanted her safe, but last night they had stayed awake until the small hours, not only making love, but talking. He had enjoyed that part, too. He had married a lively, intelligent woman, and she made herself understood only too well, once he'd had the time to listen to her, really listen.

He would not have her feel trapped, but he needed to stay close to her. Wearing their black armbands, they would venture into what few entertainments society offered. He would take her to see the sights she had yearned for when they had first arrived. St. Paul's was on their list for today. He wanted to take her to his house in the country before they went to Haxby for the August house party. However he feared if they did not find out who was behind the attacks on her and her father, he would not have that opportunity.

So they would move matters forward. A few appearances, with him by her side and the redoubtable Tranmere accompanying them, and some judicious words dropped in certain corners should move matters along.

And even meeting the Duke of Northwich. Bile rose to his throat when he considered meeting the man who, despite his oath of allegiance, was scheming to restore the Stuarts to the monarchy and to control them when they did so. But he would do it, even consider Northwich as a human being and not a villain to be bested, an enemy to defeat.

Unlike his mother, he did drink coffee in the mornings. Not that, technically, it was morning. Most of the household had been up and about long before breakfast was served at noon. He had stayed in bed with his wife, but nobody commented on that. After all, as he'd said to her as he rolled her on to her back, they were only doing their duty.

Never had anything felt less like duty and more like the greatest pleasure he had ever known. Every time they made love, the experience improved.

Marcus shifted, settling his unruly body into a more comfortable position. How he could still want her after—but if he continued to think that way, everyone at table would know, once he got to his feet.

He turned his thoughts back to Northwich. Ah, yes, that worked. Idly, he picked up his mother's discarded gossip sheet. The print was tiny. No wonder she needed the lorgnette. He was almost tempted to borrow it, too.

But no. He read the first two paragraphs and winced.

Val snatched the paper from him. "Oh, this must be good to have you all wrapped up like that. Oho!" He read aloud, to the great delight of Marcus's siblings. "Such a sight as was never seen before in the new fencing studio Domenici's. In front of the entire membership, Lord M—, previously a stalwart and admired member of society, dragged his wife and engaged in a fencing match. Lady M— proved an excellent match for her husband, gaining the first hit and changing the odds on her victory considerably. However, his lordship's superior reach eventually won the day, and her ladyship retired in confusion."

"No, I did not!" Viola cried. "How dare they? I did not retire. It was a draw!"

"A gallant gesture," Marcus said. "I would have bested you."

Viola made a sound halfway between anger and exasperation. She could not know how animated she became like this. He wished it were possible to hustle her up to her bedroom and make the best use of her fury. But he had to shift again and try to think of Northwich.

"While we do not dare to speculate on the current condition of the marriage between Lord and Lady M—, it nevertheless appears the couple share a great deal of passion. Let us hope passion has a material result in nine months' time, and not six."

"Oh!" Viola reddened, a pretty blush spreading over her bosom and up her neck to her cheeks. "How dare they?"

"I thought that was mild," Darius remarked, reaching for the toast and spreading a slice liberally with butter.

"It'll be a nine days' wonder," Lady Strenshall said in a resigned tone. "Let us pray the gossip has died down by August, otherwise we will be shooting down rumors instead of game birds."

"Not for the first time," Lord Strenshall murmured. "I wonder how Claudia is doing?"

The implication being the wilder of his female set of twins might be having the same tempestuous start to her marriage. But at least they were doing it decently in the country instead of in the public gaze.

"I have done with this," Marcus said suddenly. "I want to retire sooner rather than later." He glanced at Viola. "Since I know you will follow me or rail at me if I go without you, I intend to visit the Duke of Northwich this morning."

"We," she said calmly.

He shook his head. "Not this time. If you walk into the lion's den, he will try to take you."

"And not you?" Ignoring the protests ringing around the room, she turned to him. "You said if he was behind the attacks, he would want you dead and me alive. So I am in less danger than you."

Marcus hated that she was right. His instinct was still to wrap her up and tuck her away until he had resolved the problem. "It's a bluff. If he kills me in his house, if I disappear this morning, after telling everyone where I have gone, my father has a case to bring to court."

"But I don't want you to die!" she wailed, tears sparkling in her eyes.

"I'll go," Val said.

"No, it's my business. In any case, if I perish, you are the next heir."

Yes, Viola could be carrying his heir. It was early days, but they had been working hard at making one recently. Perhaps too hard.

He recalled the time he'd bent her over the bed. Oh, no, he could not think of that now. Throughout the days, flashes of delightful memories occurred to him, with predictable effect. Viola's enthusiastic response was an even greater delight than he had imagined. They had come a long way since their wedding night.

He knew exactly what he wanted after he'd done with this matter. If he could somehow bring the immediate danger to Viola to a satisfactory conclusion, he could take her to his house. They could spend all day and night enjoying each other—as a newly married couple should.

"I will not die," he told her now.

"I will accompany you," she said.

He should have known better than to think she would not follow him or insist on coming. Damnation, he had wanted a serious discussion with his adversary. Now he would have to moderate his language, at the very least.

* * * *

Marcus had to admit his wife looked fine in her carriage gown of rich red ribbed silk. Relatively plain, but with gold buttons, and a very fetching hat with a matching plume curled around the brim. He wished he had time to take her for a ride in the park first.

When he said so, she gave him a saucy smile. "Perhaps I will let you one day. The bills for my shopping must be horrific, but I have had little else to do."

He touched her gloved hand. "I will certainly bear that in mind. We must find you something more productive to do."

Her laugh warmed him and eased the tension ratcheting his mood.

They arrived at the grand house owned by the Duke of Northwich in good time. Several carriages stood in the square, clustered around the

Lynne Connolly

great front door, to which the knocker was still attached. Marcus had already ascertained Northwich remained in town.

He dispelled the brief touch of panic as the footman let down the steps. If he could have sent her home he would have. Why couldn't he have discovered a willing, obedient wife?

But then she wouldn't have been Viola, and that was not acceptable.

As they emerged from the carriage, the door opened, and a superior being stood inside, waiting for them. Only the slight widening of his eyes indicated he had recognized them. Since they had called in person, rather than sending in their cards, the butler would be taking a lot on himself if he sent them away. But would he?

Another insult at this stage would not concern Marcus too much. In fact, he was looking forward to the ride in the park they could fit in before dinner if the man was to do so.

But he did not. He let them in to the hall and took the cards. "It is the duke we have come to see," Marcus said.

"The dowager duchess is holding a salon today. I will enquire as to whether the duke is in, my lord."

He was in. The butler returned within five minutes. "If you would come this way, my lord, my lady."

They followed him upstairs to a small but elegant salon next to the closed double doors of the main drawing room. The buzz of conversation filtered through the doors as they opened and someone came out.

The Earl of Alconbury, Northwich's oldest son and his heir glared at them down his blade of a nose. His lean olive-skinned features rarely reflected his mood, which was generally one of sour displeasure. Today was no exception. He said nothing, but bowed his head to Viola and followed them to the room.

Polished mahogany furniture upholstered in dark blue gave a masculine air to the room, but it was still one a woman could enjoy. Not that either he or Viola were in any mood to enjoy décor. Resentment that such bitter enemies had such a pleasant way of living filled him, when he considered the unhappiness the Dankworth family had brought to so many.

Northwich rose to greet them, an urbane smile creasing his face, one that did not reach his eyes. He bowed to Viola but pointedly did not salute Marcus. Marcus remained upright and waited until Viola rose from her curtsey.

"I had not realized we would be on your list of bride-visits, else I would have called," the duke said. His dark gaze flicked over Viola. "Although I have not seen you so close before. I would most assuredly have paid a call, had I believed we would be received. Please, do sit down." He gestured to two chairs set a little apart.

Divide and rule. Marcus led his wife to the sofa and helped her to sit.

Alconbury took one of the spurned chairs, draping arms over the elaborate carving in the pose of a king. His father retook the chair he had vacated when they entered the room. "I take it you do not intend to drop in on my mother today. Her literary salon has almost ended, in any case. Would you like me to send you an invitation?"

"You can send one," Viola said. She stared at Alconbury. She had never met him before, of course, not even at the few social events they had attended recently.

Most hostesses knew not to invite both families to any but the largest events, and with the young ladies all launched, large balls were rare.

Alconbury watched with his customary concentration. Marcus had not had much direct communication with the man, for obvious reasons, but he had never underestimated the man's sharp intelligence.

"We could exchange pleasantries all afternoon," Alconbury remarked. "But your time is probably as limited as ours. If you have business with us, we will listen."

"Yes, you will," Marcus replied, not in the least disconcerted by his abruptness. He was cut from a similar cloth, preferring to get to the point, unlike his cousin Julius, who delighted in the obfuscatory remark. "You have caused my wife considerable distress. I will take your insults no longer. I'm here to ask you in a civilized tone to leave her alone. Or I will ensure you do."

Alconbury spoke first. "And how do you propose to do that?"

"Any way I can."

Northwich smiled, cool as a cat in a patch of sun. "I doubt it. You are known as a man of utter integrity. Would you dare to break that reputation?"

Marcus reached out and took Viola's hand. "For my wife, yes. Without a doubt."

The duke raised a dark brow. "Indeed. I heard it was a love match. I would not have credited it had I not seen for myself."

Marcus swallowed. "It is a matter of caring for my own. Had you attacked my sisters, I would have acted in the same way."

"Attacked?" Alconbury said sharply.

"Do not presume ignorance." Contempt filled him when he swung his gaze to the man. "You wish to deny what you have done?"

Viola squeezed his hand. He assumed from distress until he looked at her. But his wife was furious. By now he knew the signs—the blazing eyes, her luscious mouth tightened into a hard line.

"How dare you, sir? You had my father killed, and you can sit there and deny it?"

Alconbury shrugged and spread his hands in a gesture of helplessness. Feigned, of course. "I take part in so many attacks I cannot imagine which one you mean. You will have to remind us."

Marcus growled low in his throat. "The attacks on my wife, one of which proved fatal to my father-in-law."

Silence reigned for the time it took a conductor to bring down his baton. "I was under the impression that was a sad accident." Northwich flicked a glance at his son. Was he asking him if he had taken the initiative, or warning him?

"You were?" Marcus let his cynicism show in his voice. "I understood you had spies everywhere. Could it be we fooled you for the last twenty-six years?" Ah, damnation, what had he said?

The light of understanding flashed in the duke's eyes. He turned his full attention on Viola. "Yes." He drew the one word out longer than necessary. "I understand now."

While Marcus called himself fifty kinds of fool, the duke examined Viola closely. Had he really not known until that moment?

She did not react by fidgeting or any other ill-bred action. She behaved like the woman she was, sitting up straighter and staring back.

"An insolent child," the duke remarked casually.

"I could say the same thing," she said. "Considering my birth is superior to yours."

Oh, yes! As a Stuart princess, she would be revered in this house.

The duke sighed heavily. "Sadly you have made yourself useless to me."

"Not as much as you would like me to believe," she answered. "If you dispose of my husband, you may have another shot." She gazed at first the duke, and then his son. Alconbury had his head tilted slightly, his eyes narrowed as he examined her with no attempt at good manners.

If she took offense, she didn't show it, only stared down her nose at the duke. "If any harm comes to him, I will burn the papers in my possession. That will make me useless to you."

"My dear, I appreciate the effort." The duke paused, stared again. "It really is a remarkable resemblance. Have you met your father?"

"I shared the same house with him for many years," she said. "He died recently."

If he had not been sitting so close, Marcus wouldn't have seen the slight tremble of her fingers, controlled almost immediately. His heart burst with pride for her.

"Don't try to tell me you had no idea," he said. "Are your spies slipping?"

"I don't have as many as you seem to think." The duke kept his attention on Viola.

Not what Marcus wanted. He would have tried another provocative remark, but the duke spoke first.

"I'm surprised not to see your cousin Julius Caesar here."

Marcus had suffered so many taunts on his own name, the sneering way the duke said his cousin's name barely registered. Was the duke trying to make him storm out? Or was this his usual nature? "Viola is *my* wife, not his. And before you concern yourself, my name is Marcus Aurelius. I do not appreciate the familiarity to myself or to my cousin so I would prefer you did not use it."

"I daresay." The duke waved his concern away with a careless wave of his hand. "You, however, came to see me. While I will offer you the courtesy of entrance to my house, any other consideration is mine to give." He smiled, a thin curve of his mouth, the fleeting expression soon gone. "Feel free to leave at any time."

"We will," Marcus assured him. "We only came to show you what you cannot have. Or would it have been your son who had the honors?"

Alconbury glanced at Viola, but said nothing. He returned his attention to Marcus. "That hardly matters, does it? You seem to be accusing us of attacking your father-in-law."

Yes, of course. Had he lived, Gates would have been so. But had he lived, Marcus wouldn't have married Viola. He would have taken one of the society maidens his mother had been throwing his way. He'd almost settled on Lady Myra, a cold but beautiful woman who knew her business well. She would have made a perfect marchioness. But Marcus had never wanted perfection. He'd just thought he did.

"If not you, who?"

"You know the answer to that," the duke said softly.

"Then I suggest you ask him if it is of his doing. Otherwise, I will be forced to hold you responsible."

"And that is supposed to—what, put the fear of God into me?" the duke asked. The smile returned. "Better men than you have tried. However I am, as you see, unmoved. My dear…" In one smooth change of tone, his voice turned low and caressing as he turned to Viola. "At any time you may come to me. If you need help claiming your birthright, I will help you. I wish you had sought my help before you considered such a drastic step as marrying an Emperor." He made a scornful sound at the back of his throat. "Emperors of nothing. But he may be your consort one day."

She laughed, such a joyous sound in this grim atmosphere. "I'm only the daughter of a estate manager, sir, as half of London will tell you. All of it by now, I suppose."

"And reputation is all, is it not?" He sounded so gentle now. This man had such a seductive, persuasive tone. That was why he had escaped the fate of so many others of his kind. The rebels in the forty-five had lost their land, their titles, and their good names. But not this man.

"Sometimes it can be."

"Unless one has evidence to the contrary," Northwich continued.

Ah. Did he have evidence? Had he somehow found one of the documents, the copies of the birth certificates, or the marriage certificate? The latter would be the most devastating paper for him to have found. But not the original. In some quarters only that would be accepted. Certainly if he wanted to persuade the House of Lords to his side.

That alone led Marcus to believe he did not have the all-important paper. If he had—but he needed a child, too. One of the legitimate children of James Stuart, to press the claim. Preferably a presentable one. Preferably a son, but a girl would serve.

Not this girl. Never this one. Marcus did not ask the question the duke had all but invited. He had never concerned himself with getting too close to this man before. He'd been content to avoid him, while the problem of the children did not belong to him. He would support his cousins, but at a distance.

No more. He would die rather than allow this man to gain control over Viola. He would break her and then discard her. The man took wiliness to a new level of competence.

The duke leaned back, resting his hand on his cheek. "Tell me why you are so opposed to legal attempts to restore the succession. Nobody is discussing illegal moves any longer. Obviously, war is not possible. But can you not see the family has a claim?"

"You wish to usurp the throne?"

"No."

"Then perhaps you wish to conquer?" Marcus said icily.

"No. Merely restore the rights of those who were usurped in their turn. I believe the Stuarts would agree to make peace, so long as they are acknowledged."

Viola added her mite. "So that they can force the royal family into exile?"

"The Hanover king is ailing, his son is dead, and his grandson but a child," the duke said. "Britain is headed for another war. Added to which, I have heard young George is only of moderate intelligence. If that."

"He's far from an imbecile," Marcus put in. "He will cope with kingship very well. The first of the Hanovers to be born here and to speak English as well as he does German, if not better. Is that what concerns you? That he will prove the most popular of monarchs?"

"Or the most compliant," Alconbury added. "Do you really want King Bute to run the country?"

Bute was the Princess of Wales's trusted advisor, and rumor had it, her lover. He was a Scot and a Tory, and most of the House of Lords opposed him. And a great number of the House of Commons, too. "He's a Stuart," Marcus said. "I would have thought he was an agent for the disgraced royal family."

Northwich sneered, his upper lip lifting slightly. "He has not enough intelligence nor the strength of character. There are many Stuarts in Scotland. Not all of them are loyal." He did not say to what.

They made treason sound reasonable. Marcus had had enough.

"You obviously have no intention of answering my questions." He stood and extended his hand to Viola, drawing her up to join him. "Our business is done. Come after me or anyone under my protection, and I will make you very sorry for it."

"Do you think I am unaware of that? Or your father has not made the same threats in his time?"

"Not a threat, but a promise." With his wife's hand tucked in his, Marcus took his last look at this man. He would destroy everything that made the country stable to gain power for himself. "As you might discern, I have a more personal stake in this matter. I will not hesitate, and I will not necessarily use the law to achieve my ends." He turned to lead Viola from the room.

"Devil take it, what a bloodthirsty youth!" were the duke's parting words. "I wish you were mine, and I never thought I would say such a thing of any Emperor!"

Marcus did not stop to address the parting shot, but strode from the room. He was eager to put this house behind him, for good, if he was lucky.

"A word." He had been so intent in leaving, he had not noticed Alconbury had followed them out.

Sighing in exasperation, Marcus released Viola's hand and turned around.

Alconbury regarded him from under heavy-lids, a characteristic he had seen before somewhere, although the similarity eluded him.

Marcus resisted the urge to push Viola behind him, but gripped her hand tightly.

"I understand you frequent Domenici's," Alconbury said.

He met the man's stare. "I am a member, yes."

"So am I. I merely wanted to inform you I plan to go there tomorrow afternoon. You might want to remember that." He glanced back at the door to the room from which they had just emerged. It was closed. He lowered his voice. "Although if you do go, I'd appreciate testing your mettle."

He sketched a bow and walked away before they could respond.

Viola held her peace until they were inside the carriage and on their way home. "What did he mean?"

Marcus sighed. "I have no idea. But I will go."

"Not alone."

"No, not alone."

Chapter 17

Accordingly, the next day, having ensured Viola was fully engaged on a round of visits with his mother, Marcus made his way to Domenici's. He had not thought to grace the establishment so soon, having decided to allow the furor to die down. But if he wanted to know what was going on, he would have to go. He prevailed on Darius to accompany him, as a witness, and because Darius was less of a rattle-pate than his brother. Not Julius. Julius and Alconbury hated each other. Even had they not been from feuding families, they would have hated each other. If there was more history there, Marcus had no idea what it was, and he had a strong feeling he did not wish to know.

The hush in the conversation going on when they entered the academy told its own story. Nobody had forgotten the sparring or Marcus's unusual behavior. They could hardly have done so, when town was not teeming with new scandals. He was stepping into the building for the second time in a week.

Conversation started up again. Someone called, "I expected you to arrive with your new sparring partner, Malton!"

Marcus chose to ignore the sentiment.

Someone else did not. Alconbury, already in shirtsleeves, stepped forward. "Malton has a new opponent today."

Without warning, he tossed a sword across the space between them. Not a small sword. A saber. "Do you use daggers, Malton?"

"I have been known to. I thought that was your weapon of choice?"

"Sometimes." Alconbury served him the same trick with a dagger. Marcus showed his teeth, baring them in a simulacrum of a smile.

He handed the weapons to a silent white-faced Darius, while he stripped off his coat and waistcoat. They were too fashionably tight to help him in this fight. Alconbury tilted his head to the padded jackets on the wall. He was not wearing one.

Impatiently, Marcus shook his head. "The day is too warm for one to be of use."

If Alconbury tried to kill him now, he would do it with half society watching and bearing witness. Was this his intent, to push a duel on to him? Marcus determined to defend himself, and no more. Alconbury would not find him rising to the challenge.

Alconbury performed the salute, his saber slicing through the air with a lethal hiss. Cold-faced, Marcus returned the favor.

At least the tips of the swords were blunted. If they had not been, Marcus would have chosen the vest, because a "fencing accident" could clearly prove fatal and have no serious consequences. With his father, Alconbury could probably get away with murder. But not from a man whose father was the Marquess of Strenshall. Marcus's father would not rest until he had justice for his son.

Alconbury must know that.

With a gleam in his eyes, Alconbury tested him, struck his sword away, and went in for an easy dagger thrust. Marcus fended him off with no trouble. Marcus took his turn, trying a sideways sweep. Alconbury laughed as he slid his dagger down Marcus's, with a swirl that threatened to push Marcus off-target.

"I brought a message," Alconbury said, "But I could not resist the challenge." He lunged.

Marcus retreated, only to advance when he reversed the attack with a twist of his wrist.

Neither man was out of breath.

Around them, the spectators shouted the odds and laid bets, the normal practice in this place when two adversaries engaged. "A messenger boy?" Marcus taunted him.

"A message from myself. First hit?"

One hit with those weapons would do the job. Marcus nodded. "By all means. I will try not to draw blood."

Alconbury laughed. "You can try."

The men circled each other, each looking for an opening. Alconbury stumbled, and Marcus took his chance. He drove forward, a flurry of clashes pushing Alconbury back. Unexpectedly, Alconbury regained his footing and struck. He'd been bluffing.

Marcus backed up, trying to regain the impetus. He engaged the sword, and as they came closer, Alconbury swept his dagger in a wide arc. Marcus whirled his weapon around and in, locking the two men together.

Their faces were close. Kissing close. Alconbury bared his teeth in a gesture of ferocity. He roared and then added, *sotto voce*, "We were not responsible for the attack on your wife or her father," and sprang back.

That was the message? "Am I to believe your word?"

"Do what you will with it," Alconbury said, and attacked again, beating Marcus back.

Marcus was ready for him this time and defended ably, meeting each blow with one of his own. They struck with bone-jarring force, trading attack after attack. Sweat dampened their shirts, the fabric clinging to their bodies.

They came close again. Both were breathing heavily. "Take care of your wife," Alconbury murmured. "The other party has agents in the country. They can attack from anywhere."

"Then it's as well I do, too." He would send more people searching for the agents. He tended to believe the man after the second warning. He would not want to see Viola dead, because he must know who Marcus would turn to first. And he would stop at nothing.

The notion of his wife's death made him hesitate. Only for the fraction of a second, but enough to have Alconbury draw his blade along his sleeve. The sharp edge sliced through the fabric and touched his skin, delivering a long scratch.

Alconbury drew back, waiting for acknowledgment. Blood seeped from the wound, staining the already ruined shirt.

Marcus lowered his sword. "A palpable hit."

Alconbury raised a brow. "But we are equally matched. I have no idea what made you falter, but I was watching."

The thought of his wife dead. Would Alconbury know that? He'd spent most of the visit Marcus had paid him watching him and Viola closely. An observant man, then, and an intelligent one. A shame he was on the wrong side.

Marcus shoved back a strand of hair that had come loose, amused to see his erstwhile opponent doing the same. Like him, Alconbury wore his own hair tied back, a developing fashion among young men. Alconbury's hair was a darker shade than Marcus's own, nearly black, and his dark complexion indicated the time he'd spent abroad.

Darius helped Marcus. He folded back the rags of his sleeve and bound a clean bandage around the wound, which was not serious. Marcus was not sure how he'd explain it to Viola. Tell the truth, probably, since his wife seemed to see past every falsehood he tried to fool her with. Not that he had tried much recently. He knew when he was beaten. He thrust his arms into the sleeves of his waistcoat, and then his coat, as light as the tailor could make it, but still a substantial garment.

Alconbury took care of his person himself. He appeared to have nobody with him, although the family had its adherents.

He snapped a bow to Marcus and Darius. "An enjoyable bout, gentlemen. I have another appointment to see to, and I must go home and change before I do so. Good day."

They returned the bow.

"Come and have a glass of brandy," one of their acquaintances called across the room. "I won a hundred guineas on you, and I decided my man on the toss of a coin." He patted his pocket. "A lucky coin."

Nothing loath, Marcus crossed the room to the long range of windows, where a low table held a collection of decanters. He accepted a brandy. The fine-cut glass caught the sunshine, and he looked away, temporarily dazzled.

Outside, Alconbury was crossing the street, a crossing-sweeper industriously clearing the way for him. As he did so, Marcus's cousin Helena emerged from the milliner's, the same one Viola had been in that day. He smiled, remembering her fire, and watched Alconbury hesitate, bow, and then stride on. Helena stared after him.

The man was only being polite. Perhaps Marcus's family had misjudged him.

Marcus turned away and put a smile on his face, lifting the glass to his lips.

He must be mad, thinking like that, with his wife in danger and that man still at large. Alconbury was a member of the family that had opposed not only the Emperors, but the monarchy.

What was he thinking?

* * * *

"What were you thinking?" Viola, in a fine rage, hurried to help Marcus out of his coat. When she saw the long bandage, blood staining the white folds, she went cold and had to clutch the arm of the chair Marcus was sitting in. "Marcus!"

"It's a scratch," he said negligently.

"I thought he was warning you off, not inviting you to fight him! Was it a duel?"

"Certainly not. Duels are illegal. Merely a way of releasing excess energy and testing each other's mettle. The tips were blunted."

"Obviously not well enough." She hurried to the corner of the bedroom and poured some hot water from the can resting there into a small bowl.

Hastily, she collected clean cloths, a towel, and a salve, as well as a clean rolled bandage. Tears threatened to fall from the shock of seeing her husband so marked. "You could have died. He could have killed you, and they would have called it an accident. I know they would have."

"Be easy," he said, in a soothing tone.

She was far from easy. With hands that shook slightly, she untucked the end of the bandage and began to unwind it.

He put his hand over hers. He was not shaking at all. "I swear it's not a serious wound. I only subjected myself to the bandage because I did not want to stain one of my favorite coats."

The bandage was a light one, but she put no store by that. "You were hurt, Marcus. What if you were killed?"

"Sweetheart, I cannot hide away in the hopes I will come to no harm. I cannot preserve myself."

She stared at him, disbelief washing through her, anger simmering. "Then why do you expect to do that to me? You wanted to keep me immured in this house forever."

"Until we found who wished you harm."

She shook her head. "What if we never discover that? Will you wrap me up in footmen and lock me in luxurious houses with no chance of roaming free? When I went to the stables this afternoon with the intent of taking a ride on the Park, the grooms informed me there were no horses available. I could quite clearly see one, the piebald, and I know I can handle her. Did you give those orders?"

Yes, he had. She just knew it.

"I wanted to ensure your safety."

She exposed the wound. It was as he said, a superficial scratch. But men had died from such things once infection set in. "I will bathe this and apply salve every day until it is better."

He sighed. "You know how much I enjoy your touch. If I have to cut myself to receive such treatment, I might well arrange to do so, and keep a wound constantly on my person."

Smiling despite her concerns, she shook her head, her curls bouncing about her neck. "You do not have to go to such lengths."

"I know. We spend every night curled around one another, yet I still want more. Your touch is all I need, my lady, to make me better."

Now he'd made her laugh. "Such foolishness!"

She would not rest until she had seen how badly he was hurt. "For all I knew, you might be one of those men who suffered wounds until they could not bear any more. By then it would be too late. I've seen that happen twice on the estate. Once a ploughman sliced his leg with a scythe so badly he had to fasten the bandage tight around him. The wound festered and he lost the leg. He was fortunate not to lose his life. Another man considered his knock on the head from a fight at the inn a small thing, even when he had repeated dizzy spells for two days afterward. A week after his injury, he dropped dead in the fields."

"I remember the last one. A villager, was it not? A man who the neighbors considered permanently sotted?"

"Yes, but he was not." She took care to bathe Marcus's wound thoroughly. In trying to scare him, she'd scared herself.

"Every day," he said softly and kissed her forehead while she was attending to him, "I am of all things grateful this business brought me to you. I will not fail you, Viola."

"I know you will not." When she glanced up at his dear face, he was smiling so warmly she caught her breath. "You never fail any of your family."

"You are more than family. You are my wife."

They exchanged a look so long and so sweet, she considered swooning from it, like the heroine in one of the novels she used to devour. The ones that went through trials and tribulations for the men they loved. She'd do that. Before, she'd considered their exploits foolish, risking their lives unnecessarily. She'd recently read *Clarissa*, who was pursued relentlessly by a blackguard who eventually took her virginity and left nothing in return.

Marcus had taken her virginity. If he'd asked, she'd gladly have given it to him, even before they were married. In that inn room, she'd wanted him to, but he had refrained. She loved him for that. No, that was wrong. She just loved him. "Marcus?"

He touched the underside of her chin, holding her steady while he kissed her. While Marcus's actions outside the bedroom were those of a gentleman, inside their chamber he turned into the most passionate lover she could wish for. In a few other places, he was a veritable pirate, a marauder. Perhaps he'd waited for the sanctity of marriage, but he was certainly making the most of their union.

And she most certainly loved him for that.

He nipped her lower lip and then soothed it with his tongue. "You are delicious, sweetheart." He nipped again. "And I find I am not in the least hungry for anything but you."

"Lady Honiston is coming to dinner. We barely have time to change."

"Lady Honiston," he murmured, his lips so close to hers she felt every movement, "is a prosy bore. She is also not expecting all the family to dinner. She's an old friend of my mother's, not a formal guest. Val will have taken himself off already. He can't stand her. I shall plead the exhaustion of the day, or maybe I do not wish to leave my wife, who fainted at the sight of my blood."

Jerking back, she exclaimed, "Marcus, how dare you say such a thing!" Although the sight of his blood had not been pleasant, she was far from fainting.

"Then I will not say that. You have no right to be so irresistible, my sweet. Come."

"But the bandage!"

"Hang the bandage. I promise not to get blood on the sheets."

Her eyes widened. But a wicked idea entered her head, one that would give the wound a chance to begin to dry up while she kept him busy. She fumbled at the fall of his breeches and found the first button. Six in all, three on each side. He went still, watching her as she unfastened them one by one. She reached inside and found his underwear, shoving it aside to get to the bounty beneath.

He was half erect already, and as she closed her fingers around his length, he completed the process.

"How could I have ever thought I could live without you?" he asked the ceiling.

She had never seen him this close. He had been used to taking her in bed, ensuring her comfort and loving her until he was satisfied she had obtained the pleasure he wanted to give her. Making love that way was making her lazy, so much she had almost forgotten her resolve to learn every inch of him.

Recalling what he had done on their wedding night and several times thereafter, she licked her lips. His groan gave her the deepest pleasure imaginable.

"Let me see you, sweet," he said, as he pulled at the fastenings of her robe.

The robe she had donned before changing for dinner was fastened with two elaborate frogged toggles at the top and a sash around her waist. It was the work of a moment to get them undone, and then she had only her underwear on. He had returned from the fencing school just as her maid was helping her undress. She had considered an hour sitting on the window seat with her embroidery before Marcus had come in. Now she had something much better to do.

Bending her head, she cautiously swiped her tongue over the shiny head. Her husband tasted salty and musky. The tiny opening at the top emitted a pearl of clear liquid. Greedily, she claimed it.

He groaned softly. "Viola, is there no end to the surprises you bring me?"

She hoped not. She wanted to be the one giving him surprises for a long time to come. At first his superior knowledge had made her give the lead to him. But his tutelage had been so very successful, she felt confident in this venture of her own. She sucked. Another groan was her reward, and another elusive taste of the most intimate part of him.

Running her tongue over him, she explored the rest of the head, the flange beneath it, and the rest of his rigidly erect shaft. When she emitted a wholly involuntary "Mm," a thump made her look up, still with his cock head in her mouth.

He had jerked his head back, hitting it against the back of the chair. But when he looked down, their eyes met in such a deep connection, with such intimacy, she would have been happy with that alone.

Lifting his hand, he cupped it around the back of her head, threading his fingers between the waves. Several hairpins fell to the floor and over her clothes. "So very lovely," he murmured. "You look so beautiful like that. I've dreamed of you doing this to me."

If her mouth had not been full, she might have asked why he had not requested it of her. Perhaps ladies didn't indulge, but that was yet another reason why she was not a lady. Only a woman enjoying her man, exploring him.

She cupped her palm around the furry sack, the balls moving at her touch. Gently, he pressed her head, showing her what he wanted her to do. Up and down, stimulating him with her tongue. Enjoying the expression on his face and what she was doing to him, she continued without further prompting. He did not look away again, but kept his eyes on her, so she could see his reaction to everything she did.

"That's it," he whispered. "Oh, my sweet, you are—" He broke off with a laugh. "You are my wife. I love seeing you like this. I love what you're doing. As if a thousand caresses touched me at once. You are drawing me out, every part of me." He ended with another groan.

Industriously, she moved her head, copying the motion he'd urged her into and adding touches of her own.

He gasped, and in a sudden movement jerked her up, his hands under her arms. "On me," he said. "Now."

She needed no more prompting. Sweeping her skirts up around her waist, she got to her feet and climbed on him. She draped her legs over the arms of the chair while he curved one hand around her waist to steady her. Then she thrust her feet under the chair arms, dangling so they nearly touched the floor. She found if she pushed her toes down, she could move on him the way she wished.

Holding his cock, she guided it inside her, the way she had done that first night. But this time he slipped in easily. "You're so wet." His words, although explaining something self-evident, added another layer to their lovemaking. She knew she was wet—her thighs had grown slippery as she'd sucked him and she'd rubbed them together to gain a measure of relief.

"I love watching you. So intimate," he said, his voice husky and rough-edged.

She followed his gaze and watched him entering her body, sinking deep. And she accepted him, swallowed him up and settled around his shaft like an embrace. The most intimate embrace of all.

"Don't leave me," she said, the words torn out of her. "Please, Marcus, I couldn't bear it."

"I won't. I swear it." Drawing her head down, he kissed her and moved inside her, swirling his hips so he connected with all of her. His tongue slid into her mouth, imitating his actions below. Despite her feverish excitement, she did not initiate a harder, more insistent rhythm but was happy to let him set the pace.

Marcus took his time. His kiss developed into a series of flickering licks. While he did not slam into her with the power he was capable of giving, his sinuous strokes brought her up. She gasped into his mouth as tingles spread through her, insistent waves of arousal, increasing to irresistible power.

He moaned in return and kissed her in a series of seductive touches, light licks, pressing his mouth against hers and then retreating so they barely touched. Tilting his head to one side, he kissed her again, and she responded, taking him with as much need as he was taking her.

When she swiveled her hips, she created a new way of driving them both mad. His sharp, "Ah!" told her all she needed to know. Holding on to the arms of the chair, she did it again and found her rhythm so she could continue without thinking overmuch. Her senses opened to him. He smelled of fresh soap and even fresher male; he tasted of Marcus. The small sounds he made when he thrust inside her were essentially masculine, grunts and the like. Viola nestled closer to him, pressing her breasts against his chest.

They moved as one, towards the same end, their private hair meshing, their bodies colliding with each deep impact. Flinging her arms around his neck, she took her weight on her toes, so she gained a different kind of leverage.

The world froze, teetered on the brink, and she came.

An explosion of wet heat trailed fiery intensity in its wake. Helpless in the storm, she held on and heard his responsive cry.

His shaft pulsed, pushing his essence into her body, deeper and deeper until it reached the heart of her.

She stilled, half-laughing with sheer joy, her hair trailing over his face.

Putting his hands on her waist, he urged her away and gazed up into her eyes. "I don't think Lady Honiston will see us tonight."

In a moment she recalled the identity of the lady. Ah, yes, the dinner guest. "No," she said softly. "She probably won't."

They enjoyed each other for a little longer, their closeness a blessing to them both, before he lifted her away. Wetness bedaubed her thighs, the result of their mingled juices.

"Lovemaking is messy, isn't it?" Lifting her skirts, she tottered over to the washbasin and picked up the cloth.

"Let me," he said, coming up behind her.

He unfastened and unhooked, getting her naked with a swiftness she had to admire. He was so deliciously competent. When she was naked, he washed her from her neck to her toes, abandoning the washcloth to soap his hands and rub them over her breasts. He teased and tweaked, sending fresh prickles of awareness through her. "You're a wicked man," she murmured.

"And you love me for it," he said, and kissed the side of her neck.

"Yes I do."

The world stilled. Taking her shoulders, he turned her to face him. "And I love you," he said. "Truly. Nothing is complete without you."

"Yes." She could do nothing but agree with him. She could hardly remember a time when she did not want him and love him in some fashion. Although she had never loved him as intensely, as all-consuming, as she did now.

A smile curved his lips as he kissed her, as softly and sweetly as their first touch. "I love you, Viola. When I think what I could have missed, what I so nearly did not have—" He drew her close, heedless of her still wet breasts.

"I never—I always loved you."

"Always?" He drew back, his eyes widening. "Since we were children?"

"Yes. Although I would have said nothing. I always knew you were meant for greater things. I only wished your wife would give you the happiness I wanted to." She laughed, a little awkward now she had made her confession. "Not that I wandered around pining for you. That came later, after we'd spent the night together at the inn. Then I knew for sure what I would be missing for the rest of my life."

"But you're not." He touched the end of her nose with his finger and then kissed the spot. "I nearly threw away so much. I wish I could say the same. But I looked on you as more of a pet, someone to play with. When they separated us, I was angry. But my family brought me to realize I was doing you a disservice, too, if I let you follow me around all the time. You were not unhappy, were you?"

"Only at first. Then they put me into lessons with Dru, to encourage her, and I think as some manner of consolation prize. It worked, to a certain extent." He wanted to know he had not made her unhappy. He had, but she had never let herself dwell on it, telling herself firmly she was foolish for wishing for what she could not have. Except she could. The transition from estate manager's daughter to princess to countess had been an odd journey, but she welcomed it. She would not be the person he loved if she had not.

"So we will be happy, will we not?"

Of course they would. Nodding eagerly, she burrowed against him.

Chuckling, he eased her away and took her to the bed. "I've not finished with you yet. Climb in. I'll give orders for supper to be served in your boudoir, and then I'll come back to you."

She had not meant to sleep, but she drifted away dreaming of him and what he would do to her next. And what she would do to him.

He did not disappoint her.

Chapter 18

Tousled but happy, they awoke in the morning to kisses and joyous lovemaking. They had made love during the night, sometimes she beginning their loving and sometimes him.

After they had done, he curled her into his arms and claimed another kiss.

Staring into her eyes, he caught his breath. "I have an idea. Only because I am desperate to have you to myself, you understand."

Delighted in his trust, Viola listened and agreed with him. Their plan was reckless, but it had a greater degree of success than anything else they had yet thought of.

"Give me leave to visit Julius and pay a few more calls. We can be ready in two days," he said.

* * * *

At last, he could do something, and with his wife's cooperation. Marcus made his plans very carefully. The two days gave him time to tell everyone he met he was leaving town, taking his wife to his villa in Leicestershire. Two days was just enough time to make a fuss, not enough for elaborate plans. Unless one happened to be an Emperor of London. In that case, he could visit, spread the word, and have everything in place in no time at all.

He had employed the use of the family's best traveling carriage, promising to deliver it back unharmed to his mother. "Or I will buy you a new one. Just think of the fun you could have replacing it, Mama!"

Lady Strenshall gave him a narrow look. "Yes, just think!"

They set out early, so as to make the first stop in plenty of time. Several innkeepers had been warned to expect them because this time they travelled in state—a coach in front, carrying the lord and lady, and behind them, another coach with her maid, his valet, and other necessary servants.

"That is a beautiful riding habit," he remarked, handing her into the vehicle. "I don't think I've seen it before."

"Nor likely to again," she responded. "The silver braid is falling off already."

"Ah." He spotted a worn patch on the elbow. "If you don't mind me saying so, it is still better than the one you wore on our flight to London."

She smiled slowly, a reminiscent faraway look in her eyes he delighted to see.

"Do you still have that?"

"My maid threw it out. Otherwise I'd have worn that one. I had to send another maid to collect this one. The superior Frenchwoman who now attends me would have nothing to do with it."

"What did you tell her?" he said, fascinated.

The footman outside shouted to the coachman, who shouted back to him. They called to the horses, and Marcus and Viola were on their way. A slight bump pushed him forward when one of the footmen leaped up behind.

"I told her I had taken a fancy to it. I passed it in the town carriage, and I wanted it the moment I saw it. She sniffed. By the way, she is no more French than I am."

"I guessed," he said dryly. The woman's command of what was supposed to be her native language was not extensive. But she had proved a good maid, so he cared little what airs she affected.

Apparently Viola thought the same way, because she had sent Dubois ahead yesterday to ensure she reached the first inn on time. The maid in the carriage behind them was a new one, expressly employed to help her mistress on the journey. A hulking girl, and one who galumphed in skirts, unable to balance her hooped petticoat properly, but she was adequate.

They travelled through the streets of London, taking their time, while Viola pointed at various sights, demanding to know what they were.

"I did promise to take you to more sights," he said regretfully. "Next season I will for sure."

"Or we could come in the autumn, when town is less crowded. I can't promise we will have the house to ourselves, but it will certainly not be as crowded."

She sniggered. "You call that crowded? A house where everyone has his own room and even his own private parlor?" She rested her chin on her hand. "My father and I lived far closer than that, and our house was considered spacious by most of our neighbors. We were lords of the village, did you know that?"

He shook his head, glad she was finally talking about her father. He took her hand, a habit he was finding pleasant to the point of addiction. He vastly preferred it to the formal hand on arm pose they were supposed to affect. Why had he constantly done what society expected of him?

Because, before Viola, his duties had worn him down. Before, he'd taken his duties seriously and worked every hour he could to ensure he did nothing wrong. Viola had liberated him from that way of thinking. He no longer fretted his father would find him wanting. He had someone to talk to, someone who put him above all others.

Viola.

He would not say she saw him without fault. That would not be good for him in any case. Her robust arguments, her lively intelligence, and the fact he never knew what she would do next all served to keep him on his toes. He would not let her down, but that included making her laugh and enjoying life to the full.

They passed the inn where they had arrived in London on their way up Ludgate Hill, and he tightened his hand around hers. "I meant to marry you after our first night," he confessed. "I would not have done it otherwise."

"But you—you didn't—" she took a breath. "You left me intact."

"To give you a choice. I had worked so hard to ensure we travelled secretly, it occurred to me you might like to stay Miss Gates for longer." He turned his head and smiled at her dear face. "While I'm glad you didn't, I wanted the choice to be yours. That is your doing, my love."

"How so? I never told you to do anything. You seized the opportunity to travel on the coach without any prompting. I would have hired a chaise or found shelter in someone's home. I would probably have gone to my aunt's in York. But when you said you wanted to take me to London, I couldn't resist."

"If the first coach to leave the village had gone to York, I might have escorted you there," he admitted. "But already I didn't want to leave you. You would have been safe there, and I would not have worried about you while I set about discovering who attacked you. I didn't want that. Already I did not want you to leave my side."

"I didn't want to," she said, her cheeks flushing rosily. "If that was the last time I had with you, I wanted it all. I had determined to seduce you."

He raised her hand to his lips and kissed the ring he'd placed there on their wedding day. "I'm glad you did." He let his mouth quirk up at one corner. "Very soon, I'll show you how much."

The glow in her eyes almost made him draw down the blinds over the windows and show her right now.

They turned right and headed through the city towards the outskirts and the Great North Road. They passed Spitalfields Market, the traders standing under the makeshift canopies, bellowing their wares so loudly Marcus gave up talking when they passed it. Fruit was piled high next to stacks of cabbages and other vegetables. "Spitalfields feeds much of London," he said when he could make himself heard again.

"I've never seen so many strawberries in one place before."

"I should have stopped and bought you some."

She shook her head. "Soon we'll have the real thing, from the country. We had a garden at Haxby, and I grew strawberries and raspberries in it."

"I liked the sweet peas," he said, recalling the tranquil space where he'd spent hours talking to Gates. He would be a sad loss to the estate as well as to his daughter. Marcus would do his best to console her. She was bound to have a renewal of grief when she saw what was left of their home. But he would not take her until next month. They had earned their holiday from everything except each other. The house he was taking her to was a small gem in the countryside—modern, airy, and full of light colors and summer furniture.

He wanted to see her lying against the silks of the bedcovers in the bedroom. Preferably naked.

His mouth went dry when he recalled the vision of her. He had never known a woman more generous with her body or so adventurous. "I must be completely idiotic, because I never realized how utterly beautiful you are. Why did I not see it before?"

"You needed your eyes opened," she said. "Which I did. I always knew how handsome you are. But I didn't know how wonderful your body felt against mine. At that point, I decided to do everything I could to hold you, but I did not know anything."

"You're a fast learner."

He would have drawn her closer, except the coach stopped with a jerk. He glanced out of the window. They had stopped outside a busy inn.

Throwing up the window, he bellowed, "Why have we stopped? It surely isn't time to change the horses?"

"No, my lord, but I'm not happy with the rear wheel," the coachman yelled back. "It doesn't seem completely steady to me. I'd rather ensure it was safe now before we cross the Heath. I don't want to have to stop there."

The Heath was far too dangerous to stop and mend a broken wheel. "Very well. See if there is a private room available, will you?"

The footman hared off, returning with the welcome news that a private parlor awaited them.

"How long will it take you?" he asked the coachman.

"Hardly any time at all," the man said. "I don't think anything is seriously wrong, but I want to check the axle."

"I see." He shrugged, making the gesture dramatic. "Then let us know when you have done. I'm anxious to be well on the way before we have to stop for the night."

"Yes, my lord." The coachman tugged his forelock absently, his attention already on the errant wheel.

The room proved to be a small parlor at the back with a very small window that had not been uncovered from the night before. Candles flickered on the tables and in the sconces. As they entered, the occupants of the parlor rose.

They appeared a parcel of ruffians, their clothes worn and nondescript. But instead of recoiling and taking Viola out of danger, Marcus strode forward and took the hand of the dark-haired tall man. He hauled him into his arms. "Ivan, my friend, thank you for doing this. And you." He turned to his other cousin. "Tony, I can't believe your new wife allowed you to come to help."

Now her eyes had become accustomed to the light, she recognized Darius and Val amongst the company.

Antoninus shrugged. "She said I was not to hurt myself, or she would hurt whoever did this to me." Turning to Viola, he executed a bow. "Antoninus, Earl of Hollinhead at your service. I'm the younger brother of Nicephorus. Tony and Nick to you."

"But you have an earldom?" Usually only the eldest son in a family held a title.

"My wife's father held the title, and the crown was good enough to invest me with it, once I married her. I was perfectly happy as Major Antoninus Beaumont, but I fell in love with a woman with a past."

"Another couple in love?" Viola said.

"It appears to be a fatal trait in the Emperors." Tony heaved a theatrical sigh. "I fear for the unmarried cousins."

Marcus slapped his cousins on the back. "I appreciate this."

Val and Darius grinned.

"Our pleasure," Darius said. "A great pleasure."

"And I'm supposed to remove my clothes in front of you great hulking men in this tiny room?" Viola demanded, hands on hips.

"I'm sorry, sweetheart. I didn't realize this room would be so small." He had not. Would the landlord give them another room?

Viola was already undressing. But even when she stripped off the jacket and skirt she was perfectly correctly attired. Except for the lack of a hoop. She surprised Marcus when she turned the skirt upside down and pulled at a thread. The hem came down. "I sewed it roughly last night," she said. "I assumed none of you would be my height. You will have to stoop when you climb back in the coach. So who is to be me?"

Ivan waved at her. He was the shortest of the group, which was not saying much. The Emperors had considerable height, all of them.

Under her petticoats, Viola had on a pair of breeches.

Marcus nearly grabbed her and called the whole affair off. The sight of his wife dressed in that fashion gave him ideas he really should not be having at this time. He closed his eyes and sucked in a breath, concentrating his mind once more. But the sight of Viola in those breeches—damnation!

Ivan did not look half as attractive in the riding habit as Marcus's wife had. But her careful selection of the outfit showed when he buttoned the jacket, which was loose on her. It barely fit him. The hat would cover his head. Ivan's dark hair matched Viola's, dark and tied back in a queue, and he'd shaved particularly well. He would do.

Heedless of his cousins and brothers, Marcus took Viola in his arms and kissed her. "Take care, my love," he said. "I'll be with you soon."

Nobody said a thing. She clung to him for a minute. "You're the one who must take care."

He moved closer and murmured words for her alone. "Don't take off those breeches."

Her cheek heated next to his, so he held her a moment longer before he released her.

The door opened, admitting the coachman. "All right and tight, my lord," he said. "I gave the footmen permission to wet their whistles before we start up again." The coachman nodded and left the room.

Time for the switch.

With one last glance back at Viola, Marcus left the room with Ivan and his brothers, passing the two footmen on the way. They did not acknowledge each other, even though one of them was the redoubtable Tranmere. Together with Darius and Val, they would form an escort for his wife. The only way Marcus would allow her anywhere near this action was if she promised to be safe for him. Tony and Darius stopped at the door, showing remarkable skill at blending with the crowds rushing to get on the coach that waited in the yard. Their coach waited just outside the doors. Swiftly, Marcus and Ivan took the short distance to the coach and climbed in.

At the last moment, when the street was thronged with people, Tony and Darius leaped in, one after the other. Darius slammed the door behind him. He sat on the floor, and complained as the coachman drove off. "Throw me a cushion, can you? Much more of this and my arse will be too sore for me to stand."

"And you traversed half Europe with the army?" Marcus snorted, but tossed a cushion down for his cousin.

"What do you think they will send?" Ivan asked.

"They might not send anyone. We made enough noise about our leaving, but they could have given up. If we are not attacked, I'll take it that nobody wanted us enough to take us when we present them with a sitting target." He took care not to look at Tony on the floor. "I am praying they try to take us on the Heath. A single coach, how can they resist?"

Viola, Val, and two of Marcus's strongest footmen would ride for their house. Not the one in Leicestershire, but another smaller house owned by Julius, one he was careful to retain as a private residence. It lay barely ten miles from London.

Even that ten miles had worried Marcus, but he could not work out how to get his wife back to the London house without anyone seeing. Particularly as they did not know who was watching them. Julius had promised to keep a watch, or rather, put his mysterious "people" to watch them, but he had reported nothing so far.

Too late now.

They would be on the heath very soon now. Nobody would attack them before that. The Heath was just too tempting a target. As, Marcus hoped, were they. To overcome the people they had with them, the Pretender would need a troop of some size.

"How do we introduce Viola to Imogen?" he asked Tony.

"As Viola and Imogen. They have certain physical similarities." Tony paused. "So much so that I miss Imogen more now. She is waiting for me. They are not so foolish. They'll guess. Imogen will be overjoyed to have a sister at last. I hope Viola will be, too."

"Since she recently lost the man she still regards as her father, I think she will be delighted to find she is not alone anymore." He paused. Even if Imogen and Viola took instant dislike to each other, Viola would never fear that melancholy fate again.

They were within a few minutes of the Heath now.

Sparse trees and scrubland adorned this bleak area north of London. Once they had passed the Spaniards Inn, they would be on Hampstead Heath, a notorious area for highwaymen and footpads.

Their luck held, and no coach waited by the inn. Sometimes coaches would wait until several came along, and then they would band together for safety. That was the last thing Marcus wanted. He drew his pistol and laid it on his lap. On the floor, Tony noiselessly drew three swords and laid them where they could reach them easily. He had a beltful of pistols, two one side and three the other, looking like nothing so much as a pirate readying to board a vessel.

Even then, a stray shot from anyone lying in wait for them could prove fatal.

The coachman had a prearranged signal, and so did the footmen.

Half way across the heath, Marcus despaired. Surely they would not have to continue as far as Leicestershire?

But a yell and the sound of thundering hooves from outside told them they had been right, and their attackers were upon them.

"Stand and deliver!" came the words that fooled nobody.

Highwaymen generally worked in ones and twos, but approaching the coach now was a veritable phalanx of men on horseback. Marcus counted six as he waited for them to come within range. "Don't forget I want one taken alive."

"Shame," Tony said.

The coaches came to a halt, seemingly obedient to the command of the men confronting them. They all wore their hats pulled down low rather than masks and sported clothes more suited to the ragbag than a person, no doubt in character.

The coachman drew the horses to a halt.

In contrast to their appearance, the weapons they held were lethal in appearance, modern and well cared for. Most had other weapons thrust in their belts.

"When I give the word," Marcus said. "Attack. If they are highwaymen, they deserve this fate. If not, they deserve it anyway."

"What do you do if one of Northwich's sons is among them?"

"That is his problem. We are attacked by highwaymen, we must defend ourselves."

"To the death," Darius said grimly.

That almost came true when a bullet pierced the coach at the level of the doors and whistled out the other side.

Darius gave a strangled yelp. "The bastard caught me!"

He had spoken too loudly. Another shot came through the window, too high to hurt anyone. They could not stay in here. They were sitting ducks.

Tony had his hand on the door. He counted. "On three. One, two, three!"

At that instant, he opened the door and leaped out, a pistol in each hand. Darius, his sleeve covered in blood, crouched behind him, holding his pistol higher. One of the men outside screamed and fell from his horse on Tony's first shot.

Highwaymen would have turned tail and run for it. These men did not.

Marcus aimed his own weapon at one of the men and managed to wing him. The damned pistol shot to the left, but at least he'd rendered one side of the bastard harmless.

He grabbed another pistol, cocked, and fired it. The store under the coach seats held a dozen. Then they would have the satisfaction of hand to hand fighting.

His pistol refused to discharge. If he had not dropped it in the same moment, he might have had his hand blown off. The pistol fell to the scrubby ground outside the coach, already a mess of black powder and flames.

One of the horses screamed and bolted, its rider clinging on for dear life.

From a tree they had just passed, another rider galloped out, his black horse going full tilt. Were there more?

The six men who had lain in wait for them were shocked, but fought back. They whipped out their weapons as fast as possible, but they were no match for Tony. The ex-soldier had two of them off their horses and writhing on the ground before they'd had a chance to fire. One shot went over Marcus's head as he followed his cousin and brother from the coach.

Ivan had a sporting rifle and a shotgun behind him. He stayed in the coach, hampered by his skirts, but perfectly able to hold a gun to a man's head.

Marcus flung himself across the short distance and dragged one of the men's feet from his stirrup, disturbing his balance as he was about to fire. He kicked back, catching Marcus in the ribs, but his shot went wide, lost in the scrubland of Hampstead Heath.

Marcus gasped and clapped his hand to his side, but fought on. He had his sword in his hand, but instead of slashing the rider, he cut the girth under the horse's belly. The man teetered sideways, unseated, but as he went down, Tony shot him. He was dead from the hole in his head before he hit the floor.

They had killed them all, except for the one that got away.

The melée had given them no time to think. Five men lay dead on the ground. Tony kicked at one disconsolately. "No doubt about it. My aim is as true as it ever was. Perhaps their bodies will show us something."

"That's hardly likely," said someone from behind them—a voice Marcus knew.

Lord Alconbury was in the process of sheathing a wicked looking saber. He had the reins looped around his wrist and a pistol in his other hand. Once he'd sheathed his sword, he changed the reins to his free hand and unhurriedly shoved the pistol in a pouch of his saddle. "Excellent shots," he said calmly.

The man who had tried to escape was sitting on his horse, his head down.

"You think to kill us personally?" Marcus asked.

Alconbury rolled his eyes. "I told you. This is none of our doing. This is the Pretender's idea, and in my humble opinion, a foolish one. Which is why this fellow will return with you and admit it for me. I want no part of this ham-fisted affair. It would offend me if it were put at our door. My father is too subtle to throw men at a plan like this. He would have known what you were at instantly, as did I. I merely wished to prove this fact to you. This is your prisoner, gentlemen. Do with him what you will."

Calmly, he turned around and cantered across the wide stretch of ground between them and the inn on the edge of the Heath.

Tony made haste to motion the man off his horse with a twitch of his pistol before handing his weapon to Darius. He strode across to fasten their prisoner's hands behind his back. The man stubbornly refused to move until he shoved him in the back.

Then he came out with a torrent of Italian. They had not even the wit to employ an English speaker. Nothing would have proved his guilt as much as that, someone speaking the language of the court in exile.

Marcus beckoned to Tony and murmured to him, "I'll have him talking before we reach the house, and I care not what language he uses. I presume the others have nothing to identify them. We shall report the unfortunate incident on our return to town."

"We'll do that," Darius said. "No need to even say you were there. According to our story, your wife was taken ill and you decided to cut your journey short. Tony and I decided to go ahead to Leicestershire."

"And what about me?" Ivan demanded.

Darius snorted. "If you think I'm taking you to Leicestershire looking like that, you had better think again."

Marcus turned his back on the carnage. The men were evidently dead. Their horses nuzzled at their bodies, but they would leave the animals here. The next traveler along would find them. The air stank of blood and burning powder, a pungent, offensive smell he would probably associate with this scene for some time to come.

"I have business ten miles away," he said. "This is done."

Chapter 19

Viola had not ridden astride for some time, but she found the task easy once she recalled her childhood racing around the estate. Once learned, never forgotten. She hardly noticed the distance as she rode, surrounded by her protectors, for ten miles. The journey was uneventful, and in other circumstances, she would have enjoyed it, but anxiety for her husband took all pleasure away for her.

If she had been less concerned, the house they arrived at would have enchanted her. A riverside villa, the sun warming its honey stone, greeted their eyes. The man at the gate swung it open for them, as if expecting them. Of course he was. Marcus had been meticulous in his preparations. He would not have been Marcus if he had not.

Her stomach in knots, she let Val help her dismount, gave him a brief word of thanks, and let Tranmere take her indoors.

They entered by a side door into a cool, black-and-white marble tiled hall. A maid bobbed a curtsey. "Good afternoon, my lady. May I show you to a room where you may change and refresh yourself?"

"Thank you."

The cantilevered stairs led to a broad corridor painted cream with landscape paintings adorning the walls—very restrained and not at all like what she would associate with the flamboyant Julius. This appeared more like the home of a moneyed Cit or a well-to-do gentleman.

Tranmere and she followed the maid to a set of double doors.

The maid opened them with a flourish and bowed her through. "You need to get something to drink and perhaps rest," she said.

The redoubtable footman shook his head. "I'll stay here, my lady, until somebody comes to relieve me. Master's orders are to guard you until he comes, or until we receive news."

Her heart sank when she heard the rider. That meant he didn't know if he would come or not, the implication being he could be killed. Her throat tightened in anticipation of tears she refused to allow to fall. Not yet. Not at all. She refused to think of the alternative.

A simple but pretty caraco jacket and petticoat were laid out on the bed. The jacket was in that shade of forget-me-not blue that was almost Julius's calling card, although this was an outfit he would never wear.

The maid helped her wash and change and did Viola's hair in a simple but effective style. Viola sat in the chair like a statue, letting the maid have her way, uncaring of the effect.

After ascertaining Viola did not want anything more, the maid bobbed a curtsey. "Refreshments will be served in the back parlor, if it please your ladyship. Or I can bring them up here. Lord Winterton has arrived, and he says if you feel up to it, could you come down."

Julius might be able to allay some of her fears. Not at all fatigued, Viola got to her feet and followed the maid down a broad staircase to a room on the ground floor. She found herself in a sunny, spacious room with windows that opened directly on to a terrace. For the first time today she registered it was a fine day. The sun beamed down on a lovely garden that stretched as far as the Thames.

Forcing herself to smile and remember her society manners, Viola dropped a curtsey. Julius stood, and took her hand. That was when Viola realized another woman was standing near a broad sofa that faced the windows.

Her looks reminded her of someone. The dark hair and long nose gave her a moment's thought. Until she realized she saw something very similar in the mirror each morning.

Her heart skipped a beat.

"Imogen, Lady Hollinhead, may I introduce Viola, Lady Malton? Viola, this is Imogen. Your sister."

Viola swallowed and stared at the other woman. Since Imogen was likewise staring at her, this seemed admissible, but she would have done so had it been polite or not. Sister?

Imogen recovered herself first, and smiled. "My husband is helping yours. He was a soldier and he's your husband's cousin, an Emperor."

Viola nodded. "Antoninus." She knew the name, but little else.

"We live in Cheshire, but we decided to come to London to attend to a little business. And to allow me to do some shopping, of course. But Tony raced off to Julius's, and here we are, roped in to another of his schemes." She did not seem perturbed, but rather, amused.

If her husband had been a soldier, perhaps Imogen could cope with this terrible worry better. Viola nodded. "I—I'm pleased to meet you. Also a little shocked. Are there any others?"

"I was shocked too. I had no idea I was anything other than Imogen Thane until recently. According to Julius, we have a brother and a half-sister, the result of the Old Pretender's union with another woman."

"He got around," Viola said dryly.

Imogen sat down and glanced at the space beside her. "Won't you sit?"

Grateful for the chance to sit while she recovered from the news, Viola took the spot. She thanked Julius when he placed a dish of tea by her side. "I didn't know about this house."

"No," Julius said. "Few people do. It is my retreat. But if you wish, it can be yours for a while."

"Thank you. It's lovely," was all she could think to reply. "When will we know?"

"Soon, I hope. If they are forced to continue the journey, they will send a message to us by fast rider. That will give us an idea of what is going on." Julius sat in a chair opposite and crossed his legs. "Whatever happens, Viola, you are safe. We will not allow anyone to hurt you."

"Do you think I care for that?" Visions of Marcus hurt, shot, or speared through with a sword kept nagging at her, pushing themselves unbidden into her mind.

Julius raised a brow.

"I apologize," she said quickly. "I should be mindful of all you've done."

Unexpectedly, support came from the lady on her left. "No, you should not." Imogen covered her hand briefly in a gesture of comfort. "It's perfectly natural for you to worry. But with Tony there, they are unlikely to come to much harm."

While she admired Imogen's trust in her husband's prowess, Viola was not so sure. But recalling Marcus's skill with a sword made her feel better. "He's no mean bladesman himself."

"He is not," Julius agreed. "And they took every precaution. I am hoping they capture someone alive. I still have no idea who instigated this foolish attack, although I suspect the Pretender rather than the Dankworths. The Dankworths are more subtle in their attacks. This kind of brute force is not typical of the way they work these days."

So at least one of them could think properly. Yet while what Julius said made sense, Viola could not wish for anything except the safe return of her husband. "Do you know how soon we will know?"

Julius shook his head. "Not precisely. The journey from the Heath to here will take an hour, more likely two, even in this weather. How long did the ride take you?"

"Just under an hour." They had set off well before they reached Hampstead Heath. "The inn was packed, and we managed to switch passengers. We waited for twenty minutes before we set off, to give the coach a head start."

The door opened to admit Val, who waved Julius back down into his seat and found one of his own. "That was a superb job," he said, and bowed to her.

"She's eaten up with worry," Julius remarked.

Val laughed, the unfeeling idiot. "I honestly don't think you have any reason. They have a coach full of weapons and abundant skill, as well as the element of surprise. While it was an honor to escort you here, I did wish I could remain and join in the fun."

"Fun?" she almost screeched. "How can it be fun?"

"To defeat our enemies?" Val pursed his lips. "Oh, I daresay I could find something to smile about. They will not prevail, I assure you." He was smartly dressed now, in contrast to his disheveled appearance earlier. "We should hear before dinner. I say, Viola, you will have to get used to such matters. Although, given your prosy husband, you might well go for the next fifty years without any further excitement."

Excitement? But Viola felt honor bound to protect Marcus. "When he fought me at Domenici's, I saw no prosiness."

Val brightened. "And wasn't that something? I have never known my brother provoked in such a way. Town could talk of nothing else for a week. I could almost believe we were cut from the same cloth."

"You will drive any woman demented in a week," she said.

"Val's betrothed is in the unfortunate position of being expected to tame him," Julius observed.

Val made a sound of disgust. "As if Charlotte could do anything of the kind! She is immensely forbearing, but neither of us intend to make our betrothal permanent any time soon."

Had he found someone who would agree to a false proposal? His parents were exceedingly keen to see their wayward son settle to more suitable behavior. Perhaps Val had agreed to marry the unfortunate Charlotte merely to quiet his family for a time. Having not yet met the saint Charlotte sounded like, Viola was unable to judge. Nor, if she was to be honest, did she care at this moment. Only one person occupied her thoughts.

"May I suggest you retire for an hour or two?" Julius said gently. "You appear considerably worn by the ordeal. If you can sleep, time will pass quicker. Failing that, I would enjoy showing you my villa and gardens."

She liked that the choice would be hers. But while such worry bowed her down, she feared she wouldn't take pleasure from anything. "I would appreciate retiring. That is, if you don't mind."

"Not at all," Julius said. "Once I hear of the successful conclusion to this enterprise, I will take myself back to town. Feel free to treat this house as your own for as long as you wish."

"Thank you."

He got to his feet and offered his arm, but before she left the room, Viola spoke to Val. "Indeed, I beg your pardon for not thanking you properly and appearing more grateful. I do thank you and I will be forever under an obligation to you."

"Oh, not forever; never say that!" the incorrigible Val said. "I shall probably make my way back to town with Julius, as there is a promising young fighter I'm anxious to see at the cockpit."

Viola shuddered at the mention of cockfighting. It was not her idea of a good evening's entertainment. Nobly, she said nothing. After all, she owed Val a great deal, despite his brushing her obligation aside.

Upstairs, the maid helped her out of her clothes. She lay down in what was admittedly a very comfortable goose feather bed, but she was sure she would not sleep. She had agreed to come upstairs, aware she would be no company for anyone in her current state. Best to stay here and bite her nails until news came.

She had not slept much last night, and she feared tonight would be the same. Worry and unaccustomed frustration at not knowing bore on her nerves. If she closed her eyes for a moment she could at least rest them.

She awoke when the bed sank as someone sat on it.

Flinging the bedclothes aside, she hurled herself into his arms. "Marcus!"

He closed his arms around her, holding her tight. She burrowed in, hearing his chuckle, feeling it reverberate through her. She would never let him go. Ever. "Oh, Marcus, I should never have let you go!"

"What is this?" he said, drawing her away so he could gaze down at her face. "My love, you surely did not worry about me?" But he appeared pleased, for all that.

"Yes, of course I was! What happened?"

"They attacked us on the heath and we captured one." He paused. "Well, at least Alconbury did."

"Alconbury?" Tears forgotten, her jaw dropped open.

"He said the act was nothing he wanted to be involved with and wished to prove it to us. I think there was more to it than that, but I have no idea what that might be. One fled, and he scooped him up. The man told us nothing, but we were too eager to secure him and deliver him to Julius. In any case, he babbled in Italian, talking about the true king and other such nonsense. It seems clear he was part of the Pretender's contingent. The Young Pretender. We now have a useful weapon," he said with much satisfaction. "I wonder what the Old Pretender would think of his son's activities?"

She had not considered that. "You think the old man would take it amiss?"

"I know so. He's a wily bastard. He will use any tools he can find. That, my love, includes you. A shame I spoiled his ambitions by marrying you. But not for me." Cupping her face, he kissed her.

He'd washed, and he'd removed his outer clothing and was now wearing a robe of a dazzling crimson color.

"What time is it?" she said when she could.

"Nearly nine. I did not wish to disturb you, though I sent a maid to sit with you and to fetch me the minute you awoke. Julius has gone, taking his prisoner to another place. Probably London, since we will have to clear up the mess from the Heath. I'm afraid we left a few bodies behind us."

She should feel sorry, she really should, but she could not. Not when her husband was safe in her arms.

"I have something for you." Reaching behind him, he drew out a rose and handed it to her. A yellow rose.

Viola caught her breath. "Where did you get that?"

"In the garden, here. Julius has a yellow rosebush. He gave me permission to take one. He's going to instruct his gardeners to send a graft for us. We may plant it in the house I'm taking you to, our private residence."

Tears misted her eyes. She brought the rose up and smelled the sweet, heady fragrance. "Thank you."

Gently, he took the rose from her and dropped it into the bud vase by the side of the bed.

She watched him, wide-eyed. "We have the house to ourselves?"

"Except for Tony and Imogen. Val, Ivan, and Darius took off with Julius. But Tony and Imogen have decided not to return to town, but to their house in Cheshire. I prevailed upon them to defer their trip for a few days, so you may get to know your sister." He regarded her tenderly. "How do you feel about gaining siblings?"

"I always thought there might be some. The Old Pretender was not known for celibacy, after all. Rumors of his affairs reached even us." Even now she could hardly believe her good fortune. For she counted it so when she could regard herself as not alone in the world, as she'd feared.

She patted the pillow next to the one she'd used. "I want you, Marcus." So happy she could express what she wanted to this wonderful man, she touched him. He was hard, his breeches not concealing how much he wanted her. But he wanted her more than physically, she realized with a surge of her spirits. He truly loved her, as she did him.

"You are not hungry?"

She laughed. "For you."

Without further delay, he released her and undressed swiftly, while she did the same, removing her shift, which was all she had left on. She left the covers where they were, half tossed down the bed. Unashamed, she displayed herself to him.

"Where are the breeches you wore?" he said roughly, a harsh edge to his voice.

"I don't know." Belatedly, she recalled he had asked her to keep them.

"It matters not. We will find you another pair. You will wear them for me, will you not?"

Wonderingly, she blinked at him. "You found them exciting?"

"Immensely. I cannot explain it myself." He threw his last garment, his shirt, aside and stood before her as blatantly naked as she was.

Sliding into bed, he took her into his arms and rolled over her, surrounding her with his heat. "Then we are to celebrate. But I insist you eat something."

Playfully, she bit his shoulder. "I could eat you."

He groaned. "You do not know what you're saying, my love. Or perhaps you do." He devoured her with a kiss, but she responded in full measure, eagerly opening her mouth for the invasion of his tongue.

Pausing to test her readiness, he guided himself to her and plunged deep, giving a deep-throated groan. "I love you, Viola. I always have, and I always will. I was merely foolish in not knowing it before."

"I always knew it," she said. "And I will love you for the rest of my life."

After his first thrust, he made love to her gently, making it last a long time. They were in no hurry. They had all the time in the world now.

She dropped her head back, letting him see every change in her face, keeping her gaze firmly fixed on his. "Will I drive you mad, as your brothers suspect?"

"I daresay you will. I doubt we will always see perfectly in harmony."

He groaned as she gasped and held on to him, her body quivering with aftershocks as an orgasm took over.

They lost themselves in kisses, their hearts and minds as one while they loved each other. Every time he came down to touch her, her nipples came into contact with his chest, adding further stimulation to her sensually saturated body.

The first pulse of his shaft inside her triggered another heated peak. Viola shuddered in his arms as he came, hot and deep.

When they had finished, he kissed her, and still kissing, still inside her, he rolled her with him. They lay side by side, lost in each other.

He stroked a lock of hair away from her face. "My love, at this rate we will give my father his heir in no time," he murmured, his lips close to hers.

"I'm a few days late," she confessed. "That means nothing," she added hastily, "Especially with the worry you've caused me."

He touched her lips, smiling when she kissed his finger. "It's a good sign. We have time, sweetheart."

She sighed in happiness. "Yes, we do."

Meet the Author

Lynne Connolly was born in Leicester, England, and lived in her family's cobbler's shop with her parents and sister. She loves all periods of history, but her favorites are the Tudor and Georgian eras. She loves doing research and creating a credible story with people who lived in past ages. In addition to her Emperors of London series she writes several historical, contemporary and paranormal romance series. Visit her on the web at lynneconnolly.com, read her blog at lynneconnolly.blogspot.co.uk, find her on Facebook, and follow her on Twitter @lynneconnolly.

Keep reading for a special sneak peek of the first Emperors of London novel

Reckless In Pink

Like the royals for whom they were named, the Emperors of London family have enemies and rivals of their own...

As a soldier for the Crown, Dominic is charged with locating the Young Pretender to the British throne so he can be tried as a traitor. But his mission is altered when he meets Claudia Shaw, an intriguing young woman who has inherited a house of ill repute. In an effort to protect Claudia from her own recklessness, Dominic finds himself allowing the Pretender to slip away...

Claudia is one of the Emperors of London, but her family despairs of her impetuous behavior. And try as he might, the disciplined Dominic cannot quite curb her excesses. In fact, she soon drags him into her adventures— and toward a passion neither can resist. But when a deadly secret comes to light that puts their lives, and their love, at risk, Claudia won't allow Dominic to sacrifice himself. She is determined to have him—even if it means getting the Young Pretender out of the way herself.

"Lynne Connolly writes Georgian romances with a deft touch. Her characters amuse, entertain and reach into your heart."
—Desiree Holt

A Lyrical e-book on sale now!

Learn more about Lynne at
http://www.kensingtonbooks.com/author.aspx/31603

Chapter 1

"Are you sure you do not wish to return, Major?" General Court asked. "Now your family business is concluded, I would have welcomed you back. Your conduct was exemplary on the Continent."

Dominic shook his head. "I would hardly say my family business is concluded. I am the only male left to continue the line."

The general brightened, his ruddy face glowing. "Then once you beget an heir or two, we may expect you back?"

"Once I marry, perhaps." Dominic could see that in his future—marrying a suitable woman, begetting an heir, and then leaving her in peace to continue his career.

The general harrumphed. "Then hurry up and do it. We need experienced officers like you."

Dominic recalled a number of times when his superior officers had intimated otherwise. He glanced around the splendidly appointed room, with its display of silver on the sideboard and fine spirits in the glittering crystal decanters. If he didn't know better, he'd assume the General lived in this luxury all the time. However, he'd seen the man thigh-deep in mud, bellowing instructions to his men, refusing to leave the field until they were all safe.

He was no longer one of the general's officers and hadn't been so for six months. Ever since his parents had begged him to come home and find a wife. He'd done the first part but had yet to achieve the second.

He blamed himself. His two male cousins had been the heirs to the title, after him. Now they had died, and he was the only hope for his house.

Restlessly, he got to his feet. "If that's all, General…"

"No. Sit down."

Sometimes the man forgot that Dominic was no longer under his command. He let it pass and sat back down on the hard wooden chair provided for visitors. The full skirts of his woolen coat padded his arse somewhat, but he'd known worse hardships than this. Not recently, though. "May I be of further service, sir?"

The General gave him a hard stare before picking up a piece of paper and tossing across the desk. "Take a look at that. Tell me what you see."

One side was travel-stained, obviously a letter, with a seal hanging off one side. The address was a house in the City, Spitalfields to be exact. He turned it over and read.

"This is from Charles Stuart? The Pretender?"

"It is. Rallying his supporters in England."

"Have you visited the address?"

The General grunted his assent. "I sent someone last week pretending to be a seller of pots and pans. All this damned sneaking about makes me itch. Army intelligence is one thing, but this cloak and dagger stuff isn't what a gentleman should occupy himself with."

If the world were well organized and everybody told the truth, a military man might prefer to see the enemy and engage with him rather than run around lying. However, the man's professed bluster hid a devious and intelligent mind, so while the General's speech amused Dominic, it did not fool him. A gentleman didn't skulk around and spy, but somebody had to.

"Nobody seemed suspicious," the general continued. "It was the premises of a silk weaver and his family. The man did business from the house, but he had no reason to side with the Stuarts. His family were Huguenots, and they believe in pursuing the Protestant cause."

"Stuart converted to the Anglican church a few years ago," Dominic felt obliged to point out.

The General nodded. "For all the good it did him." He finished the glass of port he'd poured for himself when Dominic had refused refreshment. "The house is owned by the Duke of Northwich."

Dominic sucked in a breath. The Duke, the head of the Dankworth family, had long been a thorn in the side of the Crown. Long-time supporters of the Stuarts, the Dankworths had nevertheless evaded serious charges. Dominic reminded himself frequently that intrigue was none of his business, anymore. However, he did find himself wondering what the devious family was up to now.

"Why should that be a surprise?" He took another look at the letter. It referred to mysterious events, full of phrases like "our business" and "the parcel." Nothing new.

"The parcel referred to in that letter is a person. The Young Pretender, no less. Are you interested now?"

Sunlight streamed in through the dusty windows across the desk. The air was redolent with lavender and spices used by the housekeeping staff no doubt to clean and add fragrance to the air.

The world was normal and continued the same way, except that it had shifted a little to one side. Dominic began to understand the general's intent, and he didn't like it. "Why would I be interested?" he said smoothly. He put the letter down gently. He had affairs of his own to deal with, much less government concerns.

"We would like you to look into the matter. The government would be extremely grateful to you."

"I'm sure they would." Because he had seen the Stuart pretender when he was still a serving officer, so he would know him again. Dominic hadn't been wearing his uniform at the time and had choked down his distaste of subterfuge long enough to discover what his superior had wanted to know. He obeyed orders, but he hated the work. Lying stuck in his throat. He had particular reason to dislike it.

The General indicated a neat pile of papers stacked on the desk. "You are in a position to help us now."

Dominic had had enough. He had better things to do than listen to the general sidle around the subject. "What do you want?"

None of his London acquaintances would have recognized the sharp tones, the decisiveness, but they hadn't known him in the army. He hadn't served in a fashionable regiment, nor had the public honors he'd received been any more remarkable than many others. When he returned to London, he became someone else. Not the officer, but the aristocrat and the man of fashion.

The General didn't appear surprised at Dominic's incisive tones, but then he was better acquainted with Dominic the officer. "I want you to locate him. It shouldn't be beyond your capabilities. This time we have had enough of his dancing around London. We want Stuart in custody, and if necessary we will bring him to trial."

Dominic sucked in a harsh breath. "If you will forgive me for saying so General, that is a mistake. He is flaunting himself in order to get arrested. It's just what he wants."

"If he had heirs, if his brother weren't a Cardinal in the Catholic Church, we might agree with you." The back of the General's comfortable leather padded chair creaked alarmingly when he leaned back. Since he'd returned to London, he'd gained quite a lot of weight. The sedentary life obviously didn't suit him. "However, the hope of the Stuart Cause rests on him. We would prefer to put an end to that. It works both ways, St. Just. The line effectively ends with him, so if we take him, we have the family."

That made alarming sense. But a trial would encourage the kind of support the country could well do without at a time like this. With an aging king and a young and inexperienced heir in thrall to an unpopular advisor, the time was ripe to tip the scales back in the Stuart family's favor, if a person had a mind to do it. "If I see him, I'll inform you. Will that do?"

The General regarded him in silence for a full minute. Dominic knew better than to interrupt him, and he hoped General Court knew better than to press him further. Both men understood what that meant. Dominic would go hunting, and he'd find his prey, but if anyone asked, he'd never met Stuart, not even heard of him.

Eventually, the man nodded. "Very well. I appreciate your help."

"I hope you do." He would not forget the favor. Dominic would make sure of it.

Dominic left the room. He hurried down the stairs, more than glad to put the dust of this building behind him.

Someone calling his name interrupted him. "St. Just!"

Damnation. Pinning an affable smile to his face, he turned, letting the skirts of his coat swing gently around him. "Why, Malton, what a pleasant surprise! Do you come here on a visit, or business?"

Lord Malton grimaced. "Business, but nothing vital, as it transpires. I was merely surprised to see you."

He waved carelessly in the direction of the stairs, taking care to keep the movement elegant. "A social call. A man I used to serve under has returned to London. Paying my respects, don't you know."

"Ah." To Dominic's relief, Malton appeared to accept his explanation. His visit here had become annoyingly clandestine. "Is your business concluded?"

Not at all. "Completely." Dominic offered a smile and paused at the stand by the door to collect his sword. This set of government offices didn't even allow gentlemen to carry the mostly decorative swords. Dominic's was more than decorative, made of fine flexible Spanish steel. "Are you heading into town?"

"To Bond Street. I have to collect my sisters from the drapers'."

Dominic had planned to walk to St. James's, but abruptly he changed his plans. "Your sisters are up from the country?" Malton belonged to a large and influential family. Known as 'The Emperors of London,' they were a force to be reckoned with. Especially with regards to the

Dankworths, supporters of the Pretenders, young and old. The family feud was so old nobody recalled its origins. It had renewed itself in force when the Dankworths and the Emperors took opposite sides in the Jacobite conflict. The Emperors could prove useful to him in his current quest.

Dominic was acutely aware of his lack of supporters. In the army he'd had a complete network of allies. Here, if he were found on the wrong side, he had no doubt the authorities would arrest him and cart him off to prison. If they needed a scapegoat, he provided the perfect subject. Most definitely he needed friends. Someone who knew more about this civilian battle.

However, despite Malton's cordial greeting, he and Dominic were only socially acquainted. Dominic sheathed his sword and clapped his hat on his head, then glanced into the mirror by the desk to adjust it to his satisfaction. Malton dressed soberly and behaved responsibly. Dominic did what he liked. Released from army discipline, he'd enjoyed spreading his wings once he got to town. As the heir to a wealthy and influential title, he was in great demand.

He had no doubt that was why Malton had invited him to meet his sisters. Dominic was not a philanderer, more a card player and a man who enjoyed all forms of entertainment, respectable and decidedly otherwise. However, he never toyed with society ladies. They might expect more than he was prepared to give them.

Malton and Dominic walked out of the offices into glorious sunshine. Dominic glanced up. "A pretty day, is it not?"

Malton nodded curtly. "Indeed, sir. Spring is well advanced, although last month it seemed as if it would never arrive."

They walked down Horse Guards in the direction of Bond Street. Up St. James's Street, with its burgeoning clubs, and past the palace, where the Royal Standard fluttering from the gatehouse proclaimed the King was in residence. A rare event, since his majesty preferred the more modest comforts Kensington Palace had to offer.

Dominic remarked as such to Malton and received a nod in return.

"I believe his majesty wished to greet the Ambassador of France. He'll scuttle back to Kensington as soon as he can." Malton smiled. "I do not begrudge him his comforts. The longer we can keep him healthy the better, would you not agree?"

Sounding him out, no doubt. "Indeed." Dominic had no hesitation in concurring. "It gives the Prince of Wales more time to mature into his role. I fear a king still in his minority could cause problems for the government."

"He is a promising child, but I fear far too ready to listen to his mother's favorite." Malton hesitated delicately before the last word, intimating that the Princess of Wales and Lord Bute were more than royal patron and favorite. Most in London considered them lovers.

A political situation that would be coped with, unlike the advent of a different branch of the royal house. "I don't pretend to understand politics." Dominic waved his handkerchief to illustrate his point. A fine lace-edged piece of linen, it would probably be ruined if he put it to any practical use. "It is all far beyond me."

"I'm sure you would cope." Malton sounded so smug that Dominic spared him a glance. No, he wasn't mistaken. Clearly, Malton considered Dominic as the intellectual half-wit he preferred people to think him. A man more interested in fashion and gossip than anything serious. The pose was beginning to pall, but it had taken a year and a half for it to do so. It might prove useful for a little while longer. When people underestimated him, they were more likely to talk freely in his presence. Consequently he heard much more of the gossip before others did.

"I find other matters more interesting," he said, lengthening his vowels to a fashionable drawl. "Surely gossip about the Princess of Wales and her lover is old news. May we discuss Elizabeth Chudleigh's latest exploit?"

They did, Malton discussing the subject easily enough, until they reached Bond Street. At this time of day, the fashionable and the wealthy thronged the place, from the boxing saloon at the end to the florist's at the other. While Dominic would have preferred the fencing-master's studio, Malton took him straight past it to the drapers' shop two doors down.

The curved bay window with its bull's-eye glass panes revealed swaths of fabric, a few toys strewn across it. His gaze met fans, handkerchiefs, and a particularly pretty necessaire, the separate elements of pen, paper, scissors, spread for the admiration of the customer. Dominic spared it a glance on his way inside.

Three ladies sat at the broad counter to the left of the door. Another counter stood completely opposite, and at the end, bales of fabric were stacked.

Dominic groped for the ribbon tied at his waist and lifted the quizzing glass he kept at the end of it. Surely he was seeing things. "You said sisters," he murmured. "You did not say twins."

Or beauties, for that matter.

"I omitted that part, didn't I?"

If he didn't know better, Dominic would have detected laughter in Malton's voice. So far his acquaintance with the man hadn't revealed a sense of humor. Despite Malton's enjoyment of his surprise, Dominic considered himself a winner here.

The two young ladies seated in chairs before the counter were slender of figure. However, their breasts swelled invitingly above their bodices, and they possessed clear-complexions. Both were possessed of heavenly blue eyes. They had lively features, although one bore an air of serenity, and her gown was a little more subdued than her sister's.

The other, the one with the slight smile curling her lips, intrigued him. Something about this one drew him. She wore pink, which should not have suited her with that red-gold hair, but it did, enhancing her slender loveliness. Dominic would not call either lady a beauty, not in the accepted society sense, but they were lovely enough to create a sensation if they wished to. Their chins were slightly too pointed, their noses too large. He liked them; they added character.

While Malton performed the introductions, she watched him. He only looked away when his bow required it, and then glanced up and found her challenging gaze fixed on his. He flicked her a hard stare, before he recalled himself and allowed his lids to droop over his eyes in his usual society manner.

Her eyes widened. "I did not meet you in town last year, Lord St. Just. I would have thought you very hard to miss."

She scanned his red coat, matching waistcoat, and spotless white breeches. Gold buckles adorned his shoes, with the tiniest of diamonds and rubies, and his sword hilt was encrusted with jewels and engraving. The fact that good Spanish steel was sheathed beneath may have passed her scrutiny.

Showing no sign of insult, Dominic took her careful observation as a compliment. He flourished his hat, which he'd taken off when performing his bow. "You are too kind, Lady Claudia."

She made a sound in the back of her throat that could have been the start of a derisive snort. Except for that tiny sound, Dominic would never have known she was laughing at him from her gracious smile and nod. She'd was probably been taught from the cradle to hide her true emotions. "My lord, it would be difficult to miss such magnificence."

"The color is rather engrained in me, I fear." He straightened up. He, too, could don a public mask. After all, what was his whole appearance but a mask? "I was until recently taking the King's shilling."

Gratification swept through him in a warm tide when her eyes widened. He'd won an open, startled reaction from her, enough to make him want to see more. He wanted to get to know her better.

She was the first woman to affect him in this way since he returned to England.

"You were a soldier?"

"If your brother had introduced us formally, he'd have mentioned that I am Major Viscount St. Just." Ignoring Malton's muttered apology, he concentrated on her. "I am home now because my two cousins sadly perished last year, leaving me the sole hope of my house."

"The only male heir," she murmured. "Now you come to mention it, I do recall something about that. I beg your pardon, I should have paid more attention, and I am indeed sorry for your loss."

He hadn't meant to make her feel guilty. "I barely knew my cousins, I regret to say. I had a lot to arrange when I came home, so I decided not to come to town last season. My parents remain in the country."

Leaving him to hunt down a bride, something he resented. He hadn't meant to marry for years yet, and he was doing his best to deter them, but it was proving difficult. Society understood the value of the estate he stood to inherit and the necessity of marrying and begetting.

Once he'd done that, he could consider returning to the life he loved, in the army.

For the present, he had a delicious distraction. He could only consider her as such. Someone of her temperament would probably not agree to remain quietly in the country while he went back to war. He needed someone sweet, docile, and happy to rusticate. Not this handful of trouble. Even now her eyes danced with mischief.

Now she'd softened a little toward him, he saw that more clearly. "Were you in one of those pretty regiments, the ones that dance attendance on court and curry favor with foreign dignitaries?" she asked. "You would be a credit to them."

He almost laughed, but contrived to keep a straight face. "No." He would give her no guidance. Let her discover for herself. "Discussing the past can be tedious, can it not?" He gestured to the pretty display on the counter. "Have you made your decisions, or may I assist you in any way? My mother tells me I have an excellent eye for color."

The laughter disappeared, and her mouth flattened. Disappointment? Perhaps so. Perhaps he should not think of getting to know her at all. "Except for the green. I dislike it. It's so predictable to put a red-haired woman in green, don't you think?"

He picked up the fabric, a delicate silk in a shade of green he privately labelled puke-colored. "It slips through the fingers nicely."

As her hair would, did she ever let him near it. The notion came to his mind unbidden, as did the notion of stroking her skin to discover if it was as satiny as it looked.

A fine sheen smoothed over it when the sun came out from the clouds and streamed through the broad shop windows. It turned her hair into a ball of fire, and then the light went, disappeared behind its cover.

The shock numbed him. He dropped the fabric and reached out, touched her arm between her elbow-ruffles and her wrist.

She gasped and drew her arm back. Startled, wide eyes met his, but he said nothing. Just stared. That contact had changed everything for him, although if anyone had asked him what "everything" meant, he couldn't have answered.

"St. Just, are you feeling well?"

Malton's gentle query brought him back from wherever he'd gone.

With a short laugh, he shook his head to clear it of the odd emotion he had difficulty describing, even to himself. Exhilaration and a sense of rightness, of things falling into place was the nearest he got to it. Like at the end of a long military campaign.

"I'm sorry, a moment's inattention. That is all." He recalled the topic of conversation. "I think, madam, there are different shades of green. While I have no doubt you would appear charming in apple green or the green of beech leaves in springtime, this green is definitely to be avoided."

"Hmm." She touched the spot he had lately been, letting the material slip through her fingers.

Dominic braced himself against a threatened shudder. What if she touched him with such delicacy? A shiver racked him. He froze his features, fighting for control.

"I believe you are right, sir," she said softly. "This fabric is not for me."

She flipped the stuff back so it folded in on itself, revealing the ivory beneath. "Nor this one. Sallow skin and ivory do not make a good combination."

"Not sallow. Creamy," he said. Her skin reminded him of nothing more than a bowl of cream fresh from the dairy, whipped for a special dish, ready to enrobe and enrich a dish of fresh strawberries. It would taste best taken from her skin.

He took a hasty step back. This highborn lady was not one he should be dallying with. How could he let himself think such a dangerous notion?

Rebuking himself for a fool, he picked up a piece of fabric at random. The shopkeeper had created a brilliant display by tossing rolls of expensive fabric across the counter, so it lay in gorgeous disarray. The piece in his hand had cherry-red stripes. He pushed it aside and found the only one on the display that he considered worthy of her. "A green like this one." This was stiffer taffeta, a rich green that would flatter her, the color of mint leaves. It held a cool quality that would counter her fieriness.

"Why you are right. I hadn't considered this one." The minx gently removed the taffeta from his grasp and cradled it against her cheek. "It is a little rough."

He suppressed a sigh of longing, when he considered how soft that cheek would be.

She knew it, too. Her eyes flashed wickedly as she blatantly checked his response to her flirting.

He rallied. "Certainly not to be worn next to the skin, for sure," he agreed. "Though it would make a wonderful sacque. It would drape extraordinarily well."

To his relief, he rediscovered his society mask. The idea of her in that puke-green silk made him bilious. "I would love to make a gift of it to you, but I fear you would take such a personal token amiss."

One side of her mouth quirked up, and a dimple appeared. "Indeed I would not, sir. As you said, it would come nowhere near my skin."

The vixen handed the stuff to the avidly listening shopkeeper. "I'll take this. Send it to my mantua-maker, if you please. Madame Cerisot. Send the bill to Viscount St. Just. I beg your pardon. Send the account to Major Viscount St. Just."

He smiled. She was not trapping him into any more flirtation. From now on, he would do his best to avoid her until he'd thoroughly analyzed the odd feelings she evoked in him. The stirrings of lust, certainly, but anyone looking at these two would consider that. No, the more tender, gentle emotion with which he was entirely unfamiliar. Except with his parents, and that was an entirely different case. No similarities at all.